Prospero's Daughter

Nancy Butler

D0348640

A SIGNET BOOK

SIGNET
Published by New American Library, a division of
Penguin Putnam Inc., 375 Hudson Street,
New York, New York 10014, U.S.A.
Penguin Books Ltd, 80 Strand,
London WC2R 0RL, England
Penguin Books Australia Ltd, 250 Camberwell Road,
Camberwell, Victoria 3124, Australia
Penguin Books Canada Ltd, 10 Alcorn Avenue,
Toronto, Ontario, Canada M4V 3B2
Penguin Books (N.Z.) Ltd, Cnr Rosedale and Airborne Roads,
Albany, Auckland 1310, New Zealand

Penguin Books Ltd, Registered Offices:
Harmondsworth, Middlesex, England

First published by Signet, an imprint of New American Library,
a division of Penguin Putnam Inc.

First Printing, May 2003
10   9   8   7   6   5   4   3   2   1

BOLD AS LOVE

Miranda wanted to tell Morgan how much his appearance pleased her, had always pleased her, but it would be totally improper to say such a thing. Though she didn't know why that should stop her—her daily encounters with him were hardly high on propriety.

"You look very fine today," she said brightly, trying not to blush at her boldness. "I've grown used to seeing you only in dark colors."

"The devil cloaked in darkness," he quipped. "And I am a cawker for not paying you the first compliment. I can only plead in my defense that the sight of you this morning was so delightful that I became hopelessly tongue-tied."

"Fustian," she retorted, getting some of her nerve back. "And besides these are merely borrowed feathers."

Morgan said in a low, rasping voice, "It was not the feathers I was admiring."

Heat swept over Miranda. Not the blushing sort that skimmed up from her chest, but a truly sizzling heat, sweeping upward from deep inside her.

She was nearly breathless and a little fearful. He rarely came this close, rarely spoke in such an unguarded tone. But here he was now, virile and powerful. No teasing tormentor, determined teacher or fledgling friend, but a man . . . in his rugged, very potent prime.

For the Ladies Who Lunch—
Shirley, Lois, Donna, Anne, Karen and Tracey.

The very instant that I saw you, did
My heart fly to your service; there resides,
To make me slave to it.

. . . . mine unworthiness, that dare not offer
What I desire to give, and much less take
What I shall die to want.

—William Shakespeare
The Tempest

Chapter One

He was going to have to kill Ronald Palfry.

It was either that, Morgan Pearce mused, or spend the rest of his life waiting for Ronald to get to the point. He sorted mentally—and most pleasantly—through several lethal options while his doomed dinner companion rattled on in his usual long-winded fashion.

The two were dining—at Ronald's insistent request—at Watiers, whose excellent suppers Morgan normally enjoyed. This one was sitting in his gullet like a sullen lump; irritation made a very poor sauce.

"What did you say?" Morgan's brain suddenly snapped back into focus; he had a feeling he'd just missed something vital.

"*I said*," Ronald recited dutifully, "the General's decided to write his memoirs. And he wants you to have a gander at the manuscript. You being in the book business now and all."

"No, not that," Morgan said with a flick of his hand. "The other part. The part you managed to muffle with a mouthful of venison."

"I . . . I told my father you'd go up to Windermere and have a look at the book in person."

Morgan set down his fork and frowned. "That's what I thought you said."

Ronald's perpetually merry expression tightened as he ran one hand through his crop of curls, dislodging not one wheat-colored ringlet. "I know it's a dashed imposition, asking you to leave London so near the start of the Season."

"Hang the Season. It's Grambling House that's my concern.

You know I only sold out because my uncle was ailing and needed my help."

"Well, he ain't ailing any longer," Ronald pointed out. "Looks fit as a fiddle to me. And things appear to be well in hand at the publishing house."

"And so they shall continue to be. Leaving now is out of the question." Morgan returned to his veal chop, then after a moment said more evenly, "If your father truly wants to meet with me, we can drive up there in July."

Ronald's face turned soulful; Morgan could have sworn his lower lip actually trembled. "I . . . I fear he'll have lost heart by then. The book is all that's keeping him going these days. You know how it is . . . retired soldier . . . at loose ends. Writing this memoir's been like a tonic to him. Only trouble is, he can't decide what to put in and what to leave out. Thing's turned into a lumbering behemoth."

Undaunted by Morgan's deepening scowl, Ronald continued, "What he requires is someone like you, who is canny about such matters, to help him pull it together." He looked down at his plate, and then swiftly up again, his expression now one of heartrending entreaty.

Morgan knew exactly what was coming—the fatal stroke.

"I promised my father you'd do it, old fellow. That you'd do it for *me*."

Morgan should have been used to it by now. They replayed this same scenario whenever his friend required a boon of him, anything from recommending a first-rate boot maker to introducing the lad to a toothsome actress. "This is for Ronald Palfry," Morgan would remind himself at each new demand. "Friend, brother officer—and the man who saved my life."

Whether this last item was true or not was immaterial. Ronald *thought* he'd saved his major's life in Spain, which amounted to the same thing. In his eyes, Morgan owed him a debt of honor.

Morgan often—and devoutly—wished Lieutenant Palfry had chosen to answer the call of nature behind a different tree, one whose branches did *not* harbor a French soldier. Or that, at the very least, he hadn't let Ronald go on thinking he'd grappled with a real live sniper in that valley outside Travertina. Yet he had, because—well, the reasons were complicated. And once you were party to a deception, even a benevolent one, you were never really quit of it.

Ronald was too much of a gentleman to actually mention the debt aloud, but it was there, implicit in every requested favor. This one, however, was bordering on the extreme.

"It's not just my concern for Grambling House. My sister has finally set a wedding date with Waverly—for late June—and I'm to help her with the arrangements."

Ronald was immediately distracted by this new bone. "That must be a bit of a blow. Hard to believe she's really going through with it. Waverly must know how things stood between her and Phillip DeBurgh."

Morgan's jaw flexed. "I refuse to discuss my sister's tangled affairs, Ronald, not even with you. Suffice it to say I have both the publishing house and Kitty's wedding to keep me here—"

"—and Lady Farley's boudoir," Ronald interjected darkly. "Let us not forget that. Don't fob me off with excuses, Morgan. You've three assistants to run Grambling House for you. As for your sister—she has the entire Waverly clan at her disposal. It's Lady Farley who's keeping you leashed in London. And though far be it from me to come between a man and his paramour, rumor has it her husband's on his way back from Vienna."

Morgan idly studied the set of his shirt cuff. "I've heard nothing to that effect."

"*You* don't hang about in diplomatic circles."

He eyed Ronald dubiously. "Oh, and you do?"

His companion puffed up at once. "Bertie Chitwood's brother is friendly with Lord Alpington's secretary. Alpington is recalling Lord Farley, according to Bertie."

"Yes," Morgan agreed as he chewed thoughtfully on a bit of roasted potato. "I can see that that's a reliable source. Wasn't Bertie the one who swore he saw Napoleon Bonaparte on the Isle of Wight ferry last winter?"

Ronald refused to become flustered. "I'm merely advising you, man to man, that you might want to play least in sight when it comes to Lady Farley. Her husband is rumored to have killed two men in duels of honor—"

Morgan nearly snorted. "When was that? During the reign

of Queen Anne? Good God, Ronald, the man is seventy if he's a day."

It suddenly became clear to him that this whole Windermere visit was a ruse, and he now understood why Ronald was being so insistent. It all went back to that damned sniper incident.

Immediately after his "heroic" act, Ronald had hatched the cork-brained notion that he was wholly responsible for keeping his major out of harm's way. The brash officer known to his troops as Mad Morgan now found himself forced to practice prudence in battle.

It was one thing to rush headlong into the fray when he had only his own skin to worry about and quite another when a stubborn young subaltern remained glued to his side. His worst fear was that Lieutenant Palfry would intercept a fatal sword thrust or pistol ball meant for him. Morgan certainly didn't want that on his conscience.

Of course, if he throttled Ronald himself that was a whole other story—and the likelihood of such an outcome was increasing daily. Even after they'd both sold out and returned to the relatively tame haunts of London, Ronald insisted on dogging his footsteps, a blasted guardian angel in blue superfine and tasseled Hessians.

He leveled his fork at his friend as if it were a weapon. "Don't think I haven't sussed what you're about, inventing this excuse to send me from London merely to keep me safe from a jealous husband—one who probably can't even *lift* a pistol without a footman to assist him. You're starting at shadows . . . as usual."

Ronald's eyes narrowed. "I haven't *invented* anything. My father specifically asked me for your aid. It just happens it's a timely request."

"Timely be damned."

"Besides," Ronald said, "if you're so in need of female company, I take leave to remind you that I have two sisters still at home, Bettina and Ariadne."

"Still at home, eh? Trust me, you're not going to tempt me away from London with your spotty sisters."

"For your information, they're both diamonds of the first water. It's true they haven't got a brain between them, but you've got more than enough for one person in that head of yours."

"Thank you . . . I think."

"Come on, old fellow." It was practically a whine. "Say you'll do it. Mad Morgan Pearce was never one to back down from a challenge." His eyes brightened. "Besides, I understand military reminiscences are all the crack, now that the war with France is ended. Grambling House might actually stand to make a profit."

Morgan glared at him. "I don't need you to tell me my business." He pushed his plate away and snatched up his glass of claret. His companion watched with cautious anticipation as he emptied it, and then ran the ridge of his knuckles over his chin several times.

"You needn't spend more than two weeks up there," Ronald coaxed, sensing a chink in his companion's armor. "That should be plenty of time to get my father back on track. Anyway, he's eager to show you around Windermere, so it won't all be burning the midnight oil."

The trouble was, Morgan reflected, he liked burning the midnight oil. It was the reason he had agreed to take over the reins at Grambling House after his maternal uncle suffered a mild apoplexy—even though it flew in the face of his father's lifelong edict that Pearces did not engage in trade, not even a refined, gentlemanly trade.

Ronald wasn't much better; he seemed to think it was all a foolish lark, one Morgan would soon tire of. But he hadn't. He fancied he'd made quite a difference there in the past months, enough that he didn't want to lose his momentum by turning things over to assistants.

Still, what Ronald had said was true. Grambling House *could* use a vigorous memoir. General Sir Janus Palfry's military career spanned decades. He had seen action in the war with the American colonies and in India, and his cool head in the face of fire was legendary.

A memoir definitely had merit. But not if it required him to spend weeks away from London. His life had finally fallen neatly into place and he was not in any hurry to alter the balance.

He was about to utter a flat and final refusal when he made the mistake of glancing at Ronald. There it was again, that look of earnest expectation Ronald had worn outside Travertina. It reminded Morgan of a spaniel pup he'd once owned—the same limpid brown eyes, the same unspoken promise that a "no" was tantamount to heartbreak.

"Oh, very well," he said at last, trying not to sound sullen. "I'll go to Palfry Park if it will make you happy. We can travel up to Windermere, and then—"

"Oh, no," Ronald interjected quickly. "I'm not going with you. I've dozens of commitments in London over the next month. Plus, I'm promised to dine at Carlton House in a week's time. Can't disappoint the regent now, can I?"

Morgan muffled a curse when he realized that Ronald, never much of a tactical wizard on the battlefield, had somehow out-maneuvered him, aided as usual by that infernal debt of honor. It was his own fault, though. If only he'd told him the truth four years ago in Spain.

Fate, as he was rapidly learning, had a very peculiar sense of humor.

Kitty Pearce swiped idly at a stray tendril that kept tickling her nose as she bent over her work. The window in her uncle's parlor was open and a delightful breeze occasionally wafted past the escritoire where she sat writing out wedding invitations.

Morgan would be here any time now to go over the pages she had marked in *La Belle Assemblée*. Trousseaux were tricky things—too much lace and adornment on a gown and Waverly would think her a parvenu; too little and he might fear she had Quakerish tendencies.

Thank heavens her brother possessed that certain je ne sais quoi required for choosing the perfect trousseau. One had only to view him, even with a sister's jaundiced eye, from across the dance floor or while driving in the park, to understand why all her female friends begged for introductions. It wasn't just the superb cut of his clothing that drew them, but the wide shoulders and lean, soldier's body. And then there were those in-triguingly gaunt cheekbones, the toll of six years of hard campaigning, and the dark eyes that could dance with devilish mischief even while his other features remained composed.

Poor Morgan. Unlike her, he'd never understood his own physical allure, and so from his youth had taken great pains with his wardrobe, as though the lily needed any gilding whatsoever. It made a dangerous combination—the elegant, refined tailoring and the wild, gypsy looks. And when his dark beauty had been paired with the golden radiance of Phillip DeBurgh, why the two of them—

"No!" she cried, throwing down her quill and leaving a haphazard trail of ink on the blotter. She had promised herself not to think of him, not ever. That chapter of her life was over. There was a bright, promising future ahead of her now. No more days of worrying and fretting, no more nights disrupted by despair.

She ripped up the invitation card she had ruined and took a new one from the pile, inscribing the next name on her list in a determined yet feminine script.

"Steady as a rock," she said, noting her writing hand approvingly.

There was a soft tap on the door and Morgan came into the room. She'd been sure her composure had returned, but the guarded expression on his face set her heart to thudding again.

"You're looking well," he said as he leaned down to brush a kiss over her cheek.

"I'm afraid I can't say the same for you. What is it?"

He perched on the edge of the desk, took up a bronze paperweight shaped like a pomegranate and began to study it as though it held the secrets of the universe. It was an old trick of his, she knew, one he'd mastered whenever he was called before their father. He'd toy with his riding whip or a book, anything to avoid displaying his feelings openly.

"Look at me, Morgan," she said

He raised his head and met her eyes. "You're not going to like this, Kitty. I've promised Ronald Palfry that I'd go up to Windermere. His father's writing a memoir and Ronald wants me to get the old fellow sorted out."

She gazed off thoughtfully into space and nodded sagely. "Of course Ronald's needs must outweigh my own. I am merely your sister, after all, and Ronald is . . ." She paused dramatically. "What exactly is Ronald to you, Morgan, that you always seem to drop everything at his request?"

Her brother shrugged and almost grinned. "An infernal nuisance?" He set down the paperweight. "Look, Kit, I know the timing is awkward, but I hope to be back in less than three weeks. You soldier on here till then. . . . You've still got Aunt Dorrie to help you. And it's not as though planning a wedding is exactly a drudgery."

She frowned and her fingers twined and twisted on the blotter. "You were supposed to be here to give me moral support. To distract me."

Morgan cocked his head. "I rather thought that was Waverly's job."

Her frown turned ominous. "You know to what I am referring."

She saw the sadness, the defeat, pass across his face for an instant, and her expression softened at once.

"Perhaps that's why I need to go away, Kit," he murmured. "As I said, you've got Waverly and your wedding plans to keep your brain occupied and out of trouble. But not a day passes at Grambling House that a line in a book or some idly spoken jest doesn't remind me of him."

"I know," she said, reaching out impulsively to grip his hand. "Though I've always been better than you at pushing away the unpleasant parts of life."

He rose then, still holding her hand. "So do you forgive me for going off to Windermere?"

"Only if you promise to bring me something nice when you return."

He thought this over. "How about Ronald Palfry's head on a platter?"

She gave a quick, gusty laugh. "I think I should like that enormously."

"Bloodthirsty wench," he said. "Now I'm off to pay my respects to our aunt and uncle. And remember, Kitty, I shouldn't be away above three weeks. I trust you can hold the fort till then."

* * *

"I am turning into a damned sponge," Morgan muttered as he clung to his seat while his coach battled through a teeming downpour, rocking and bucking along a muddy, furrowed lane on the outskirts of Windermere. His valet, wisely, said nothing.

It had been nearly a week since he'd set out for Palfry Park in a hired post chaise, accompanied only by the stalwart Hodges. The rain had fallen unceasingly since they left London, and it seemed to Morgan that a particular spidery black cloud had hovered directly overhead for most of the journey—like the vengeful hand of some Greek deity—resulting in a soggy dampness that quickly permeated the interior of the vehicle.

Morgan wished he'd opted to make the trip on horseback, the method of travel he'd grown used to in Spain. Weathering spring showers out in the open wasn't nearly as bad as enduring the cramped confines and stomach-tilting gyrations of a pitching coach.

Now that he was nearing his destination, he had to admit he was in a definite funk. Not even the glorious vistas of the Lake District were able to stir him. Perhaps six years on the Peninsula had made him immune to the restorative effects of bucolic scenery.

Everything chafed at him—his annoyance at leaving his duties at Grambling House, his regret over parting with Lavinia Farley, his frustration with Ronald in general. There was also his secret relief—and subsequent guilt—over getting away from Kitty and her convoluted affairs of the heart. For the next few weeks at least, he wouldn't have to watch her fling herself into frenzied plans for an ill-advised marriage. He might have been heedless on the battlefield, but unlike his sister, he never rushed headlong into romantic entanglements. Mad Morgan they might have named him, but he wasn't *that* mad.

Not that he was immune to the lures of the fair sex. The light skirts of London had welcomed him with open . . . arms . . . when he returned from Spain. And then, two months earlier, Lady Farley had glided into his sights at a dinner party, with a whisper of silk and trailing the heady scent of gardenias. He'd become increasingly obsessed with his work at Grambling

House, and she had offered the perfect distraction. Lavinia Farley gave burning the midnight oil a whole *other* connotation.

She'd appeared to him a rare prize, beautiful, accomplished and intelligent. And furthermore, possessing that most desirable of *objets* . . . an absent husband.

Of course, if Ronald's source in Whitehall was correct, Lord Farley might be halfway home by now. Even if it were true, the man probably wouldn't arrive in London for weeks yet—his lordship's generation subscribed to a leisurely mode of travel—and Morgan could have spent that time happily installed in Lavinia's bed. Instead, here he was, pledged to play nursemaid to an aging soldier with literary aspirations.

The words "lumbering behemoth" insinuated their way into his brain, and he sighed.

There had better be something worthwhile in Windermere, he grumbled to himself, something to repay him for abandoning Grambling House, his sister *and* the luscious Lavinia.

Because if he had come all this way to look at a pile of unpublishable foolscap, Morgan swore he was going to drive straight back to London and draw Ronald's cork for him.

Debt of honor be hanged.

The rain stopped abruptly as the coach turned onto the level drive of Palfry Park, and Morgan at once let down the window. A lone beam of sunlight had broken through the lingering clouds, bathing the distant house in a shimmering golden glow. The limestone facade appeared so pale and so luminous that it might have been the finest Italian marble.

The estate, Morgan knew, had been constructed in the days of the first Hanover king. During the reign of subsequent Georges, the family had added several embellishments, most notably a colonnaded walkway on the southern facade and an ornamental lake in the parkland. The grounds and gardens he observed from his window were manicured to a fault, every flower bed, hedge and swaying poplar trimmed and tamed into regal elegance. Morgan thought it resembled an artist's idealized depiction of a country house—rather too good to be true.

"Probably deathwatch beetles in the wainscoting," he muttered as the post chaise drew up at the front door.

Sir Janus himself came out onto the semicircular porch with Lady Palfry, wearing a cherubic smile, a half step behind him. "Welcome, sir. Welcome," his host called out. "And look—you've brought the sun. There's a proper omen for you."

Morgan had met them last autumn, when he and Ronald first arrived in London. The General appeared much the same—a robust sixty-five-year-old, with a head of thick white hair and flyaway eyebrows that framed flinty blue eyes.

Morgan alighted from the chaise, praying his boots didn't squish as he went up the stone steps to the porch. His host and hostess drew him into the front hall, where a pewter-haired butler relieved him of his greatcoat and hat. They then whisked him into a warm, sun-drenched parlor, where a pretty maid in a ruffled apron brought in tea and cakes. The tea was piping hot and the cakes tasted of marzipan and clotted cream. Morgan felt the soggy damp recede almost at once. It was as though he had wandered into a sublime, comforting dream.

His pleasure did not diminish when the daughters of the house appeared. Miss Bettina Palfry, flaxen-haired and pansy-eyed, made her curtsy to him, and then dimpled charmingly when he complimented her on her home. Miss Ariadne Palfry, nearly her sister's match in height and form, was blessed with toffee-colored curls and sparkling hazel eyes.

Morgan settled into easy conversation with the General and his wife, but did not miss the admiring glances sent his way by their daughters. Although they were too young to interest him in any serious way—even as a youth he'd had little interest in unfledged misses—he had to acknowledge that Ronald hadn't exaggerated. The Palfry sisters were paragons.

When the topic shifted to London, the girls grew animated. "How I envy you, sir, living in the capital," Bettina said breathlessly, her eyes widening. "We have neither of us been farther afield than Chester."

"But our father has promised to take us to London within the year," Ariadne added with a twinkle to the General. "Haven't you, dear Papa?"

He responded with a smile. "I will indeed, but only if you are still unattached, puss. Which seems most unlikely." He turned to Morgan. "You may wonder why my girls have not had a proper come-out in London, but I never saw the sense of it. They've more beaux than they know what to do with here in Windermere."

"Fortunately, our neighbors offer frequent entertainments," Lady Palfry explained as she leaned forward to refill Morgan's teacup. "And we attend the monthly assemblies in town, so my girls never lack for opportunities to meet other young people."

"The two most sought-after young ladies in the district," the General pronounced.

"I sometimes worry that so much attention will turn their heads," Lady Palfry confided. "But I know my girls—they are as good-hearted as one could wish."

Sir Janus nodded. "That they are, both of them always out and about—visiting the sick, assisting with the local charity fetes, helping with the floral arrangements in our little church. They take after their mother, there."

"I do love my roses," said Lady Palfry with a wistful smile. She turned to Bettina, beside her on the sofa, and touched her fingertips to the girl's cheek. "Especially *these* roses . . ."

"Oh, Mama," Bettina said with a blush as she lowered her eyes. "What will Mr. Pearce think?"

"Mr. Pearce is charmed," Morgan answered truthfully. "I'm sure you and your sister are the belles of the Lake District."

Ariadne shifted toward him. "If I may be so bold, Mr. Pearce, we would like very much to invite you to a party at the squire's home later in the week. We've made especially sure that you are to be included."

The General harrumphed. "No need to go, Pearce, if you mislike that sort of flummery."

"It's not a problem," Morgan said. "I believe I might enjoy such . . . flummery . . . very much."

The sisters beamed at him.

Chapter Two

After a week at Palfry Park, Morgan was convinced he had found a secret window into a perfect world. So perfect that he remained a bit incredulous.

The family treated him as an honored guest and did everything to see to his comfort. His bedroom was large and tastefully appointed, his feather bed the sort he had dreamed of in his bivouac in Spain. The General's cook prepared meals that would have honored royalty, his wine cellar was outstanding and his stable boasted several raking hunters that had been placed at Morgan's disposal.

Most amazing was the endless affability of the family members toward each other. This was a welcome novelty to Morgan, considering he and his own father had not spoken in over six years. Sir Janus doted openly upon his daughters. Their mother smiled with tender pride whenever she regarded them. Yet in the face of all that unstinting parental approval, the Palfry sisters had somehow remained free of conceit.

It was positively unnerving.

He'd attended the squire's party two days earlier—a tame affair, but he'd managed to enjoy himself. The young ladies, most of them bosom bows of either Bettina or Ariadne, had not let his relatively advanced age deter them from flirting with him and dancing with him and generally making him feel like the catch of the century. The young men had questioned him about his experiences in the war, and then hung upon his every word. One local lordling had paid special attention to Bettina, and Morgan suspected a betrothal was not long off.

Morgan's only disappointment at Palfry Park turned out to be the General's memoir.

Someone once observed that budding soldiers made the worst scholars, that the last thing they desired was to bury their heads in books. By Morgan's reckoning, Sir Janus had not been near a book in the last twenty-five years. His manner of writing was slavishly eighteenth century—stilted, pedantic and top-heavy with long-winded rhetoric.

Definitely lumbering-behemoth territory.

Ah, but the man had some remarkable stories to tell—of years spent in the American colonies, where he had been impressed by the vast resources of the daring young nation . . . of his time in India, living in the cantonments, battling mountain bandits or mutinous maharajas. He had a trunkful of anecdotes about Arthur Wellesley from the days before he became the national craze and endless stories of brave officers and notable statesmen now in their graves.

The good stuff was in there all right, but it needed badly to be distilled.

Morgan knew he could be perfectly truthful and tell his host that the book needed more doctoring than he was able to furnish—and head back to London with a clear conscience. Yet the thought of another tedious journey was not tempting. He was content to dwell in the comfortable bosom of the Palfry family for another week or so. Meantime, he would offer Sir Janus a quick tutorial on writing engaging narrative prose.

Since the wet weather continued that first week, Morgan ended up closeted with his host for most of the daylight hours, the two of them honing the existing portion of the manuscript. He was often astonished by the man's razor-sharp ability to recollect people and events from his distant past and further impressed by his unassailable good nature.

Generals, in Morgan's experience, were not known for their lamblike manner. Crusty, curt, autocratic, imperious . . . all were more fitting epithets for the breed than the word affable. Sir Janus had to have a backbone of steel somewhere under all that bonhomie, else he'd never have lasted a minute on a battlefield. But Morgan had yet to see any sign of it.

After six days of solid work, the General's rewrites were

starting to shine. Morgan expressed this sentiment aloud from the study table, where he sat reviewing the latest pages.

"It's all your doing, Pearce," Sir Janus said, clapping him on the back. "Advising me to write as though I were telling the tale in the mess tent is what did the trick. It's rougher, more earthy than I would have liked—"

"Earthy sells books," Morgan interjected dryly.

"—but, by Gad, it's finally reading like a proper story."

"It is, indeed," Morgan said as he rose. He set his hand on the stacked pages and added, "After I leave for London next week, you'll do fine on your own."

"Nonsense," said the General, his untamed brows furrowing. "You're my lucky charm, old chap. It only started coming together after you arrived here. Nothing like a fellow soldier to understand what the story required. No, no . . . I want you to stay on until I've finished."

Morgan felt a shiver of disquiet. The General's epic was barely half done. "It would certainly please me to see it through to completion, Sir Janus, but I can give you only another week at the most. You will understand that there are things I must get back to in London, responsibilities, obligations . . ." *Lady Farley's bed.*

His host appeared not to have heard his protest. "And my girls are all atwitter to show you off. You were such a success at the squire's party, I fancy they've lined up dozens of entertainments for you."

Morgan mustered his severest expression—the one that made his troops shiver down to their boot tips—and said again that he absolutely had to return to London in a matter of days.

The General's genial manner dropped away in an instant, and he countered, no surprise, by reminding Morgan tersely that Ronald expected him to stay on until the memoir was completed. "My son has indicated that you are in some manner greatly indebted to him."

Morgan drew a breath and muttered, "He . . . he believes he saved my life in Spain."

Crossing his arms over his broad chest, Sir Janus purred, "And is that the way of it?"

Tell him the truth! Morgan's brain screamed. *Let it finally be over. This ridiculous farce has played out long enough.*

Morgan opened his mouth to explain and had an instant vision of Ronald's soulful eyes. He swallowed once, then nodded.

Sir Janus tipped back his leonine head. "Well, there you have it. Nothing more to be said."

Morgan wanted to cry out that indeed there was a great deal more to be said. To remind the arrogant old despot that he had a business to run in London, for God's sake. But it was pointless to argue, not after the holy name of Ronald had been invoked.

He excused himself before his temper was fully roused and went quickly from the room.

So much for wondering if the man possessed a sturdy backbone. Honed Toledo steel had nothing on Sir Janus.

The sun had finally reappeared an hour ago, and Morgan decided a brisk walk in the fresh air was what he needed—something to work off his anger in a more productive manner than lobbing a fireplace poker at the General's head.

He emerged onto the roofed colonnade, growling slightly as he set off along the shaded area, head bowed, hands knotted behind him. Frustration was his least favorite companion, and he knew if he didn't wrestle it into submission, his remaining time at Palfry Park would end up an exercise in resentment. His most pressing question now was how long that might be.

He tried to conjure up some emergency that would offer him an immediate escape back to London. Kitty's wedding came to mind, but it was not until the end of June. The thought of cooling his heels in the country for another month or two gave him a sinking feeling in his gut. How many insipid neighborhood entertainments among a callow set of youngsters would he have to endure in that time? For how many more days could he stand being closeted with Sir Janus before his temper flared and he ripped up at the man?

Lord, he'd never once felt as constricted by army life as he did right now.

When he reached the end of the colonnade, his gaze was drawn beyond the adjacent hedged path to a grass allée bordered by high, sculpted yews. It was a noble prospect and, since his own family home in Surrey was a modest pile, Morgan knew he should have felt some admiration for the beauty of the garden. His current anger with its owner, however, made him view it in a slightly different light.

He recalled certain deadly tropical plants that lured unsuspecting insects into their depths with honeyed droplets. Once caught in the sticky sweetness, the poor creatures could only struggle to exhaustion. He thought of the enticing, honeyed comforts of Palfry Park and saw them now as a trap. He'd been lured, and he'd been caught.

Oh, he was definitely going to kill Ronald Palfry.

Stepping down from the colonnade, he rubbed fretfully at his brow, trying to soothe away the uncomfortable sensation of being held captive here against his—

Morgan uttered a low grunt of surprise as he collided with the back of a hooded Bath chair. It slewed forward several feet and a startled cry rose up from the interior.

He quickly sprang after it, reaching for the handle.

"Sorry," he said as he steadied the chair, then leaned around the raised hood. "I'm afraid I didn't see you sitting beside the hedge."

He assumed the female drawn back in the shadows was elderly, but when she spoke her voice was youthful—and tart. "You must have been woolgathering. I'm rather hard to miss."

He peered closer, trying to make out her features. Her face was pale-complected and thin, the bones standing out in sharp relief. A fringe of brownish hair feathered her brow, shaded by a severe black bonnet. Her gown was also unrelieved black, a heavyweight wool with the collar fastened high against her throat.

At his open scrutiny, she turned her head away.

"Please, sir," she said. "Please go about your business. My maid merely went to fetch my lap rug."

He stood upright and looked off down the allée of yews where the bright sunlight was making short work of any lingering dampness on the grass. "Not sure you need a rug. It's come on quite warm."

He heard her sigh. "They fear for me to take a chill."

"It's April, ma'am. And though there is a slight breeze, it's nearly balmy."

She made no comment.

He wanted to get on with his walk, but didn't think it right to leave the woman unattended. It was obvious her limbs were unsound—her hands, lying inert in her lap, were covered with square muslin mits tied at the wrist. The toes of her slippers, which showed at her hem, were canted slightly toward each other. He'd seen enough soldiers suffering from paralysis to recognize the symptom.

Who the devil was she? He'd been here a full week and had heard no mention of another guest or an infirm relation staying at the house. It was as though the woman had dropped from the sky—Bath chair and all.

"Perhaps you will allow me to push you down the avenue until your maid comes along." Without waiting for permission, he began to propel the chair along the path. "If you begin to feel chilled you must tell me, and I will take you back inside at once."

More likely she would faint from heat prostration, he thought, wondering at her need for that winter-weight gown. It was, however, the least of the mysteries that surrounded her.

They were halfway down the avenue when a voice called out. Morgan stopped and turned. A serving girl with a lap rug over one arm was hurrying toward them across the grass. She shot him a look of irritation as she closed the gap. "Bless me, sir, but it gave me a start when I saw she was gone from the path. There's no way in heaven she could have moved the chair herself."

The girl *tsked* crossly as she spread the rug over the woman's knees. She then drew a heavy black veil from the brim of the bonnet and arranged it over her face.

"Can't even do this much for herself, poor cow," the girl said over her shoulder, tugging at the woman's collar button, which had come half undone. She stood upright and turned to Morgan. "I'll see to her now." She gave him a narrow look when he didn't retreat. "Sir?"

Something perverse in his nature rose up. A moment ago he wanted to be off on his walk; now he refused to be dismissed by this snip-tongued servant who spoke about her mistress as though she weren't there. "I believe I will see to the lady."

She looked at him assessingly for a moment, then shrugged. "Suit yourself. But mind you, don't tire her. She's peevish at the best of times."

Morgan waited until she had gone, then crouched down in front of the chair. "I don't wonder you're peevish, ma'am. I'd hate like the devil to be prodded and poked at by impatient servants."

The woman made no response at first, and then a hoarse whisper rose from the depths of the chair. Morgan leaned closer. "Pardon?"

"I said, *Go away.*" The husky voice contained a surprising amount of resolve.

Morgan rocked back on his heels and set his fist against his chin. "That puts me in something of a quandary. I can't very well just abandon you."

"Don't fret yourself. Alice often forgets me out here, leaves me among the plantings like . . . like a garden gnome."

He'd detected a distinctly wry note to that last comment. At least she wasn't beyond seeing some humor in her situation.

"I am used to being alone," she added. "It's no hardship, I promise you."

Morgan stood up slowly. It was clear she wanted him gone, and he was loath to force his will on anyone so defenseless. But then curiosity overrode good manners. He returned to the back of the chair and again began to wheel it along. He didn't want a solitary walk any longer; he'd much rather discover the identity of this mysterious woman, the dark secret harbored in the midst of the perfect Palfry household.

"I see there's an ornamental lake up ahead," he said when they reached the end of the allée. "Screened by that copse of beeches. Perhaps you might enjoy the view. My name is Morgan Grambling Pearce, by the way."

He waited for her to offer her own name, and when she didn't respond, he said, "I am here to help Sir Janus compose his memoirs."

"Ah, then you must be a hired secretary."

"Of sorts," he said with a chuckle, refusing to be baited. "I wear many caps these days—secretary, banker, taskmaster, father confessor. I am a publisher, you see."

She said nothing.

"Are you perhaps a relation of Sir Janus or of Lady Palfry?" he ventured.

"Not so you would notice," she said under her breath.

He growled softly in vexation. She was not going to give an inch. Still, there were other ways to get to the bottom of things. Once he was back at the house, he would ask his valet to investigate. Hodges was a veritable wizard when it came to ferreting out belowstairs' gossip.

Morgan pushed onward, following a graveled path that led out from the beeches and continued around the lake, which was bracketed at either end by the soft, green blur of willows. On the opposite shore sat a trellised folly, modeled in the Oriental style, its onion-domed roof gleaming white in the sun.

"Let's set a course for Cathay, shall we?" he said. "I've always wanted to visit China, but I've never been farther east than Ibiza. My father did once threaten to ship me off to India, when I was sent down from Oxford for some prank that escapes me at present. But the exotic East was not to be my lot—I was destined for the Iberian Peninsula. The war, you see. Made me quite fit for publishing, however. I learned to keep my head down during a heated volley, whether artillery or authorial."

He rattled on in this bluff, nonthreatening fashion—as though he were trying to soothe a skittish horse—hoping to ease her into some response. It was to no avail; his charge gave no indication that she was even listening.

It occurred to him at one point that she might have fainted from the heat, swaddled as she was in layers of wool. He halted the chair and moved around to view the woman. Her head was listing back against the hood and it was nearly impossible to make out her face through the opaque veil.

"How are you faring in there?"

When still she made no answer, Morgan's concern grew. He reached in and raised the veil with both hands, setting it on the brim of her bonnet.

"You are not to touch me!" she cried in a voice that mingled panic and pique.

He stepped back at once. Her eyes had widened in alarm as her hands began to stir in her lap. Morgan noted it with surprise, those mitted hands fretting against black worsted.

"It's all right," he said. "I meant no disrespect. Still, if I can't see in through that veil, it's likely you can't see out very well. And this is quite a pretty lake. A shame to view it through a scrim."

"I do not go anywhere unveiled," she said in a low voice. "Alice was preoccupied today, which is why she forgot to adjust my bonnet before we left the house."

"Well, that's daft," he said without thinking.

"Necessary," she countered.

"Are you in mourning?" She did not acknowledge the question. "Or merely eccentric?"

Her eyes narrowed as she uttered, "It should be clear to even a simpleton like yourself why the veil is necessary."

Morgan observed her as best he could within the shadowed confines of the hood. *Perhaps she suffers from a wasting illness*, he thought, and his mind recoiled at that, because the lady in the Bath chair was clearly not old—not yet thirty, he suspected—and her angular, gamine face held some remnant of lost beauty.

"I *don't* see," he said softly. "Only that you are ill . . . or have been ill. Surely the good sunlight on your face is what you require, not hiding away behind a layer of gauze."

She angled her body forward, away from the protective hood, and turned her face to the right. He did see then, and nearly groaned. The outer ridge of her left cheekbone was noticeably flattened, as though from a heavy blow. A network of faded, pinkish scars radiated back from that place, toward ear and temple.

She faced him full on now, chin upthrust, her eyes challenging him not to be disgusted, not to look away in distaste. Morgan didn't lower his gaze, but could think of nothing to say.

"At least I've found a way to make you stop talking," she observed. "That's something. Now, please, take me back to the house."

"How did this happen?" he asked.

Her eyes flashed again at his boldness. In the sunlight they were striking—pale woodsmoke gray rimmed in deepest blue. The wisp of brown hair upon her brow had taken on a golden cast, like gilded fruitwood. He was struck again by the potential for beauty.

Then her mitted hands fumbled upward, in a futile attempt to pluck at the veil, and he was reminded that the possibility of beauty was only an illusion. Beneath those muslin mists he suspected her fingers were curled claws.

"Leave it," he said, gently taking her wrists and setting her hands in her lap. "You don't need the veil. Not with me. And I won't pester you with questions any longer. I won't even speak, if you prefer. But let us finish our walk around the lake, and then I will take you home."

She lapsed again into silence as he wheeled her along the path. It was easy work; he imagined she weighed little more than a child. He paused when they reached the folly and asked her if she would like to sit on the enclosed wooden bench.

"Oh, yes," she drawled. "I will just scamper up those steps. . . ."

His teeth ground. "I was thinking I might carry you. I expect you're a featherweight and I'm not exactly in my dotage."

"I assure you I am fine. But don't let me stop you . . . since you have come all this way to view the lake."

Stifling a sigh of annoyance, Morgan went up the shallow steps. He didn't give a fig about the lake, but he was damned if he'd let her know it. He braced his hands on the intricately carved railing and leaned out over the path. The cattails and eelgrass that grew in profusion along the shore would make it nearly impossible for the chair-bound woman to see the water, so for lack of anything better to do, he began to describe the view—the elegant manor house on a slight rise in the distance, the sculpted avenue of yews marching in precision down to the graceful stand of beech trees.

"There's a family of ducks on the lake. Teal, I believe, though I'm not sure . . . I never went in much for blasting away at waterfowl. Six little ones in a row behind the parents, no make that seven. One of them has fallen behind his—"

"Mr. Pearce," she interjected, "this tiresome running narrative is hardly necessary. I am not blind, only crippled."

"And peevish," he added before he could stop himself. "Don't forget that. I fear it may be the worst of your many ailments."

He couldn't see her face—the chair was turned slightly away from him—but he fancied her jaw had just dropped.

He came swiftly down from the pavilion and set himself in front of her. Leaning forward to look her square in the eye, he said intently, "I have a friend who lost a leg on the Peninsula. Another lost the use of his arm. I, myself, have a rather interesting scar from shrapnel . . . in a place I will not discuss, out of respect for your maidenly sensibilities. It's a bloody business, the waging of war. But the men who survived it felt lucky just to be alive. Now I'm thinking that whatever occurred to you to leave you in such a state might very well have killed you. You could dwell on that fortunate happenstance the next time you are tempted to take out your disagreeable humors on someone who *simply wants to entertain you*."

He bowed once, and before she could make any reply he went striding off. When he got to the turning in the path, he pivoted and called back, "I'll send Alice to fetch you. Wouldn't want you to catch your death of cold out here."

Miranda watched the man disappear from view at the far end of the lake. It was minutes past that before she stopped trembling. No one had ever spoken to her in such a way. It was true that Alice was brusque with her at times, and that she and the other servants often addressed Miranda as though she were a half-wit. Sometimes she wished it were true, that her wits had been as damaged by the accident as her body. Then she wouldn't have been so aware of her limitations, of the vast, incomprehensible difference between her former life and her current existence. Existence was a good word . . . what she experienced these days was hardly a life.

Alice came eventually, wheeled her back to the house without a word, only grumbling to herself about "high-handed gentlemen." Mrs. Southey, Miranda's other caretaker, was waiting in her bedroom on the ground floor. She lifted Miranda from the chair and settled her in the bed. The two women undressed her, replacing the layers of wool with a flannel nightgown and a heavy robe. All this was accomplished without a word of conversation.

Miranda sometimes wondered if their need to swathe her in layers of clothing was an attempt to obscure her emaciated condition. She always looked nicely padded once they were through with her.

After they fed her a supper of broth and toast, Mrs. Southey brought in her glass of porter—wretched stuff—that the latest physician had promised would build up her stamina. What she required stamina for, Miranda was sure she didn't know.

The servants left her then, the bellpull pinned to her mattress within easy reach of her stiffened fingers. It was six o'clock in the evening and her day was over. Bettina and Ariadne would have only just begun changing for supper, and here she was, tucked up in bed.

There was a time shortly after the accident when Leanne, the eldest of the three sisters, would come to Miranda's room before the evening meal, to show off her newest gown or to discuss her latest beau. Miranda was still too weak to be enthusiastic, even though she'd been grateful for the company.

Then Leanne had married one of her suitors and gone off to live in Chester. Bettina and Ariadne had never given her a look-in since she'd come here. Which was not such a bad thing; even when she'd been hale and upright, Miranda found her younger cousins a trial, one more empty-headed than the other.

Their brother Ronald was another story. He at least could carry on a reasonably coherent conversation, and he'd always found ways to make her laugh. But Ronald was off fighting in Spain; he had been since just before her accident. She prayed every night for his safe delivery—out of genuine affection and also because once he returned to Palfry Park, she would again have a diversion.

She wondered if Ronald knew Mr. Pearce, if they had served together in the war. It might explain how the man came to be working with the General. Perhaps he had been a senior officer in Ronald's regiment. He certainly possessed an officer's bearing, the proud set of the shoulders, the arrogant tilt to the chin.

A pity this notion hadn't occurred to her earlier—she could

have asked Mr. Pearce for word of her cousin in Spain. They might even have gotten off to a better start.

But, no, she'd been too flustered by him to be cordial, and he'd ended up barking at her beside the lake, as though she were a raw recruit. It had been very upsetting. No one ever raised their voice in her presence. Hushed whispers were the order of the day or, more usually, complete silence.

Still, now that she could look back at it more clearly, their exchange had also been rather bracing. Nothing had so much as raised her pulse in the past three years, and then, in one brief encounter, Mr. Morgan Grambling Pearce had set her heart to thumping and her stomach to churning. She'd felt such a compelling desire to leap out of her chair and box his ears.

She smiled ruefully as she lay there in the near darkness. Mr. Pearce was safe from such retaliation on her part—she'd never, *ever* rise up from that wretched chair. Furthermore, she had a notion he'd steer clear of her in the future, which was fine with her. She certainly never wanted to see him again. Not only had he railed at her and shaken her out of her comfortably benumbed state, he had also made her feel a complete gorgon. Oh, not intentionally. He'd actually been quite kind at first.

But she was aware of how badly she suffered in comparison to even average-looking people. It had been near torture to find herself weathering the scrutiny of a man like Mr. Pearce, who was tall and well muscled, with a lean, almost fierce face and dark, vividly bright eyes. She'd felt like a wizened, withered gnome in truth. How could she not—he was her exact antithesis: robust and vital. And talkative. Mr. Pearce was very talkative.

There was a time when she'd have relished conversing with such a man, one who was educated, well traveled, most likely bookish. Papa had been bookish, God bless him. He'd passed his love of the written word to her, set her to writing essays as a child, a pursuit she'd never outgrown. Even now, she still composed passages in her mind, little snatches of insight and observation. Much good they did anyone trapped inside her head, she thought sourly.

She could not recall the last time she'd held a quill pen in her hand. Had it been the morning of her journey? Had she written a farewell note to her friend in the village, or perhaps to her beau, off studying at Cambridge? It was quite likely—she'd intended to be away from home for over a month. That morning would remain forever hazy, though; there was no one left to edify her. Her friend had never come to visit her afterward and her fickle beau had likewise found other pursuits more compelling than calling on an invalid. Miranda hadn't been back home since the day she and her parents set out. The house had been let to a merchant and she'd come here to live with her father's cousin and his family.

Three years of their benign neglect she'd endured. It could go on for decades longer, she feared. Her constitution was strong, all the physicians assured her, even if her limbs were virtually useless. Short of fasting herself into the grave, she saw no way out of her situation.

It occurred to her now that if Mr. Pearce had *truly* wanted to be kind, he'd have done well to tip her out of her Bath chair and into the deep end of the lake.

The lady would have been gratified to learn that their encounter had likewise shaken Mr. Pearce. It took fully an hour for Morgan to calm down. He spent the time on horseback, riding over the north parkland, trying to comprehend his cavalier treatment of the woman in the chair. He suspected some of his anger at the General had been deflected onto her, but that didn't begin to explain the intensity of his outburst.

It was not his habit to harangue women; there were better persuasions a man could use on the fair sex, and he was adept at most of them. Something about this woman had riled him out of his usual polished manners, enough so that he'd startled himself by mentioning Phillip to her—a matter he'd thought safely shelved far back in his brain.

He saw now, with sudden clarity, why the woman had struck such a tender nerve. She reminded him of Phillip, of course. Not only in their similar infirmities, but also in their refusal to accept even the smallest of kindnesses. Morgan feared he had made a cowhanded mess of things with his friend—although ultimately Kitty had been the one to suffer for it—and he'd be a fool, twice over, to consider coaxing this lady out of her sullen anger as he'd tried to do with Phillip. He was done with knight errantry. All he required now was a simple answer to the question of her identity. Once he was back at the house, he would send Hodges to do a little fieldwork. And that would be the end of the matter.

Chapter Three

"Jacob Runyon's daughter?" Morgan repeated as his valet helped him on with his coat.

Hodges, a rangy young man with an appealing thatch of light brown hair, nodded.

"I know that name. Runyon was an essayist. Republican sentiments and a nice way with a metaphor. I believe my uncle published a collection of his work while I was at Oxford."

"The same man," Hodges said. "Of course, you couldn't know that Runyon was a connection of Mr. Ronald's. His father's cousin to be exact. Which is why the young lady was brought to this house."

"And how did she come to be in such a wretched state?"

Hodges looked solemn. "It's all very sad. Four years ago it was . . . Miss Miranda and her parents were traveling to London, where the young lady was to speak before a literary society. It was early evening, three days out from her father's estate in Cornwall. The coachman had whipped up his team—he wanted to make the posting house before nightfall—so they were traveling at some speed when they came to the bridge."

Morgan winced.

"Not a large bridge, I am told, just a high wooden span over a small river. But a portion of the roadbed had been washed away by a severe storm. A barrier had been placed before the entrance with a sign posted to warn travelers to take the ford. That's the worst part, that there was a passable ford only a dozen yards from the bridge. But some boys had apparently moved the barrier as a prank. The Runyons' coach went across the span at a fast clip and pitched sideways down into the river, where it broke apart."

Morgan gave a low, ragged groan. "Miss Runyon was able to recall all this?"

Hodges shrugged. "Who can say? T'would be a blessing if she could not. This tale came from one of the two coachmen apparently. They both jumped clear of the coach before it fell."

"Lucky devils."

"The team of horses had also managed to stay on the bridge, so the coachmen unharnessed two of them and rode ahead to the posting house to alert the constable. Neither man thought to stay behind with the coach, they couldn't believe that anyone had survived. But when they came back, the rescue party found Miss Runyon amid the wreckage, trying to hold both her mother's and father's heads out of the water."

Morgan grimaced. He was beginning to wish he hadn't pried.

"But Jacob Runyon and his wife were both dead," Hodges said softly. "And Miss Runyon so badly injured that no one expected her to live. Yet she managed to, somehow. The local vicar's family took her in until she was well enough to travel here."

Morgan sat heavily on the edge of his bed and shook his head. "Hard to believe she's blood kin to this family. She's been relegated to the care of servants by all appearances."

"It must be difficult for the Palfrys," Hodges pointed out. "To see her in the state you described, I mean. From all reports, she was a lively, engaging young lady and something of a scribe in her own right."

"She's a wraith now," he said gruffly. "Hardly more than skin and bones. And lively only when she is crossed."

"They say in the kitchen that she never recovered her appetite and eats barely enough to keep a sparrow alive."

"And does she never take meals with the family or join them after dinner? Do her cousins read to her or try to entertain her?"

Hodges's expression darkened. "According to Daisy, the parlor maid, Miss Runyon might as well live in John O' Groats for all the attention that is paid to her by the family. A physician comes by every other month to attend to her, and she has two

caretakers, Alice and Mrs. Southey, a rather strapping woman
who is responsible for lifting her. That seems to be the extent of
the Palfrys' concern."

"It makes no sense," Morgan muttered. He sat staring into
space for a moment, then shifted his gaze back to his valet. "I
recall that before the army, Hodges, you started life as a footman. So tell me . . . back then, wouldn't you have counted
yourself lucky to be placed with a family like the Palfrys?"

Hodges's long face narrowed further as he mulled this over.
"On the surface of things, yes. They are good masters by all ac-
counts. The young ladies are never cross with their maids, Lady
Palfry is lenient with the household staff and I suspect the
grooms would lay down their lives for the General. But think,
sir, of the parable of the lost lamb."

Morgan blinked twice. "Perhaps you need to refresh my
memory."

"Well, to boil it down to basics, the good shepherd will go
off from his whole flock if even a single lamb has strayed into
danger, and then, after the lamb is recovered, the shepherd will
cherish it more than all the sheep who didn't stray."

Morgan paused an instant to sort this all out. "That's as may
be, Hodges," he said, "but the Palfrys are decent people. There
has to be an explanation for their continued neglect, something
the other servants have not told you."

He pushed up from the bed then, and after adjusting his
neckcloth in the mirror, he made for the door. "At any rate,
thank you for clearing up the mystery of the lady in the Bath
chair." He shot his valet a wry smile. "I know how distasteful
you find the pursuit of gossip."

Hodges bowed. "I suffer gladly to serve you, sir."

As he made his way to the drawing room, Morgan mulled
over Hodges's grim recounting of the coaching accident. He
felt a new pang of guilt over how he'd behaved that afternoon.
At the very least, he should seek out Miss Runyon and apologize.

It was no wonder she was peevish. She was treated like a
pariah by her family, a family that lavished affection upon one
another. He reminded himself that he might be judging the Pal-

frys unfairly. It was possible the lady had chosen her seclusion willingly. She definitely hadn't welcomed *his* attentions.

There was one thing Morgan knew with a certainty, however. Whether Miss Runyon's isolation was her own choice or theirs, the Palfrys behaved in public as though she did not exist. The family had never mentioned her presence to him, and neither had Ronald. They appeared to live their lives oblivious to, and untroubled by, the specter of tragedy that dwelled beneath their roof.

Morgan determined it would be best if he didn't mention their meeting to her family. If they chose not to acknowledge the lady, they were hardly likely to approve of him breaking with protocol. And since Morgan felt an obligation to at least apologize to Miss Runyon, the last thing he desired was the General ordering him to stay clear of her.

Still, he decided, it wouldn't hurt to do a bit of reconnoitering.

In the drawing room he seized the chance to engage Lady Palfry in private conversation while Sir Janus was occupied with his daughters, leafing through a book of landscape prints from America.

"Now that the sun's decided to favor us again," Morgan said pleasantly as they strolled the length of the room, "I've finally had the opportunity to see your home in all its glory."

She nodded. "It looks particularly fine in the springtime. Though if I may say so, every season favors it. Even in the dark of winter, the house retains a warm glow."

Morgan frowned slightly. He had to go carefully now; he didn't want to lie outright.

"I'm curious over one thing, ma'am. Your son's told me a great deal about Palfry Park . . . and so I was wondering about the female relation you have staying with you. I've been here a full week and have seen only you and your daughters about the house."

There was a hitch in Lady Palfry's graceful step. "Ronald ought not to have told you that," she said under her breath. "My husband's cousin is an invalid, the victim of a coaching accident that took her parents' lives. Out of respect for her modesty and her natural reluctance to become an object of pity, we do not encourage her to appear in public."

Morgan mustered a look of commiseration. "That is very sad. You have my condolences, ma'am."

"Yes, it's been a definite trial to us." As if she realized that her words sounded a trifle unchristian, she added hastily, "She is well looked after, I assure you."

"I am certain you do everything for her comfort." He stole a glance at his host, still poring over the book with a daughter at each elbow. "I was wondering, however, if I might make her acquaintance. Here among the family, of course. Her father's essays were published by Grambling House, you know, so I feel some connection to the Runyons. It might lift her spirits to speak of her father's work."

Lady Palfry appeared aghast at this; she quickly drew Morgan closer to the French windows.

"Please," she whispered urgently, "do not ever suggest such a thing to Sir Janus. The Runyon name is rarely mentioned in our home. It was a terrible shock to my husband—the loss of a favorite cousin and his wife. We do all we can to help him forget. Furthermore, Miss Runyon does not receive visitors under any circumstances. She is unfortunately quite horribly disfigured and also suffers from a paralysis. As I said, we do not intrude upon her privacy—just think how mortifying it would be for a gently bred young lady to witness the shocked reactions of others." She touched his sleeve. "It is ultimately a kindness, Mr. Pearce."

A kindness? Morgan fumed silently. He forced himself to maintain an expression of indifference as he assured Lady Palfry that he understood perfectly. He then asked after the state of her rose garden, which was a topic guaranteed to distract her from his earlier questions.

He and the General were still cool toward each other during the meal—only natural after their tiff in the study—but Morgan managed to dine with an almost normal show of good spirits. Afterward, Bettina played the pianoforte and Ariadne sang, both young ladies displaying a moderate amount of talent and a more than moderate amount of teeth each time they smiled at him. Which was often.

It was clear they were vying for his attention, but not ever in a spiteful or catty manner. They never did anything to make him view them in a less-than-favorable light, but he was beginning to think of them as the wicked sisters in a fairy story.

And no wonder—life had heaped a bounty of blessings upon them, yet they did not seek to share even the tiniest part of themselves with their cousin, not a crumb of their time or their attention. Of course, there was the General's order hanging over their heads, but he knew from his own wayward youth that children rarely let something as paltry as a parental edict restrain them.

He forced himself to shrug off his preoccupation with Miss Runyon when the sisters asked him to join them and their mother in a game of whist. In the middle of the first rubber, however, he was struck with the notion that their cousin might be distracted by card games. A wooden rack could be easily fashioned to hold her hand, and it would be a simple matter for another player to make her discards.

He'd have to see what sort of setup the General had for woodworking—

"Your bid, Mr. Pearce," Bettina said with a touch of asperity.

"Oh, sorry." He realized it was the second time she'd reminded him.

"You are uncommonly quiet tonight, sir," Ariadne remarked.

Her father looked up from his book by the fireside. "Leave the man alone, Addie. It's a wonder he can get a word in edgewise with the two of you chattering away." He then smiled at her to take the edge off his criticism.

Morgan studied his host, sitting so contentedly by the fire, surrounded by his adoring family. He tried to picture Miss Runyon among them . . . and could not. Her imperfections would be an affront to this dazzling room with its gilded, painted ceiling replete with crystal chandeliers, its tasteful scattering of graceful furnishings and its elegant, attractive occupants. Yet it was becoming clearer to him, minute by minute, that the lady in the Bath chair was the only truly flesh-and-blood person he had met at Palfry Park. It was not Miss Runyon who lacked substance; rather it was this wholly manufactured world of spun sugar the General had erected around him.

There was something far worse than deathwatch beetles plaguing Palfry Park, Morgan realized, recalling his first muttered impression of the place. If his instincts were correct, there was an inhumanity here that staggered the mind.

Morgan's favorable opinion of the Palfrys was now hopelessly sullied, and his first instinct was to pack up and drive back to London—and devil take the General's expectations and Ronald's spaniel eyes. But then he thought of another pair of eyes, smoky gray with indigo rims. It would be difficult to leave her, even though she had been a stranger to him until that afternoon. Yet she felt no more a stranger than the hundred or so nameless soldiers he had sat beside in an infirmary tent and coaxed through the darkest hours of night.

When he realized he had no heart to continue the game, Morgan made his excuses to the family and went off to bed.

Sleep wouldn't come, though. He kept hearing echoes of Hodges's vivid tale of the Runyons' accident. The speeding coach, the damaged bridge with its barrier gone, the horrible smashing and twisting of wood and metal. And the most visceral image, the one he absolutely could not shake, was of a gravely injured young woman fighting to keep her mother and father from drowning.

He recalled lecturing her that she should be thankful she was still alive. After hearing the details of the accident, he saw that it might have been kinder if she'd died with her parents. Such a weight of grief and loss—subsequently compounded with a disabling, disfiguring injury—was more than anyone should have to bear.

And then, to be placed among these callous souls, who could so blithely dismiss her very presence in their home, prating on about how they were saving *her* from embarrassment.

It was not in his nature to sit by and do nothing. Added to that was his still fresh anger over the General's behavior that afternoon. He knew if he sought out Miss Runyon again, he could both right a terrible wrong and get a bit of his own back.

The mere thought of this small rebellion against Sir Janus brought Morgan a rush of satisfaction. The man might have the

power to hold him here—abetted by that supposed debt to his
son—but Sir Janus was hardly omnipotent. Morgan felt it was
now within his own power to prove that point.

Yet the notion of scoring points off an arrogant old man was
childish, he told himself. Furthermore, Miss Runyon had survived three years without anyone rushing in to aid her, so why
should he imagine it was his duty to do so now? After his disaster with Phillip, he'd have to be an addlepated fool to meddle
in another person's troubles.

In the morning he would offer his regrets to Sir Janus, and
stand firm in the face of the man's objections. He'd shake the
dust of Palfry Park from his boots and drive away without a
backward glance.

Nothing could be more simple.

Morgan awoke at dawn, plucked from a wretched nightmare
by the first cock's crow.

Gad, where on earth had that *come from?* he wondered
blearily as he pushed himself upright on the mattress. He'd
been back in the war, in the thick of a fierce battle, where a
group of his men cried out to him from amid a twisted pile of
shattered wood, arms reaching for him . . . pleading with him
not to abandon them. But he had ridden away, deaf to their
cries, fleeing from the carnage.

He threw off the covers and staggered from the bed, as
though by leaving the site of bad dreams he could clear them
from his head. The draperies were open and he leaned, naked
and shivery, against the window frame, watching as the rosy
light of sunrise drove away the shades of night.

He rarely thought of the war these days and even less often
dreamed about it. His was not an overly sensitive nature, not
like Ronald's. Lord, the boy had quailed and quaked the first
time he'd heard artillery fire in the distance. Once the battle had
drawn near, Ronald Palfry had stood transfixed, unable to follow even the simplest commands. Morgan had cursed the cloth
heads in Whitehall who insisted on selling commissions to callow sprigs.

Fortunately Ronald settled down after a time. . . . Morgan
had seen to that. The lad had even had the sense to run for the

sergeant at arms the day Morgan was wounded, fetching the strapping old fellow to help drag him behind the lines.

Morgan gingerly traced his hand over the long, jagged scar that ran from the top of his hip to the crease of his left thigh. Not a life-threatening wound, Morgan had been assured by the company sawbones, even though it seemed to Morgan at the time that he was bleeding like a gutted hog. It occurred to him now that he might have bled to death there in the icy mud if Ronald had not kept his wits about him.

Maybe the infernal watchdog had saved his life after all.

And if that were the case, he had no choice but to stay on at Palfry Park. He owed Ronald a debt of honor in truth. One could even could say he owed Ronald's family. *All* of Ronald's family.

"Very well, my friend," he whispered into the first light of morning, "you shall see how I repay my debts. If I offer you a life for a life, I believe that should even the balance between us very nicely."

Chapter Four

Miranda was surprised when Mrs. Southey came to fetch her for her walk the next morning.

"Alice's busy," was all the woman would say.

"Wait." Miranda fretted as they went into the hall. "You've forgotten my lap rug."

"No rug," Mrs. Southey muttered. "Not today."

Miranda was secretly relieved—she hated the scratchy old thing—but she didn't approve of this departure from routine. The clockwork sameness of her life was one of the only things that gave her comfort any longer. As stifling as it would have seemed to her three years ago, she now clung to it and cherished it.

Awakened each morning at eight, she was bathed and dressed by nine, fed breakfast by ten. If the weather allowed, she was taken to the lower garden for a walk until noon. After being fed her luncheon, she would be settled beside her bedroom window until midafternoon, when she was taken on another walk.

Neither Alice nor Mrs. Southey made any attempts to converse with her during these excursions. They even refrained from belowstairs' gossip in her presence, so that she never knew what was occurring with the other members of the household. If not for an occasional glimpse of Sir Janus on horseback or of her female cousins driving out in the barouche, she might imagine herself the mistress of Palfry Park.

From her bedroom window she had a limited prospect—the brick wall of the kitchen garden and, beside it, a high row of hedges. She knew she had been given this room for a reason, not only because it was on the ground floor, but because its remote location at the rear of the house prevented any visitors from accidentally seeing her at her window.

She had long ago become accustomed to the notion that the Palfrys found her an embarrassment. She knew that Alice had instructions not to take her outside when there were guests in the house. It made Miranda wonder how the girl had managed to disregard the presence of Mr. Pearce. He was certainly not an easy man to overlook.

And yet here she was again today, being trundled down the allée by Mrs. Southey. Maybe the Palfrys had decided that since she'd already met up with their guest, the bull was out of the barn, so to speak.

Mrs. Southey kept on after the yew avenue, following the same path that Mr. Pearce had taken yesterday. Miranda didn't grow suspicious until they reached the lake.

There was a dark-haired man seated in the Oriental folly.

"Hold up a moment," Miranda said.

The woman ignored her, guiding the chair down past the willows and around to the far side of the lake. The closer they came to the folly, the more distressed Miranda grew.

"Please," she uttered hoarsely, "I want to go back to the house."

"Not yet."

The gentleman rose as the Bath chair stopped beside the shallow steps.

"Good day, Miss Runyon," Mr. Pearce said as he moved to the edge of the pavilion. "Would you care to come up here and share the view with me?"

"No," said Miranda, "I would not."

He sketched a motion to Mrs. Southey, who proceeded to lift her from the chair and carry her up the three steps. "No tantrums," the woman admonished as she settled her on the bench, which had been padded with cushions. There was also a small round table in the center of the space with a pack of playing cards on it.

"Thank you," Mr. Pearce said to her caretaker. "You may come for the lady in an hour or so."

"Very well." She gave Miranda a long look of warning before she went trudging off.

Mr. Pearce seated himself opposite her on a spindly wooden chair, and then shifted the table so that it lay between them.

"First of all," he said, "I need to apologize for yesterday. I spoke very much out of turn, and then abandoned you here beside the reeds . . . like a garden gnome." He looked across at her, his dark eyes beseeching. "I hope you can forgive me."

Miranda turned her head away, thankful for her veil. She would not speak to him, would not look at him. After a few minutes of one-sided conversation, he would grow bored and fetch Mrs. Southey to take her back to the house.

But she had forgotten Mr. Pearce's annoying ability to converse without any acknowledgment whatsoever.

"No, I don't blame you for ignoring me," he mused aloud. "I was particularly insensitive to your situation yesterday, taunting you with tales of men who survived and even prevailed over adversity. It was foolish to think a woman could rise to such heights. You are, after all, the weaker sex. Pointless of me to hope you might show a little grit."

He leaned forward. "Did you say something, Miss Runyon?"

She'd only barely managed to contain a growl by biting on her lip.

"I have a sister," he continued, "so I am not without some knowledge of female nature. You are willows in the wind, shunted this way and that by life's errant whims. Not a backbone among the lot of you. And so again, I am sorry. For expecting courage and strength where there can only be . . . frailty."

He shifted forward again. "I definitely heard you say something this time."

She turned her head to face him. "I was wondering where you put the shovel."

"Shovel, ma'am?"

"Because you have just dug yourself in even deeper than before."

He leaned back and gave her a sly, closemouthed smile. It

crinkled the corners of his dark eyes. "Ah, but I got you to speak to me, didn't I?"

He savored his victory for a long moment, then said, "You see, it's never a good idea to expect a man with sisters to fight fair. I've been coaxing Kitty out of the sullens for twenty years—since she was three. Impugning the abilities of females always works like a charm with her. With you as well, it seems."

"Your family history is of little interest to me."

He ran his knuckles pensively over his chin several times, as if trying to come to a decision.

"Perhaps *this* might interest you," he said, reaching into his pocket and setting an oblong wooden rack before her on the table. It was perhaps ten inches long, with a groove notched along the inside of the base.

"I made it earlier this morning in the General's workshop," he explained. "I was a fair hand with hammer and saw as a boy. I recall making a yar little boat to sail upon my father's duck pond."

While he spoke, he'd opened the pack of cards and begun to shuffle them. He now dealt out seven cards for each of them, placing Miranda's face-side toward her on the rack.

"Gin rummy," he announced, scooping up his hand. "I trust you are familiar with the game."

Miranda nearly cried out, fighting off a sudden, hurtful remembrance. But the image came to her, clear and potent. Winter nights, Papa playing rummy with her while Mama sat close by with her quilting frame, setting tiny, precise stitches. They were so merry, the three of them teasing each other, her father pretending to cheat, Miranda pretending to catch him at it. They would make Mama laugh so hard, she would miss her stitches and grumble over having to redo them. But she was never really angry; before bedtime she would make cocoa to take away the chill, always with an extra dollop of cream for Miranda's mug.

The aching sense of loss loomed up and nearly overwhelmed her. Miranda thrust it away. She would not, could not, let herself recall those happy times. It would destroy her.

"Why are you punishing me?" she groaned softly.

"How is this a punishment?" he asked in genuine perplexity.

"I . . . I am very uncomfortable." From the quaking tone of her voice, she knew he'd see the truth—that it was fear she was feeling. "If you have any gentlemanly consideration, you will leave me here and fetch Mrs. Southey."

He shook his head slowly. "No, I've done with running off. You forget I was a soldier; we don't shrink from battle."

"I don't want a battle," she said, wishing her veil was up so he could see the earnestness in her face. "I just want to be left alone."

To his credit, he did not badger her after that. He sighed a little in resignation as he gathered up her cards from the rack. "Not a bad hand," he murmured as he set them back on the stack. "Pity you won't play. Maybe tomorrow you'll be of another mind."

"That is highly doubtful."

He didn't speak after that, just shifted his chair around so that it faced the lake. In spite of her veil, she had an excellent view of his profile—the jutting nose, the strong chin and high brow, the compelling mouth that was now drawn up in a thoughtful frown. His was not a classically handsome face, but it stirred her. Something to do with the stark angle of the cheek, the intriguing hollow above the jaw.

At one point, the breeze from the lake ruffled his hair. It feathered like strands of silk, fine and fluid. It was a true black, without any hint of brown, and it waved slightly at the ends. Miranda had had beautiful hair once. It might have been her only justifiable vanity. Alice kept it brutally short now—it was easier to care for and dried quickly after her bath.

Mr. Pearce shifted in his chair, angling his arm up and setting his fist against his chin. His dove-gray coat stretched taut over his shoulder and the starched ruffle at his wrist peeked out another inch, showing creamy white against his slightly tanned skin.

She'd never seen a man so immaculate, not even her cousin Ronald. It fascinated her. She'd attended enough assemblies in Truro to pick out the aspiring dandy or hopeful macaroni. Mr. Pearce's mode of dress was much more understated, yet it drew the eye as surely as a dandy's swallowtail coat or his mile-high neckcloth. She wanted to blame her interest on the precise tailoring of his attire, which forbade even the ghost of a wrinkle, but she had a sneaking notion it was rather more the honed body beneath those custom-fitted layers of fabric that intrigued her.

Since this was by far the most scandalous thought she'd ever entertained, she fully expected to feel a blush burning its way up from her chest. That one was not forthcoming made her understand how greatly her body had betrayed her. Maidenly blushes were reserved for young ladies who could actually act out their brazen yearnings, at least when a proper suitor came along. Blushes were clearly of no use to crippled invalids who would never live out any yearnings, brazen or otherwise.

She began to hate Morgan Pearce for bringing her to that realization.

Minutes passed and still he said nothing, just sat there, very much at ease, staring out over the serene water of the lake. She wondered if he knew she was watching him, if he had retained that soldier's trick of sensing when he was being observed by the enemy.

He had said he would try again tomorrow. It made her think of the way he had arranged things this morning, and she was immediately curious about how he had gotten Mrs. Southey to do his bidding.

"How much did it cost you to bribe her?" she said all at once.

He didn't pretend to misunderstand. He turned to her with a guileless, unapologetic stare. "Half a crown."

"A paltry sum, considering she is risking her place by going against the General's wishes."

"Why would you think that?"

"I am not stupid, sir. I know he does not want me mingling with his guests." She tipped her head toward him. "Unless you have gotten his permission to meet with me . . ."

"No, he knows nothing about it. Not worth troubling him over it, I imagine. After all, I played whist with his daughters last night, he can hardly object to my playing rummy with his cousin today." He gave her an icy smile. "You are the one doing all the objecting, ma'am. And very little playing."

She put her head back. "I will give Mrs. Southey a whole crown if she leaves me in my room tomorrow."

He shrugged. "That might work. Though I suspect she didn't bring you out here for the money."

"Oh, you're thinking it was because she gets more free time for herself when I am not inside the house?"

"No, I meant that she worries over you being alone so much of the time—"

"Nonsense!"

He hitched one shoulder. "You would know best."

Of course she would know best, Miranda repeated to herself.

Mrs. Southey had never expressed any concern over her. She was taciturn and gruff, though never as openly belittling as Alice. Truth to tell, Miranda preferred Mrs. Southey's attentions to the younger maid's. Alice was sullen when carrying out her duties and frequently lax over Miranda's appearance, as though she knew it didn't matter one whit how her charge looked. Mrs. Southey, on the other hand, was most attentive, making sure she was pristine at all times. The woman would brush her cap of hair morning and night, and smooth lotion onto her limbs. That these actions were an expression of affection or concern had never occurred to Miranda.

She mulled this over in silence until Mrs. Southey herself came to fetch her. Mr. Pearce rose and followed them down the steps.

"Same time tomorrow," he said to her caretaker.

"Yes, sir," she replied.

"And I think perhaps we can dispense with the veil."

"Certainly, sir."

Miranda opened her mouth to protest this high-handed re-ordering of her life, but she was already being propelled away from the folly. She fumed in silence all the way back to the house.

The next morning, the routine was repeated. It did no good to scold Mrs. Southey or to threaten her with dismissal. Miranda knew she was no better than a cloth doll, easily carted about and set in place at anyone's whim. And for some unfathomable reason, Mr. Pearce's whim was to plague her with his presence.

He met them at the entrance to the pavilion, and again directed Mrs. Southey to place her on the bench. This morning he was dressed for riding, in a coat of deepest claret worn over oyster-colored buckskins. Miranda forced herself not to notice the length and contours of his thighs, but when he seated himself opposite her, she could hardly overlook the way his legs stretched out under the table, his boot soles only inches away from her slippers.

Anger and humiliation coursed through her. His posture was a mockery—no man would sit before a woman he respected in such a slouching, offhand way. Not that she'd been a stickler for manners back in Cornwall—she was something of a sloucher herself at the end of a long day on horseback. But this man galled her with every word and action, and she had no trouble finding fault with his current pose.

Her irritation was so great, that her right foot jabbed out at the sole of his boot. "You could at least have the courtesy to sit upright."

He seemed taken aback, cocking his head so he could peer under the table at her legs.

"And stop that!" she added.

He smirked at her as he drew himself upright, removing the offending limbs from beneath the table. "As you desire, ma'am."

He took up the cards and went through the same motions as yesterday, shuffling, then dealing out her hand onto the rack.

"Do you want that discard?" he asked as he leaned back, his eyes probing her face.

She turned her head away, feeling exposed and vulnerable without her veil or the sheltering hood of the chair. Surely he could not want to look at her; she was a horror.

She'd only seen her face once, soon after the accident, when one of the vicar's servants had inadvertently carried her past a hall mirror. But that brief glimpse had sufficed. She still cringed at what she'd seen—her mouth swollen beyond recognition, her left eye a mere slit, the cheek beneath it smashed and scabbed over. She was aware that some of the swelling had gone down over time, but she knew from the doctors that her left cheek had been permanently damaged. She still had little feeling on that side of her face.

No, this man could have no interest in looking at her.

Finally she broke her own vow of silence. "Why did you ask Mrs. Southey to take away my veil?"

"It is difficult to converse with a person when you can't see their eyes."

"Yet surely it is a hardship to look upon my face. I nearly swooned the one time I saw it back in Warfield."

His mouth narrowed. "It is no hardship, I promise you. You could do with a bit more flesh on you, if I may be so blunt, but there is nothing there to cause dismay."

He'd spoken in an offhand manner, but his meaning was clear. Was it possible she was not quite so monstrous as she'd thought?

"I have a dent in my cheek," she said with a stern frown.

"Yes, you do," he agreed softly. Setting his elbows on the table, he leaned in closer. "And yet I barely perceive it."

She wanted to name him a liar, but something in his expression stopped her. His eyes were full of concern, without any hint of cozening.

"'Pon my honor, Miss Runyon," he added, "you exaggerate the effect."

"And what if I tell you that I am no more comfortable than I was yesterday? Perhaps even less so. Will you call Mrs. Southey to me?"

"No."

"Suppose I say that you are bullying me."

"You may say whatever you like." He returned to studying his cards, humming a little as he rearranged them in his hand. Then he looked up and caught her staring at him. "The thing of it is, ma'am, I enjoy a challenge. The more you resist, the greater my pleasure. If you want to make me truly miserable, just humor me. I wager I'll soon grow bored if you do."

"Is that how you see me? As . . . as some sort of project to while away an hour or two? Or are you merely doing this to tweak the General?"

"Not at all, though I fancy your cousin could use a good

tweaking. The truth is, I am beginning to find Palfry Park a bit stifling. This is my way of escaping all that perishing perfection for a time."

"Because I am so imperfect, you mean?"

He gave her a toothy smile. "Perfection is really very . . . boring, don't you think? And the Palfrys are one bland dish. You, Miss Runyon, add a bit of salt to the mix. Or spice, if you like. I believe you possess that quality in full measure."

Again, Miranda wasn't sure if he was complimenting her or insulting her. This was the oddest conversation she'd ever had. Especially since she'd not intended to have *any* conversation with him. She had the inspired notion that if she pretended to fall asleep, he would have to leave her in peace until Mrs. Southey arrived. She gave a mighty yawn and tucked her head to one side, pretending to doze.

Within a minute, though, she got such an awful crick in her neck, and when she opened her eyes, he was wearing a curious half smile. It seemed so benign, that smile, but she knew he was assessing her, measuring her.

"Resistance is pointless," he said, and then nodded meaningfully toward her chair. "I hold all the cards, so to speak."

"Yes, you find in me the truly captive audience," she purred, then added with a sneer, "How lucky for you, since I expect few others can keep from fleeing away in horror once you begin to natter on and on . . . *and on*."

He laughed, low in his throat, and ducked his head once in acknowledgment of her hit. "You do bring that out in me, strangely. I am accounted a terse fellow by most who know me."

"How fortunate that I alone get to see this new side of you."

His face sobered at once. "Is it really that hateful to you? Would you truly prefer to spend all your time with sullen servants?"

"It is what I am used to."

He was studying her face again, his eyes intent, and she found herself surprisingly less edgy this time. When he spoke, his voice was soft, thoughtful. "I gather you aren't much accustomed to being with others. You might even prefer things that way. But I believe solitude eventually leeches away a person's soul. It is why even hardened criminals quake at being confined alone."

"I do not quake. I prefer to be left alone."

"No," he countered with a touch of irritation. "The Palfrys have chosen to leave you alone and you have merely adapted to it. You notice I do not say 'made the best of it,' because you must be the first to admit that is not the case."

She put her chin up. "You are mistaken; I have a very rich inner life."

"Hogwash!" he shot back, his irritation now full blown. "And even if it is true, your outer life is miserable. It makes me furious to hear your cousins prate about their benevolent acts in town, their sick calls and work with the church. They are so proud of what they have done afield, when here at home they have a perfectly good opportunity to—"

"To what?" she demanded sharply. "Look after their own charity case? Let me tell you, Mr. Pearce, I am no one's charity case. All my expenses are borne by my lawyer in Truro. For your information, I came into a tolerable inheritance at my father's death *and* a fine estate on the Cornish coast."

He half rose as he barked out, "Then why the devil are you not there in your own home? God knows you could hire someone more agreeable than Alice to look after you." He sank back to chair and added with less heat, "Surely the comfort of strangers would be preferable to the obvious neglect of your kin."

She had an answer for that, but no intention of sharing it with him.

She would never to return to Nasrannah. In her mind, that possibility had ceased to exist, as if the sprawling old house had come tumbling down and crumbled into a roiling sea.

Yet there were times at night, just before she fell asleep, when she would hear again the familiar sound of the waves sighing against the rocks, and the mewing of the gulls that followed the fishing boats home to the village below the house. Those nights she cried herself to sleep with bitter, scalding tears.

He was cruel to remind her . . . that the house still sat waiting for her, unhappy with its staid tenants who did not cherish it as her parents had, who did not bring the garden inside by the armful or fill it with music and laughter and love—so that an aura of harmony positively shimmered through its sun-washed halls.

But what was the good of returning to a house when the lives that gave it all meaning and purpose had been obliterated?

Mr. Pearce didn't say anything, but sat with his body canted slightly forward in his chair, one hand curled against his brocaded waistcoat.

At last he said gently, "Memories can be the very devil."

When he reached forward and placed a folded handkerchief into her hand, she looked at it in puzzlement—until she realized she'd been sniffling. She clutched at the fabric and tried to raise it to her eyes, concentrating on the effort.

He *tsked* slightly as he rose from his chair and slid beside her on the bench. "Here, better let me do that." He dabbed lightly at her eyes. "I believe your grasp exceeds your reach."

Miranda chuckled in spite of herself. It was something she'd not heard in years—the lilting sound of her own amusement.

Mr. Pearce did not comment on this victory, though she was sure he was aware of it. He merely returned to his chair, set his elbows on the table and pointed to the playing cards. "Now, do you want this discard? No? Then I shall take it." He made his own discard and waited for her to ask for a card.

"I cannot do this," she cried. "I don't know what imp has gotten into you, that you think you need to make me your cause, but I have not asked for your aid and I do not like it."

He acted as though she hadn't spoken, merely leaned over to peer at the cards on her rack, his brow furrowing as he muttered, "Two fours, two eights, a seven, a nine and a queen. Hmm, let's forfeit the lady, shall we?"

He continued on in this vein, making her selections and discards for her. She spent the time forcing herself not to watch him, trying to dampen her awareness of the masculine grace and power he conveyed in spite of his frivolous preoccupation with a card game.

"That's twice you've bested me," he said as he jotted the score on a gold-encased notepad.

"This is a farce," she grumbled. "You can see my cards, so

you are feeding me the ones I need to make gin. And I don't appreciate anyone letting me win."

"Then play your own hand, Miss Runyon," he said brusquely. "Else I'll start impugning womankind again, and how sad it is that they need help to beat a man at anything."

Before she could respond, Mrs. Southey appeared on the lake path.

Has it been an hour already? Miranda wondered. Perhaps the woman had decided to take pity on her.

"Tomorrow, Mrs. Southey," Mr. Pearce said. "And no mitts next time, I think."

The woman's face narrowed. "I don't—"

"I believe I know what we're dealing with here," he said evenly.

"Very good," she replied as she turned Miranda's chair about.

"Good-bye, Miss Runyon," he said. "And, please, feel free to keep my handkerchief."

Miranda realized it was still lying balled up in her lap. With a chuff of irritation, she swatted out awkwardly with her arm and sent the crumpled linen scudding into the reeds.

She was facing away from Morgan, so she didn't see the intense look of satisfaction that lit his eyes or the narrow smile of self-congratulation that curled his mouth.

Morgan lit up a cheroot and tipped back in the spindly chair, propping his boots on the carved railing. He was feeling fairly pleased with himself at the moment. It didn't require the trained eye of a physician to see that Miss Runyon was not completely paralyzed; he wondered if paralysis even entered into it.

When he was a boy, his maiden great-aunt had come to stay with his family. She had taken to her bed that first winter, complaining of a variety of ailments, and refused to get up, not even to use the garderobe. By spring, she had virtually lost the use of her legs. Her arms, likewise, had grown feeble and flaccid.

It took the cry of "Fire!" from beyond her chamber to rouse her from her bed. She had managed to totter to the hallway stairs before Morgan's father discovered him in the adjoining bedroom, fanning a small, smoky blaze in a tin bucket.

Morgan had received a proper whipping over that prank, but it had been worth it. Aunt Bertha never did go back to her bed. So far as he knew she was still alive . . . hale and crusty, camped out with some Scottish relations.

He drew in the aromatic tobacco smoke and then held up the cheroot to observe its glowing tip. He'd made a good start at lighting a fire under the stubborn Miss Runyon. A little more fuel each day, he calculated, and before long he'd make a blaze so big, she'd be able to burn that blasted Bath chair in its flames.

Moran and the General still had not made peace with each other after their brangle earlier in the week, but Morgan refused to tiptoe around the man. He'd come here to do a job and he would see it through. When he went to the study later that morning, however, he found his host deep into a new chapter, his pen slashing over the page like a fury.

"Later, Pearce," he muttered without looking up. "We'll go over this bit after nuncheon."

Happy for the reprieve, Morgan took himself off to the library and sat down to write a note to his uncle. Morgan wasn't about to embark on this campaign without arming himself with some practical knowledge, and Cyrus Grambling was just the person to locate the most up-to-date medical texts in London. The last thing Morgan wanted was to cause further harm to Miss Runyon.

He had to admit, though, that in spite of the damage to her body, her mind was unimpaired. Enough spirit lurked behind those gray-blue eyes to give him hope that she would soon learn to fight back against her limitations instead of against him.

He sealed the note and carried it out to the hall. His uncle might think it an odd request, but he would relish the chance to be doing something useful again. He'd been forbidden the publishing house by his physician, but Morgan didn't think it would be too taxing for him to hunt down a few books. Cyrus would be relieved to be back in his own element.

Which led Morgan to wonder what Miss Runyon's own element might be. Hodges had mentioned a literary society. That made sense, considering her father's facility with the written word. He seriously doubted she had kept up with her writing—it was difficult to picture her dictating her thoughts to Alice or Mrs. Southey.

She must miss it like the very devil, he thought.

He'd have to see about remedying that.

Miranda spent the afternoon in her room—watching a pair of thrushes build a nest in the hedgerow beyond her window. She enjoyed the sight of them working so well in tandem.

Her parents had been such a pair, supporting each other in all their concerns. Her mother would read her father's essays aloud in her lilting, West Country voice, and her father would help Mama sort through her fabric patches when she was planning a new quilt. Some nights they argued over political matters, incisively, often heatedly, yet always with fond tolerance. When Miranda's occasional pranks earned her a rebuke, they faced her together. It made her understand how perfectly aligned they were, even in carrying out the onerous duties of parenthood.

The greatest thing they shared, which they'd early on conveyed to Miranda, was their deep belief in magic. Not the paltry sort that humans performed to amuse their fellows, but rather the magic of place, the sort that was sunk deep in stone and that rose up from woodland and field and rocky cove.

Miranda doubted that anyone born in Cornwall did not feel those emanations, but her parents had made it their special quest to gather everything they could—books, folk tales, songs and poems—relating to the mystical history of the duchy. Paintings and woodcuts of Arthur and Merlin adorned the walls of Nasrannah, the shield of Pendragon hung above the fireplace in the library. It had been a fanciful, wondrous house to grow up in, where both parents had encouraged her to expand the limits of her imagination and to exalt in the magic that drifted upon the Cornish air currents like rich, yellow pollen.

She used to believe there was magic everywhere; that one had only to seek with the senses to find it. But there was no magic at Palfry Park, though as a child she'd thought there was. She now knew the magic she'd felt had come, not from any particular place or any particular past, but from her mother and father. It was their rare bond, their deep love, that had created it.

She realized now, with a jolt, how unbearable it would have been for either of her parents to have lost the other. Being taken together had spared them that pain.

Miranda was not a sentimentalist; it never occurred to her that they were watching over her or guiding her. Along with her belief in magic, any notions of God or heaven had departed her life the instant her father's coach careened off the damaged bridge. Yet for the first time since the accident, she felt herself being watched over by some benevolent spirit—although she could not say who or what it was.

Of course there was that other malevolent entity that kept her in its hawklike gaze—Morgan Grambling Pearce. For three days now she had been forced to suffer his badgering.

She had to be more resolute and make herself ignore him. Even if he talked the whole time they were together—and she never doubted he was capable of such a thing—she would force herself not to respond. She would be like the martyrs of old who refused to recant their faith. An apt metaphor, since Mr. Pearce's probing and provocative questions truly were akin to torture.

She had only one thing with which to combat him, and that was her strength of will. Her body might be feeble, but her brain and determination were as hale as ever. He'd learn that. And then, she prayed, he would go away.

Chapter Five

"I've something to report, sir," Hodges announced later that night as he was readying Morgan for bed. "I had it from Daisy. It appears Miss Runyon does not know that her cousin Ronald is returned from Spain. Her servants have been keeping the news from her on the General's orders."

Morgan stopped in midmotion with his shirt half over his head. "But she must know. . . . Ronald visited here over Christmas."

"Perhaps the General also ordered him to keep away," Hodges ventured as he moved forward to aid his master. "Though I find that hard to credit. According to Daisy, she and Mr. Ronald were always close—he often summered with her family in Cornwall. Still, the old man might not have wanted his son to discover how he's neglected Miss Runyon."

"The General doesn't view this as neglect," Morgan reminded him. " 'It is ultimately a kindness,' to quote Lady Palfry. He believes he has nothing to hide."

"But the General must feel *some* guilt over it, sir. Else why does no one upstairs ever speak of her? I can tell you, she is prime fodder at the servants' table."

"Well, you know how it is with generals. After sending so many men to face death, they quickly develop a hard-nosed resistance to guilt." He added with a wan smile, "It was one of the things we soldiers loved about Wellington—that he still mourned openly for his fallen men."

He was lost in reminiscence for a moment, but then his face clouded. "Still, I can't believe Ronald is a party to all this. Was he addlebrained to send me up here? Did he think I wouldn't come across Miss Runyon?"

Hodges shrugged as he drew a dressing gown from the wardrobe. "Apparently, any number of people have stayed here and not come across the lady. Her servants do not take her outside if there are guests in residence. The only reason you met her that afternoon was because Alice is mooning about after one of the grooms, and she wanted an hour to herself. She thought to leave Miss Runyon hidden in the lower garden and run off to the stables after young Barkin."

"Another little twist of fate," Morgan said with a theatrical sigh. "My life seems to be ordained by such things."

Hodges winced as Morgan reached for the robe. The sight of the jagged scar on his master's flank always gave him a start. They'd come very near to losing the major that day.

"Will you tell her, sir, that her cousin has returned?"

Morgan shook his head as he slipped into the dressing gown. "It's a choice between letting her fret over Ronald's safety or seeing her hurt by his defection. I think the former would ultimately be less painful."

His valet moved toward the door, and then paused. "There's something else, something Daisy said earlier. Your Miss Runyon has never seen herself since she came here. There are no mirrors in her room or in the hallway she passes through to the garden. From what you have told me, sir, she thinks herself a monstrosity."

"How can she not? She apparently only saw herself early on, when she probably *was* a bit monstrous, and since the family continues to avoid her, she believes she has not improved. It's illogical. . . . I mean, how can she use them as a barometer, when they haven't seen her for three years? But there is rarely logic to one's worst fears."

"There is another parable . . ."

Morgan raised one brow. "Why am I not surprised? Don't tell me you've taken a preacherly turn, Hodges."

The man blushed. "Not since I traded chapel for the army, but I do recall the Bible saying that hiding one's light under a bushel is a wrongful thing."

"And am I to be the . . . the bushel remover?"

Hodges grinned. "None better for the job, sir."

                          *   *   *

If Morgan thought Miss Runyon would soon mellow, their next encounter proved him dead wrong. He could not elicit a response from her on any topic; she merely stared unseeing into space, to the point where he wondered if she'd been drugged with laudanum. Except that he knew from Mrs. Southey that she was never given any tonics or nostrums except for a daily glass of porter.

He purposely avoided staring at her uncovered hands, which she kept buried in the folds of her skirt, but he managed to see enough. They were not desiccated as he'd feared, but the inert fingers did curve inward toward her palm.

After ten minutes of talking to himself, he wanted to shake her. After another ten minutes of mutual silence, he wanted to shake himself. What stray idiocy had convinced him to make her his cause? He could be riding out over the estate at this moment on the General's excellent horseflesh. He could be out making calls with the Palfry sisters, sitting down to tea and cake in some pretty parlor that overlooked the blue-green rise of Scafell Pike.

But, no, those were no longer options. He had promised himself that he would see this through, knowing it would not be an easy road. Three years of neglect had withered this broken blossom, and he was not a miracle worker that could revive her in a few days' time.

After half an hour had passed, he pushed up from his chair and went to sit beside her on the bench. This needed a bold stroke—and he had nothing to lose.

He reached down and took up her left hand. It sat unmoving in his palm, weightless as a dead, furled leaf. Someone, probably Mrs. Southey, had trimmed her nails to neat half-moons. She made no sound during his examination, but kept her head rigidly turned away from him.

He stroked his forefinger along her palm. No response. He tried to form her fingers into a fist, but they unclenched the instant he released the pressure.

"Fight back," he murmured. "You know you want to. You are longing to box my ears for being so forward. Or perhaps you'd rather fetch me a leveler square on the chin. I bet you were a little pepper pot when you were young. Kept Ronald under your thumb, I imagine, and bossed him unmercifully. No wonder he's not been to see you in the six months since he returned from Spain—"

Her fingers curled tight around his hand.

He waited until her grip relaxed, then set her hand again in her lap.

"Sorry," he said as he rose. "That was a low blow and I apologize. I had not meant to tell you . . . but I needed to say something that would get a reaction out of you."

Her head jolted up, eyes blazing. "Why, sir? Why is getting a reaction from me so important to you?"

"It's not important to me, Miss Runyon. It's important to you. This lamb's wool you've been swaddled in by your misguided relations has been more prison than protection."

"Yes, you're very clever with words. I could almost admire that in you, if I didn't find everything else about you detestable."

Morgan nearly reeled back at the harshness of her tone. "Detestable? Have I ever treated you as though you were inferior to me? No, I rather think I have treated you as an equal, as my peer. How is that detestable?"

"You inflict your company on me!" she cried. "And badger me and provoke me and . . . and bribe my servants to do your will. Bad enough to be the object of your pity, but it is a hundred times worse to be the object of your misplaced gallantry."

He sank onto his chair and stared at her. "You reject kindness, then?"

"I reject finding myself always at your mercy, just so you can congratulate yourself for being some sort of wretched, righteous, busybodying do-gooder."

Morgan gave a grunt of frustration and said, almost under his breath, "And yet you don't say a word against those who have abandoned you . . . but instead target me for your anger."

He felt like the poor fisherman of legend, who freed the imprisoned genie from the bottle only to receive his stored wrath rather than his gratitude.

She broke into his fanciful musing. "Can you deny that your attentions to me serve your own needs far more than they answer mine?"

"*My* needs? You little ingrate, I am devoting my mornings to you."

"And I am clueless as to why. Nobody makes time for strangers, not without some ulterior motive."

"I thought I was being generous, even selfless."

"When people are being truly selfless, they do not brag of the fact."

Well, she had him there.

Morgan fought off a frown, discarding the urge to tell her about Phillip, about his failure on that front. The subject still pained him too much. Instead, he fell back on the Ronald mythos.

"Maybe this will help you understand. Your cousin Ronald did me a service in Spain, one that placed me in his debt. It is why I am here working with the General. My interest in you is merely an offshoot of that. Furthermore, Sir Janus expects me to stay on until his book is completed, so you might consider that I, too, am a captive of Palfry Park."

She eyed him dubiously. "You have two legs, sir, in working order. You can leave this place at any time."

"No. I am bound by my honor to stay."

"A trifling reason, if I may say so."

His face narrowed. "Not to a gentleman."

"And if you do remain here for as long as my cousin requires, will you continue to harass me with these unwanted attentions?"

"Most assuredly."

Mrs. Southey came up the path at this point. He waved her away just as Miranda called out sharply for her to stay.

"There you are wrong, Mr. Pearce," Miranda said as the woman stood wavering with indecision at the foot of the pavilion. "I won't be here tomorrow. Or ever again. I've decided to complain to Sir Janus about your . . . attentions."

He raised one brow. "Indeed? And how will you accomplish such a thing? Shall you tell him during his daily look-in? Or confide it to his daughters when they seek you out for a cozy, cousinly chat?"

"I will dictate a note to him," she proclaimed. "Mrs. Southey is able to write well enough for my purposes."

His gaze shifted to the woman. "Would you abet her in such a thing?"

"Perhaps, sir."

"What if I were to offer you two guineas to refuse? I'll throw in another guinea if you convince the other servants not to aid her."

She thought for a moment, then bobbed her head. "Done, sir."

Miranda was almost inarticulate with rage. It was one thing for him to cozen her servants behind her back, but here was bold-faced manipulation. She wracked her brain for some way to combat him as Mrs. Southey carried her to the chair. Before she could form a defense, he motioned the woman away with a curt wave, then stood looking down at her with a tight expression on his face.

"You don't care for that, do you, Miss Runyon? It's distressing to find yourself increasingly at the mercy of everyone, even trusted servants."

"Even strangers," she shot back. "Especially strangers."

She wondered if she should feel afraid; a look of pure deviltry burned in his dark eyes.

"And there is nothing you can do to fight back, is there?" he continued in that soft, ominous voice.

She drew in a badly needed breath and blurted out, "I shall complain to the doctor when he comes next to visit me."

"Ah, but that's weeks away."

"I will stop eating. Then they will have to call him."

"No, they will hold you down and force you to eat."

He went down on one knee before the chair and took hold of the woven armrests. "So it comes to this. You will meet with me for an hour each morning and behave graciously—if that is at all possible for a woman determined to have the word 'shrew' engraved large on her tombstone—and you will fall in with my whims. If I wish to play cards, you will play. If I wish to converse, you will respond. Whatever I wish, you will do."

"You have no leverage with me," she cried. "No means of forcing me to do your will."

"Haven't I?" he said and drew the chair a few inches closer. "While it's true there is nothing I can take from you that has not already been stolen away by circumstance, there is something I can offer."

"I am not interested in anything you might offer me. Unless it is to go away—permanently."

He sighed. "Were you this much of a trial to your teachers? I wonder you managed to achieve any schooling at all. Yet I am assured that you are your father's true daughter, a skilled essayist in your own right. Perhaps your teachers had more patience than I do because you allowed them to see your true metal." He smiled sadly. "All I see is dross, ma'am. It is all you allow anyone to see, I fear."

She'd been purposely looking away from him, concentrating on the tiny pinpoints of sunlight filtering through the wicker hood. He now took her chin in his hand.

"Look at me, ma'am. And listen. I will make a bargain with you. If you do as I ask, I will promise to send for Ronald Palfry."

She tugged back from his touch and snapped, "What do I care for Ronald Palfry? Not one letter in three years have I had from him. Not even a note of condolence. And now, to learn that he's been in London for months without sending me word. I was deceived to think well of him. He's proven himself to be just another fickle friend."

He surprised her by declaring, "Ronald is an idiot. But that's neither here nor there. I have the power to bring him to your side, if that's what you wish."

She glared up at him. "I wish to be left alone. Clearer than that, I cannot say."

He pushed up from the chair and paced a little way down the path. When he turned back to her, his face bore a sly smile.

"Very well, you shall have your wish. And I myself will carry a note to Sir Janus complaining of my impertinence and my interference . . . providing you write it in your own hand."

"You are mad!"

He grinned. "I've heard that before. Still, the offer remains. If you want me to leave you in peace, it only requires that you pick up a pen and scratch out a few words." He cocked his head. "Shall I send your woman to fetch ink and paper?"

"You're mocking me," she sobbed. "It's horrible. Do you

taunt your friend who lost his leg to race with you, or badger the one with the injured arm to wrestle with you? No, I think not. Then why do you tease me over things I can no longer do? Why, Mr. Pearce?"

He reached out and stroked the back of his hand lightly across her cheek. "Because someone has to, Miss Runyon," he said in an odd, rasping voice. "Someone has to raise the bar . . . or you will never test your limits. And that would be such a damn shame."

Good God, how she hated him. And herself. How dare he touch her? How dare she like it?

For hours that night she'd tossed in her bed, flinging herself about under the weighty covers. Her body was so overwhelmed with a rambunctious agitation, that for a time she completely forgot her paralysis.

Now she lay exhausted, but still unable to sleep. The confused, complex feelings kept returning to her, no matter how often she thrust them away.

How gently he had held her hand . . . how tenderly he had caressed her face. It made her want to cry. It made her want to shriek in outrage.

No one had touched her that way in so very long; the sensations nearly scorched her.

Alice, Mrs. Southey, the various doctors . . . when they tended her their hands were cool and impersonal. For twenty-one years before that she had basked in the warmth of human touch—hugs and fond kisses from her parents, cousinly roughhousing from Ronald. She and her friend Clara would walk arm in arm through the village. Her beau, Francis, would hold her hand, nuzzle her hair, and on several memorable occasions, he'd actually kissed her. She'd liked the kissing part very much.

At least, she thought sadly, she'd had some small chance to experience that. There would be no more kissing in her future. Or any sort of intimacy. No strong arm around her back to lead her through the steps of a dance, no wide shoulder to lean on as she stood at the top of the sea cliffs. No hand clasping hers, warm and firm, as she climbed up the rocky path from the beach. Who would want to hold a misshapen claw?

In anger, she forced her right arm up and bit viciously at the knot that tied the muslin bag to her wrist. When it came free, she tugged the cloth away and observed the useless hand in the firelight.

It had been a very nice hand once. Papa always said she had her mother's pretty hands, deft and delicate. When they weren't allover grubby from the stables, he would add with a wink. Now the fingers curved inward, the tendons showing ugly beneath the frail layer of skin.

Experimentally, she forced herself to flex them into a full fist. And then spread them flat on the bed. She did this six times. It took nearly ten minutes and she was sweating from the exertion. Still, the final time she swore it required less strength and concentration.

Could she eventually hold a quill? Could she muster the dexterity to write a few sentences on a page? However much he vexed her, she believed Morgan Pearce was a man of his word. All she had to do was write down her complaint, and she trusted it would reach Sir Janus.

Dear Cousin, she composed in her head. *Your guest, Mr. Pearce, has greatly distressed me with his attentions. I entreat you that he be forbidden to see me or speak to me, that I might return to my normal—*

Her normal *what*? Life? Pursuits? What was there for her to return to, save the solitude of her room and the company of dour servants? And how had it come to this, that her familiar, regulated existence was now the greater of two evils? How had that sly, controlling man managed to make his irksome company preferable to the calm serenity of her former life?

She felt the urge to cry, to react with tears to the unpleasant sensation of being caught between the proverbial rock and a hard place—Mr. Pearce being the rock.

Instead, she rallied herself and did another two-dozen hand exercises.

Chapter Six

Kitty found the letter from Morgan lying half open on her uncle's desk in the study, where she had gone to look for a penknife. She'd already received a letter from her brother explaining that General Palfry had coerced him to stay on. She humphed again at the notion, as though Morgan were a lamb to be led anywhere against his will. It was all the work of that dashed, interfering Ronald Palfry—she just knew it.

Giving in to temptation, she picked up her uncle's letter and scanned it. What nonsense was this about medical texts? She prayed Morgan wasn't still wasting his time trying to help Phillip. There was no help for that one.

She set the letter aside and began to sharpen her pen, using a great deal more force than was necessary. It still rankled her that Morgan had abandoned her just when she needed him most. However was she to manage all the arrangements for the upcoming wedding? She'd still not ordered any of her bride clothes, afraid she'd make some fatal error in style or color without Morgan's sure eye to guide her. She recalled the riding habit he had given her for her sixteenth birthday—a vibrant poppy color with intricate jet buttons. When she'd worn it, all the young men in the neighborhood called her Diana and Hippolyta . . . and . . . *Oh God!*—with a sob she threw down her pen and spun away from the desk. She was sick to death of thinking about gowns and bonnets and silly furbelows. What did any of it matter now?

He had never cared how she looked, whether she dressed in the height of fashion or hung about in an out-of-date frock. Why, the very first time he'd seen her she was fresh from the dairy barn with straw in her hair and her tucker half off her throat.

He had ridden up the drive of Roselinden on a raking bay hunter and found her idling in the lane. She'd looked up at him, towering above her with the sun on his face, and all her usual glibness had drained away. She'd yet to meet a male she couldn't cozen with a few sweet words and a seductive look, yet this young man struck her silent. Even her graceful, ever-fluttering hands hung limp at her sides.

After he'd swept off his hat and introduced himself as her brother's friend from Oxford, her first conscious thought was, "No wonder Morgan thinks himself a commonplace."

Phillip DeBurgh was cut from a heroic mold, large-framed, muscular and impossibly tall. The face that gazed down at her could have graced a Roman sculpture. The same high-bridged nose, the same heavy-lidded eyes. And somehow the grin that quirked his wide mouth and the amusement that lit his clear blue eyes only added to the impression of a classical statue come appealingly to life. His hair gleamed like a polished horse chestnut, and she had such a desire to touch that lustrous cap, to set her fingers over that wide mouth and feel the warmth of his breath on her skin.

She was barely turned sixteen, but the sight of Phillip De-Burgh made her feel like a woman of great age and wisdom. She knew instantly the sum of all the yearnings and desires a woman could experience in a lifetime, and she knew, further, that here in the lane before her was the answer to every one of them.

Of course, being in truth a young and callow female, she decided not to let him see how smitten she was. Instead, she turned up her nose and informed him pertly that Morgan and her father were away from the house and that he'd do better to come calling another time.

He did not seem at all flustered by her frosty manner. He looked off toward the house and said musingly, "Do you think they'll set the dogs on me if I hang about for a bit? I mean, since I've already had the pleasure of meeting the resident cat, the hounds can't be far behind."

So he had a brain, did he? She liked that. Everyone in her

family—on the Grambling side, at least—was clever in a bookish way. *She* even read an improving volume from time to time,
when she wasn't escaping into the world of Walter Scott and
Thomas Mallory.

She told him she was completely indifferent to his future
plans—she recalled that scathing line from a delicious novel
she'd just finished—but added that she supposed he could wait
on the terrace until her brother returned.

"I have my own duties to attend to," she announced as she
began to move away from him. "So you needn't think I can
spare the time to entertain you."

"I promise you've already entertained me plenty," he said
softly and a bit cryptically.

She stopped and turned. "And what is that supposed to
mean?"

He dismounted and came toward her, leading his horse.
"Morgan warned me that his little sister was a force to be reck-
oned with. Only he neglected to tell me even the smallest detail
of your appearance. So how was I to know that the breath
would be knocked right out of my body?"

"Oh." She was dumbstruck for several seconds as this ultimate compliment flitted from brain to belly and then rippled in
a delightful shiver down her spine. She felt, at once, muzzy-
headed, hollowed out and wobbly at the knees.

"But please," he continued, "don't let me keep you from
your responsibilities. You are chatelaine here, I understand, so
you must find yourself working tirelessly from dawn till dusk."

Since she had just whiled away an hour in the dairy with the
barn cat's latest litter of kittens—and looked it—and was at
present deciding where to settle herself with her sketchbook—
which was tucked under one arm—she suspected him of some
sarcasm. Yet his face was without guile.

"I could perhaps see to it that you receive some refreshment
while you wait," she said, mustering an ounce of graciousness.

She motioned him to follow her as she set off, and forced
herself not to look back. She was comforted by the steady, muffled clip-clop of his horse's hooves as beast and master trailed
in her wake. Once they reached the house, one of the stable lads
came to take his horse. Without a word, she led her guest up the

steps of the terrace and then disappeared inside the house through a pair of French doors.

She ran like a madwoman to the front parlor, tugged on the bellpull, and then stood on tiptoe to look at herself in the large, gilt-framed mirror over the fireplace.

Great heavens and all the saints! She looked like a female hedge tramp.

There was no time to change her gown or fix her hair. She tried licking her palms to smooth the flyaway mass while she waited for a footman to answer her summons. The instant he appeared, she told him to bring cake and lemonade out to the terrace, and then raced up the front stairs to her room. She washed her face and hands, tugged on her newest straw bonnet, discarded her tucker and replaced it with a lace fichu, and lastly, drew a fine cashmere shawl over her shabby gown.

Unfortunately, by the time she made her way back to the terrace, Morgan had returned. He was now lounging against the stone wall, where he and his guest were sharing some private joke. She took a moment to observe them.

Both were dressed for riding, Morgan a slender silhouette in a slate-blue coat and black top boots, his friend a more strapping form in hunter green wearing a knotted scarf of brown and red figures in lieu of a cravat. The sun drew highlights from both the black and chestnut hair, and as their mingled laughter rose from the edge of the terrace, heads thrown back, strong, vital throats exposed, Kitty fancied she was gazing at the two most dazzling young men in the county.

She draped her shawl more gracefully around her shoulders and stepped down from the doorway, making sure to display an ample glimpse of ankle.

Phillip DeBurgh did not appear to notice.

"Oh, hullo, Morgan." she said a little more loudly than was necessary. He sketched her a wave, then returned his attention to his companion. She hovered around the wrought-iron table, now set with food and drink, and said with a brittle attempt at airiness, "I see Cook has taken care of you nicely. These lemon squares are her specialty."

The two young men barely glanced her way.

"Well, carry on," she said just before she slinked back through the doorway.

Phillip DeBurgh stayed on for supper; Papa had insisted on it when he returned from his errands. Over the meal, he made much of the young man, applauding his achievements on the cricket pitch and in the hunting field. Several times he made light of Morgan's lack of interest in any sport—it seemed to her that he was almost disparaging her brother. It was her first inkling that her father and Morgan were not in full charity with each other. Over the next few years those inklings would turn to bleak certainties.

But on this day, this rare and special day, she had thoughts only for the new guest at the table. He, alas, after that startling compliment in the lane, barely acknowledged her presence.

Morgan saw him out directly after dinner—his friend had a ride of several miles to reach New Forest, where he was spending the school break as secretary to the local member of Parliament. After he'd gone, Morgan tracked her to the library, where she was pretending to read an improving sort of book on the fall of Constantinople.

"I am afraid I don't much care for Mr. DeBurgh," she announced as he came through the door. "A bit full of himself, I thought."

Morgan moved to stand beside her, bracing his arms on the library table and grinning down at her. "Phillip told me you practically whipped him from the place. 'Proper little watch-cat,' he said. 'Tried to send me packing.'"

She hitched one shoulder. "I was here alone. You could hardly expect me to encourage a strange man."

He tugged on one of her hair ribbons. "Don't gammon me, Kit. You've been encouraging every man within a twenty-mile radius since you gave up wearing pinafores. And Phillip is hardly a stranger. . . . You've surely heard me speak of him from time to time."

She rolled her eyes with great drama. "How about every fifteen minutes? Whenever you're home from Oxford, it's been Phillip this and Phillip that . . . until I am fit to scream."

Morgan appeared undismayed. "He's a topping rider, a first-rate scholar and a jolly good friend. Oh, and one other thing.

He's got entrée into some of the more, shall we say, interesting haunts in London."

"Papa should hear of that," she said tartly. "He acted as though the sun rose and set over your Mr. DeBurgh."

Morgan was quiet after that; Kitty realized she'd inadvertently rubbed at a sore spot.

"I don't suppose your friend had anything nice to say about me," she prompted, but in a carefully studied manner.

Morgan pushed away from the table and went to the door. "What do you care, minx? You barely said three words to him all evening."

"I was just wondering. I put on my newest gown tonight in his honor . . . because he is your best friend." She sighed theatrically. "But I fear he is sadly lacking in address."

"Perhaps he is." Morgan had gripped the edge of the door and now rocked it back and forth several times. "But he mustered enough . . . address . . . as you call it, to tell me one thing." His face was now merry with some secret.

She picked up her book—Lord, it must have weighed ten pounds—and opened it to the passage she'd been scanning earlier. "If you think I am going to beg you to edify me," she said without looking up, "you are mistaken."

"No, I don't suppose it matters much to you—"

"It does not."

"—that once you've grown up a bit . . . he intends to marry you."

Her eyes darted instantly to the doorway, but Morgan had vanished. She half rose from the library table as her mouth fell open. For the third time that day, she had been rendered speechless at the hands of Phillip DeBurgh.

As Kitty knew now, it wasn't to be the last time by any means.

Chapter Seven

The morning after his ultimatum to Miss Runyon, Morgan was crossing the front hall when he was waylaid by Bettina and Ariadne.

"Our father has given us a special commission," Bettina said, clasping her hands before her. "Ariadne and I are to entertain you. Papa believes you are growing weary with all the work on his silly book—oh, please don't tell him I called it such—so my sister and I are going to take you with us on morning calls."

Morgan immediately flogged his brain for a credible excuse, but before he could come up with anything, Ariadne, sensing his intention to bolt, took him firmly by the arm. "We won't take no for an answer, sir. We've had our orders from the General."

Morgan found himself carried off in the Palfry barouche like the prized spoils of war. They visited the vicar, then a stout matron with a gaggle of intractable lapdogs and ended up at the squire's home, where Morgan was forced to endure a thorough and bloodthirsty recounting of his host's favorite foxhunting stories.

The entire time, he fretted over Miss Runyon. He'd had no chance to get a message to Mrs. Southey, who would have taken her charge to the folly at the arranged time. On the other hand, he was sure Miss Runyon would be in high alt to be spared the torture of his company for one morning.

When they reached the lake, it became clear to Miranda that the folly was unoccupied.

"Perhaps he's walking the path, screened by the reeds," she told herself, refusing to get up her hopes of a reprieve. But as they turned at the stand of willows, Miranda saw that the path before them was empty.

Mrs. Southey pushed her as far as the pavilion, but seemed uncertain of what to do next. "You might as well carry me to the bench," Miranda said. "There's often a pleasant breeze up there." After the woman settled her, Miranda pointed to the chair. "Will you sit with me?"

Mrs. Southey's mouth tightened. "T'isn't fitting."

"Please," Miranda said. "Since Mr. Pearce seems to have abandoned his mission to pester me, I'd like it if you passed the time with me instead."

The woman set herself gingerly on the edge of the chair and folded her hands in her lap.

Miranda cast around for something to say. "I believe you are not originally from the Lake District."

"No, miss."

"Somewhere far from here?'

"East, miss."

Miranda blew out a breath. "Mrs. Southey, it is obvious that you have no trouble conversing with Mr. Pearce. In fact, I infer from some of the things he's told me that you are a veritable gabblemonger."

"I . . ." the woman began, and then blushed, the bright color washing over her careworn face.

"You what?" Miranda prodded.

"I only told him that you need more looking after than me or Alice could give you." She gazed down at her meshed hands, then swiftly up at Miranda. "I told him you needed people of your own sort . . . gentry folk . . . to talk to you. It ain't natural, miss, you living your whole life in that one room with just me and Alice about."

"And so you believe Mr. Pearce is a proper person for me to talk to?"

She nodded. "He be a gentleman *and* a military man, just like my Geordie . . . er . . . that would be Mr. Southey, miss."

"What happened to your Mr. Southey?"

"Kilt, miss. In Spain. Mr. Pearce, he knew his commanding officer. Though he never knew my Geordie."

Miranda cocked her head. "I'm not sure I understand. Why would a man with a wife leave her behind to enlist in the army?"

Her voice lowered. "He lost his position in the house where we was working in Leeds; they said it was from the drinking and would not give him a reference. He went into the army then, and I came here . . . after the General advertised for a strong woman to care for an invalid lady. Then he was kilt. Two years ago, it were."

Miranda could not contain her shock. "You received notice of your husband's death while you were caring for me? Sweet heaven, ma'am, you never said a word. I . . . I am so sorry."

Mrs. Southey shrugged. "T'weren't nothing you could do, after all. And you had the world of woe on your own young shoulders."

They sat in silence, Miranda still reeling from the knowledge that this woman, whom she saw every day, had suffered such a blow and not said one word to her.

"I fear I have been so wrapped up in my own troubles," she said at last, "that I never spared a moment to acknowledge anyone else's pain. Again, I am very sorry for your loss."

The woman raised her eyes. "It helped, miss, having you to look after. I prayed every night that you would begin to improve. It gave me something to look forward to during those dark days."

"But I was destined to be a disappointment to you, wasn't I? Just sitting there in that chair, year in, year out, barely moving, barely breathing, like a great lump of suet."

"I can't say what I expected. I only thought that when you finally let go of your sadness, you would begin to mend."

Miranda gave her a weak smile. "It's not that simple. My back was damaged, broken, most likely."

"Your Mr. Pearce has a few contrary opinions on that—"

"He's not a doctor."

Mrs. Southey hitched her chair forward. "No, but he has eyes in his head, don't he? He sees what you will not. What we've all seen, me and Alice and even Daisy. You can move,

Miss Runyon, and no doubt about it. I tuck you up on your back most nights and find you curled on your side come morning. You tell me how a woman what's got a broken back can do that?"

"Perhaps I have regained some use of the muscles in my back, but it doesn't mean I will ever walk."

"Who can say what it means? These doctors come and go, and not a one of them says the same thing. Oh, I hear them talking to the General in his study. We all listen in when we can. None of them doctors can say for a fact what ails you. The one before Mr. Cheney, he wanted to stick your limbs with hot pokers to show where you had feeling left."

This was news to Miranda. "Whereas Mr. Cheney only plagues me with porter," she said with not a little relief.

"So," continued Mrs. Southey, "I don't much see that Mr. Pearce's methods are any worse than those high-and-mighty doctors'."

Miranda thought for a moment. "Since we're being open here, I'd like you to tell me something else. Did you know that my cousin Ronald had returned from Spain?"

"Aye, he was here for Christmas, but we was told not to say a word to you."

Miranda started. Morgan Pearce had not given away that little tidbit.

"Since then, I hear Mr. Ronald's had a mind to stay in London—well, who could blame a young gentleman fresh from the war for wantin' to be about town?"

"But you also think he's been staying away to avoid me."

"Mayhap he don't want to see you in such a state. . . . Mayhap he is afraid."

Miranda sighed. "Then what Mr. Pearce told me was a lie. He said it was no hardship to look at me."

Mrs. Southey reached across the table. "T'was no lie. I didn't mean it like that. Only that you be bound to that chair. You'd get your looks back, miss, if you was to eat your three squares a day. But you nibble at dry toast and sip at a thimbleful of broth. 'Tis a wonder you haven't faded away completely."

Mrs. Southey suddenly seemed to regret her bout of candidness; she drew back and grew silent.

Still, the woman had just said more words to her than over the past three years combined. All it had required was for Miranda to open the door.

"Thank you for telling me," she said softly. "I think it's long past time *someone* gave me the plain truth. And maybe Mr. Pearce was the catalyst for that, but he seems to have given up his crusade. We will have to move forward from here on our own—"

"Do you think so, miss? I mean, do you really think you can make a change after all this time?"

In answer, Miranda set both her hands on the table. Mrs. Southey's eyes widened as Miranda's fingers slowly fanned out over the surface.

"It's still very hard to accomplish," she said. "It takes a good deal of concentration—"

"But it's a start," Mrs. Southey said, a little breathless. "Oh, miss, it *is* a proper start."

Disappointed, of all preposterous things!

As much as she tried to convince herself otherwise throughout the day, Miranda knew that the instant she'd seen the empty path, her heart had twisted in disappointment. It was the reason she had begun talking to Mrs. Southey—she needed something, anything, to keep her at the pavilion in case he had been delayed.

Not that she regretted drawing the woman out. Their talk had given her more than an insight to Mrs. Southey's own tragedy. It had also shown her a number of remarkable things—first off, that the other house servants had a care for her and, further, that the doctors were not convinced of her paralysis. Perhaps most critical right now, she discovered that Morgan Pearce had been correct in his assessment of Mrs. Southey. The woman truly did have a fondness for her. And if he'd been right on that score, was it possible she could trust him enough to put herself in his hands?

A burden shared is a burden halved. Papa used to say that whenever she was blue-deviled, and it was never truer than today. She felt lighter of spirit for the first time since the accident—and all because she had passed the time talking to a raw-boned, unschooled woman. Mrs. Southey had no beauty or accomplishments, but Miranda had discovered, through the simple device of finally looking her full in the face, that she had the warmest eyes she'd ever seen. It was a beauty that did not fade, the beauty her parents had carried with them, even when the bloom of youth was gone from their faces—the light of kindness.

I am not a kind person, Miranda forced herself to admit. *I am become more ugly in my selfishness than from any scars or damage to my body*.

She saw the truth now, how for three years she had grown increasingly self-absorbed, as though her pain and loss justified her self-indulgent behavior. She recalled what Mr. Pearce had spoken of that first day—men thankful to be alive after battle. He had challenged her to prevail, as they had, over pain and adversity. She wondered if she could live up to that challenge, live up to his expectations.

Oh, but it was pointless to ponder such things. She had clearly driven him off with her harsh words and shrewish manner.

The next day at the breakfast table, Lady Palfry asked Morgan prettily if he would run a few errands for her that morning in Windermere. He acceded graciously, meanwhile chaffing at this further obstacle to meeting with Miss Runyon. He was mentally composing a note to Mrs. Southey, asking her to bring her charge to the folly in the afternoon, when the General mentioned that he'd stayed up late and now had fifteen new pages for Morgan to review when he returned.

Morgan wagered Miss Runyon would be doing a victory dance—in spirit, at any rate—when she discovered that she would again be spared his presence.

The instant he was back from Windermere, Morgan went directly to the study. He strode to the desk where Sir Janus sat writing and snatched away the page he was working on.

"We need to talk, you and I." He set the page neatly on the stack beside the blotter. "Now."

The General's head reared back, his nostrils flared and his whole manner brightened, like a bored old warhorse who senses incipient battle.

"I've been waiting for you to have things out with me," he said as he set aside his quill and rose. "And let me say, you won't be the first officer to stand toe-to-toe with me with that earnest fire burning in his eyes. Brings to mind another young fellow name of Wellesley."

Morgan nearly smiled. It was a wise man who began a debate with a compliment.

"We need to seek some accord, sir," Morgan said less combatively, "if we are to continue working together."

"It was never my intention to rile you," Sir Janus said. "You've been generous with your time and I appreciate that more than words can say. And since I have in the past been used to running an army or two, I understand fully your need to get back to your responsibilities at Grambling House."

Morgan had the startled notion that his liberation was at hand. The feeling was short-lived.

"Yet I am entreating you to stay on. I fear I didn't fully explain myself the last time. The thing of it is, I desire that this book be more than a recounting of my experiences in the army. I want it to be my legacy to all the generations of British soldiers to come, so that they might understand the times I lived through, the places I saw that will soon be gone from the world. Even now in America, so much of the wilderness I admired has been plowed out of existence. India is more changeless, but our presence there has altered . . . more blasted merchants than military men these days. Do you understand what I am saying?"

"You are seeking to write a history as much as a memoir."

"Exactly. Something of lasting value, not just the meanderings of an old soldier. And that is why I need you, Pearce. You won't flatter me or cozen me or allow me to lapse into vain ramblings."

"I will not," Morgan assured him.

"And that is why I need you here—to be my watchdog."

Morgan hesitated; he was going to ask for a quid pro quo and needed to phrase it just right.

"I believe we can reach a compromise," he said at last. "I have only one condition for staying on—I want my mornings to myself, so that I can focus on my own work."

The General appeared perplexed. "I am not aware that anything has been forwarded here from Grambling House."

Morgan wasn't surprised that his host knew exactly what items arrived each day in the post. It was going to be interesting, trying to outfox the crafty old fellow in his own lair.

"Truth is," Morgan said evenly, "I intended to leave all that behind in London. But there's a problem that's recently arisen, one that will require a deal of my attention. I've written to my uncle on the matter and am expecting a package from him anytime now."

"And in spite of this other matter, you promise to give me your afternoons?"

"Absolutely. The main thing is that you focus on your writing every morning."

"But you'll be here in the house if I need you." Sir Janus sounded not a little anxious.

"Not necessarily," said Morgan. "And even if I am, you must wait to seek me out. That is the whole purpose of this discussion, that you understand my mornings are sacrosanct. No coaxing me to go driving with your daughters or run errands for your wife. I am my own man until, say, one o' clock."

Sir Janus mulled this over, then nodded. "Fair enough. I assume you will need a place to work . . . perhaps the library."

"Don't trouble yourself over it. I have somewhere in mind already, a trifle out of the way."

"You're being fairly mysterious, Pearce."

Morgan smiled. "Not at all. You see, I understand writers, Sir Janus. The instant they know where to unearth their editor, they are clamoring for his attention. In London, I often find myself buttonholed at my tailor or my club by anxious authors needing reassurance. I merely want to guarantee that the writer in residence here will attend to his story."

"Done," he said. "And you have my deepest gratitude for

staying on. I daresay if I write faithfully each morning, I'll be finished with the book in no time."

"No hurry," Morgan said, and added softly, "Not now. Not any longer."

The next morning, Morgan sent word to Mrs. Southey that he was resuming their former schedule and would be at the pavilion by ten. As he came along the lake path at five minutes to the hour, he was surprised to see Miss Runyon already in place on the bench.

She watched him warily as he came up the steps and stopped at the threshold, shifting the parcel he carried under his arm.

"My dear Miss Runyon—" He swept her a theatrical bow. And then he cocked one eye. "Or are you merely an apparition brought on by the overconsumption of Sir Janus's excellent brandy?"

Her mouth twisted. "You're never going to make this easy for me, are you?"

He settled on the chair, laying his package on the table. "How about a bargain, then? I'll make things as easy for you as you make them for me."

"That should work to your favor. You find me this morning attempting to be docile."

He barked out a curt laugh. When she frowned, he shook his head. "No, don't scowl. You find *me* attempting to believe you. Whether we are both destined to be disappointed remains to be seen." He hitched his chair closer. "So what's brought about this sudden change of heart?"

She sniffed. "I find that I have been misled by those I trusted. And not only about Ronald. That just opened the door to other questions. I've been talking to Mrs. Southey—"

"Ah."

"—and have discovered that not one of my doctors offered any fixed diagnosis to the General. They are, to a man, perplexed by my condition, save that it is not akin to any paralysis they have ever seen."

"You were never told any of this?"

She shook her head. "When I was recuperating at the vicarage in Warfield, they said it was impossible to make a full diagnosis until the swelling in my spine went down, but that there was little likelihood I would walk again. Since then, none of the subsequent doctors ever revealed their findings to me, so I foolishly assumed that no news was bad news."

"Contrary to popular maxim," he observed. "And it never occurred to you to simply ask these learned men why you could not walk?"

She grimaced. "It's bad enough being poked at by impersonal strangers and asked endlessly about the regular functioning of one's . . . entrails."

"Oh, dear." Morgan couldn't keep a soft chuckle from sneaking out. "That's very lowering."

She grimaced comically. "You can have no idea. It did not foster confidences."

Then her face changed, the humor faded and the expression that replaced it held so much hungry hope that he felt his insides twist. "I know you are not a doctor. But you have been in battle; you have seen men suffer terrible injuries and still recover. So I am going to ask you. Mr. Pearce, as I never asked my doctors, do you believe I will ever regain the use of my legs?"

Morgan looked away, mentally sorting through the things he could say. What if he gave her false encouragement and she struggled toward a goal she would never attain? Still, where there was heart there was hope, as his mother liked to say. And Miss Runyon would be the better for it, even if she never did walk again.

He met her eyes and did not blink as he said, "Yes. I believe you will." He saw relief sweep across her features. "And to that end, I've already sent to London for a few medical texts. I also have some experience in the infirmary tent . . . saw more than one ailing fellow through a long, restless night. So I will stick things out, Miss Runyon. I promise you I will."

"All because of some piffling debt to my cousin?"

"I have other, more . . . baroque reasons, ones I will share with you someday soon." He tapped the parcel. "For now, you'll have to make due with this small gift I purchased in Windermere. I believe it's something you've needed for a very long time."

He untied the string, but before he could finish unwrapping it, she said, "Oh, please. Let me do it. You see, I've been practicing."

He slid it over and watched as she slowly flattened her fingers on the edges of the paper and pressed on them to draw them apart.

"A picture frame?" she asked as a section of gilt molding was revealed.

"Not exactly." He reached over and raised the object, turning it toward her.

He was startled when she cried out a horrified, *"No!"* and batted it away.

As he snatched it back, the mirrored surface caught and reflected a shaft of sunlight, which danced against the pavilion's vaulted ceiling for an instant.

"Oh, you are wicked," she moaned, head down now, hands curled and fretting in her lap.

"Dear girl," he said gently, urgently. "It's long past time. How will you know what you can become if you don't even know what you are?"

"Go away," she said miserably. "Just go. I was a fool to trust you."

He slid onto the bench beside her, still holding the mirror. "If you run craven now, there's no hope for you." Leaning closer he whispered gruffly, "Remember what you just said, that they'd been lying to you about Ronald?" He tipped her chin up with his knuckles and forced her to look at him. "Well, here is another untruth. Lady Palfry told me you were horribly disfigured when I mentioned your name to her."

"I *am* horrible," she said thickly. "Scarred and misshapen and—"

"Miranda—" he said to catch her attention. "Your father named you aptly. Miranda . . . so alone on your island in the aftermath of a great storm, patiently awaiting your destiny."

Her head reared back. "No, not Miranda! Not even blithe Ariel, but wretched Caliban—'a most ridiculous monster.' "

He smiled slyly. "Yes, truly Miranda—'who art ignorant of what thou art.' "

"I know what I am," she retorted darkly. "And the only destiny for monsters is an unhappy one."

Morgan felt his tolerance slipping away. "Will you trust me, for God's sake? Did you think I was lying or idly flattering you when I said your face was no hardship to look upon?"

"I thought you were daft."

He gave her an exasperated smile. "Look, then, and you will see how daft I was."

"Oh, very well," she said in the hoarse, quavery tones of a child agreeing to swallow a noxious medicine.

He held the mirror up and turned his head away to afford her a private moment.

"Well?" he said after a time. "You are very quiet."

He snuck a peek around the edge of the frame. She was turning her head slowly from side to side, and then up and down, a little pucker of concentration between her eyes and a tracing of tears on her cheeks.

At last she murmured, "Hardly the face I recall."

"But not horrible or monstrous?"

"No, just pale and thin." She sighed. "Even the scars have faded. I was prepared for something far worse."

"Mmm, I know."

"Aside from the dent in my cheek, I see little of the damage that was there earlier." She hung her head. "I see also that I have been a witless fool."

"Not a bit of it," he said. "Without being able to touch your face, you couldn't know how much of the damage remained."

"The left side is still numb—I know that from when Alice bathes it."

He *tsked* softly. "Can you bear these things, Miss Runyon? The dent and the scars and the loss of sensation?"

"I suppose I must."

"Will you relinquish the veil?"

"Only if this wretched bonnet goes with it," she said with sudden determination. "No wonder I frightened everyone."

Morgan had to stifle a laugh. Leave it to a woman to reduce everything to a matter of fashion.

"And I must see if any of my lighter clothing was brought

from Cornwall. These dark, heavy gowns were intended for mourning. I think three years is sufficient."

"I'll front you the funds if you want to order some new things from Windermere."

Her eyes gleamed for a moment, then dulled again. "It is quite pointless, Mr. Pearce. You can dress up the rag doll and put pretty bonnets on her, but she will never be more than she is."

"What's this?" he cried. "You're giving up already? You've allowed yourself but a scant minute to feel hopeful. Linger there a while, Miss Runyon, I beg you."

"It's so new to me," she said. "Three years of living under a shroud cannot dissipate in a twinkling. Let me grow accustomed to the possibilities before you ask me to act on them."

Morgan nodded. "Whatever you like."

Morgan stretched out his legs and crossed them at the ankles. His pose was relaxed, but inside his head he was again cursing the Palfrys. The more time he spent with Miranda, the clearer it became that she'd have likely made a full recovery soon after the accident—if only she'd been treated by someone with a jot of common sense. Instead, whether from ignorance or malice, she had been confined to a chair, where her limbs had grown feeble, and completely shunned by her family, which made her believe herself a deformed monster.

He hadn't a clue which problem to address first—the weakened body or the bruised spirit. Until he received the medical texts from his uncle, it might be wisest to begin with her mental state.

"If this is to work," he said, "we'll need to be fairly blunt with each other. No missish airs or gentlemanly constraints."

"I think it's safe to say we've both mastered the blunt part."

He smiled. "Perhaps I should rephrase it. We need to be . . . open with each other."

"Dangerous," she said. "I've a tongue like a whip and your questions cut to the bone."

"We will try not to draw blood, ma'am. This is not to be a conflict, but an alliance." He shifted his chair closer. "Now, we must put our priorities in order. It would help if you could tell me what you require."

Miranda lowered her eyes. Six days ago she would have assured him her every need was met. She had food, clothing, shelter, servants. But now she knew the truth; she had nothing . . . less than nothing, if that were possible. He wanted to know what she required. What *didn't* she require? Conversation, human warmth, the ability to walk and run and dance, to write till her fingers cramped, to read late into the night, to race over spring meadows on the back of a half-broken moor pony, to hunt for wild blueberries in the briar wood, to wade into the sea and retreat screaming and laughing from the surging waves. She required it all.

Finally, she answered in a whispery voice, "I want the impossible."

He crossed his arms on the table. "Start small, my dear. We'll work our way up to the impossible in increments."

She looked down at her hands, resting on the tabletop. "Very well. I want to be able to write again, to put pen to paper."

Smiling indulgently, he nodded. "I believe I can manage that."

Her eyes widened as he drew a fat pencil and a drawing pad from his coat pocket and slid them across to her.

"You see," he said. "I had a feeling. . . ."

Chapter Eight

Kitty staggered into the Gramblings' small parlor and dropped the eight assorted parcels she carried onto the sofa. She rarely minded the rather pared-down servant situation on Clarges Street, but today it would have been lovely to have a footman at her disposal as she was used to at Roselinden.

She took up a longish package wrapped with twine and began to undo it. Waverly would be here any minute and she couldn't wait to show him the fabric she had chosen for her new traveling dress. And the matching bonnet was here somewhere, the wickedly expensive one with the three iridescent peacock feathers perched rakishly on its brim. She pulled the hatbox onto her lap and opened it, congratulating herself again at finding a bonnet that so exactly matched the rich Prussian blue of the material.

Waverly liked her in blue. He said it brought out her eyes. Not exactly the most original of sentiments, but then Viscount Waverly had no need for originality. When your family had been more or less running things in the Midlands for the past eight centuries or so, you didn't need to resort to clever flatteries. Anyway, it wasn't his fault that the family hadn't produced anything even close to a brilliant offspring since the time of the Tudors. The Waverlys were steady and good-natured. That was enough for Kitty.

Morgan had once pronounced waggishly that Lord Waverly never said an unkind thing and never did a wise one. Kitty told him she knew full well that the quote pertained to Charles II and that, furthermore, the Waverly bloodlines went much farther back than the Stuart king's.

Maybe it was better that her brother had gone off to the wilds of Windermere. She was doing just fine on her own as it turned out, and she feared if he'd remained in London, he would have kept at her to postpone the wedding.

It was too late now. The last invitation had been sent out yesterday—to their aged aunt Bertha in Edinburgh. She would not come, of course, which was a pity. *Someone* from her father's side of the family ought to be at her wedding. Papa wasn't coming; he'd made that clear. Not if Morgan was to be there.

His refusal still pained her. The rift between father and son was more than six years in the past and yet showed no signs of mending. Papa had offered her a generous dowry, so she would not think he disapproved of the marriage. He had also indicated that Roselinden would be hers upon his death. It shocked her to hear him say it. It meant that everything that had been dear and familiar to Morgan for the first twenty-one years of his life would be denied him. It was the reason she'd given him preference over her father at the wedding. *She* was all he had left from those days.

And Phillip. He still had Phillip. Or perhaps it was more accurate to say that Phillip still had Morgan. No one could actually consider Phillip DeBurgh an active factor in anything these days—he had cut himself off from every part of his past.

Don't think about him, she warned herself. It was bad enough she'd had tearstains on her cheeks the last time Waverly came to call. She'd fobbed him off by blaming the particularly heart-wrenching book she was reading—as if a gothic novel was a patch on the high drama in her own life lately.

It was odd, since those early days with Phillip had seemed so wonderfully serene, as though they were on a sure path to some mutual, if unspoken, destination.

After their meeting in the lane, he'd become a regular visitor to Roselinden during his school breaks. He spent endless hours with Morgan and they usually included her in their adventures. They ranged over the countryside, Phillip and her brother behaving more like schoolboys than budding gentlemen. The three shared their deepest secrets, spoke nonsense until they fell about on the grass lost in laughter and occasionally even expressed a profound thought or two.

Phillip often teased her, worse even than Morgan did, and he never grew angry at her retaliatory attacks, holding her off with lazy good humor.

They often managed to land themselves in Papa's bad graces—for riding over a prickly neighbor's property or poaching fish from the vicar's pond or sneaking out late at night to watch a meteor shower. Every time, regardless of who was the instigator—and she was often the culprit—Morgan took the blame. Those episodes hadn't done anything to ease the breech that was growing between father and son.

She saw less of Phillip once he and Morgan were out of university. Phillip's cabinet minister had found him a position in London, while her brother had come home to Roselinden. Within the first year, it became clear to everyone, save their father, that Morgan was not cut out for the bucolic, relatively idle life of a country gentleman. He burned with unspent energy, becoming more and more like a tautly strung wire. Papa only made matters worse by tightening the reins on his finances, eventually treating Morgan like a supplicant in his own home.

When she confronted her father, he refused to discuss it.

Her brother finally rebelled full out, and slipped away to London to stay with their uncle Cyrus. When he returned for her eighteenth birthday—at her insistence—the antagonism that had been brewing for years between father and son finally came to a head.

She'd been awakened by the sound of raised voices and had hurried downstairs to huddle outside the door of her father's study.

"You're not going to break me as you did my mother!" she heard Morgan shout. "I won't give you the power. I'm stronger than she was."

"You're exactly like her," her father shot back. "Oh, plenty clever, yes . . . but you've got her secretive ways. I saw how she turned you against me. And now I find you sneaking off to London, currying favor with your lowbred uncle. You can sport all the fine feathers you want, but you'll never be a true gentleman, not if you choose to consort with men of that ilk. I always feared there was bad blood in you—"

Morgan gave a sharp cry of protest, and Kitty nearly echoed it aloud. There was no one more honorable or decent than her brother.

Then Kitty understood. Morgan must have told Papa that he'd decided to work with Uncle Cyrus at Grambling House. Seeking a career in Parliament, as Phillip intended, was one thing. But to take up a trade? To her father, that would be the ultimate unforgivable sin.

She was thinking of some way to intercede for her brother, when things escalated beyond her worst nightmares.

"I have no choice," her father declared. "I am writing you out of my will. You want nothing to do with Roselinden, so you will reap nothing from it."

No, she wanted to cry out. *That is so unfair—*

Morgan's response still haunted her. "What a disappointment I must be to you, sir. It's a pity I didn't die at birth—"

"A pity you didn't," her father snarled back. "You'd have saved us all a great deal of trouble."

Kitty sobbed out a cry of shock, and seconds later her father came thrusting out into the hallway. But she had already skittered away into the darkness.

Her brother came to her at dawn the next morning and told her he was enlisting. "Papa wants me dead," he said grimly, "and within the year, perhaps I shall be."

She trailed him down the stairs, clinging to him and pleading with him not to go, but her tears and entreaties went unheeded. He might have been carved of stone. Her last sight of Morgan was in a billowing cloud of dust as he rode like a madman down the winding drive of Roselinden.

Kitty took a mail coach to London that same day to Phillip's rooms in Mayfair.

He came into his parlor that evening after a long day at Government House and found her half dozing in a chair.

"Miss Pearce . . . Kitty!" he cried, dropping to one knee. "Is something amiss?"

She'd always thought him astute and now appreciated that

he did not protest the impropriety of her actions, but rather, cut right to the heart of the matter.

"Morgan," she said with a throb in her voice as she leaned toward him. "And my father . . . a terrible row. Papa said . . . horrible things. Morgan's gone—"

He grasped her wrists. "Gone where, Kitty?"

"He . . . told me he was enlisting in the army. That if Papa wanted him dead . . . then he would dashed well accommodate him. Oh, Phillip, what's to be done?"

He drew her to her feet and set his hands on her shoulders. "I'm not sure what I can do, Kit. He's of age, so that's no impediment. And you know your brother, once he sets his mind on something—"

"You must stop him!" Kitty cried. "You must find where he has gone and prevent him at all costs." She gripped the lapels of his greatcoat. "If you don't, I know he will run headlong into danger and die. You should have seen his face." She shivered. "It frightened me beyond anything. I don't want Morgan to die . . . you don't want it, and I swear to you my father doesn't want it. I don't know what devil reared up between those two last night, but I can't believe my father wants his son's death on his conscience."

Phillip's face grew taut. "I'll find him for you, Kitty. And I vow I will not let him throw his life away."

Kitty now heard those words as if he again stood before her. It hadn't been Morgan, however, who'd ended up throwing his life away.

With a curse, she thrust up from the sofa, sending all her purchases scattering to the floor.

"*Why . . . ?*" she moaned as she paced in agitation across the small parlor. "Why do these ghosts return to trouble me? It is over and done with. Morgan and Papa will never be reconciled, and Phillip is gone from me. He might as well be dead." She stopped pacing, and her mouth tightened in determination. "Yes, that's what I shall do. I'll convince myself that he died in Spain, oh, years and years ago. And I have been over him for a long time now. Such a very—"

"Ho, my dear—"

She looked up in surprise as Lord Waverly stepped into the

room. He was an open-faced young man, not tall, not imposing, but rather willowy and pale of complexion.

He took one look at her and started toward her with his arms outspread. "Oh, no, never say my kitten's been crying again."

"No, no," she said, dodging his advancing embrace and simultaneously scrubbing at her tears. Waverly might not have been the brightest radish in the row, but was the kindest man, the absolutely best-hearted man, and she hated it every time she distressed him.

"It was just another book I've been reading . . . another foolish book. Now, come, my lord," she said with a forced smile as she guided him to the sofa. "See what I have purchased for our wedding journey. I know how much you like me in blue."

Chapter Nine

The day Cyrus Grambling's package arrived, Morgan pleaded out of a dinner party at the squire's and settled himself in the library with the three textbooks. After fifteen minutes, he developed a serious headache and so moved on to the clippings his uncle had also sent, mostly advertisements from the London papers hawking intestinal restoratives and muscle invigorators.

Morgan suspected these curatives were more chimerical than medicinal, but there was one clipping that intrigued him. It was an article about the Ealing Clinic in Edinburgh, where a certain physician, one Samuel Ealing, was experimenting with a new, radically improved, type of artificial limb.

Morgan at once thought of Phillip. His friend had refused to be fitted with a wooden leg. Grotesque, he'd called the oversized whittled pegs, grotesque and cumbersome. The clipping featured several detailed drawings, one of an articulated wooden hand, and another of a facsimile human leg, complete with a hinged knee.

Morgan's heart started to race. A man could get his dignity back with such things. Even if they were prohibitively expensive, he knew Phillip's family would gladly beggar themselves to get him out of that damned bed. He wondered if Cyrus had sent it to him for that purpose.

He carefully copied the information from the article onto a separate sheet, then sealed the original in a folded note and addressed it to Phillip. So what if he had agreed to leave his friend in peace? This clipping was too felicitous to ignore.

His second missive was almost as much of a gamble. It occurred to him that the Scottish doctor might have some experience with spinal injuries, so he set pen to paper, describing Miss Runyon's accident and her subsequent lack of mobility, ending with the curious fact that she could move her limbs in a limited manner and sit upright without assistance.

Let the doctor sort that bit out, he thought as he sealed the note, since it still boggled his brain.

"What do the books say?" Miss Runyon inquired as he placed the three fat volumes on the table between them, causing its delicate legs to wobble noticeably.

Morgan had been pleased to see that not only was she awaiting him at the pavilion, but she had also brought along her overnight assignment, three sheets of words beginning with the letter A. Unfortunately, the words were so large that only four or five fit on each page and most were barely legible, but he was impressed.

"My uncle took my request for current medical texts seriously. These are not for the faint of heart."

"Ah, but *we* do not shrink from battle," she quoted, tossing his own words back at him.

"Battle is one thing," he noted dryly. "Page after page of obscure Latin and Greek allusions is quite another. It's no wonder physicians are a shambly lot, no two of them ever agreeing on anything. I have three books recommending three different treatments."

"No hot pokers, I hope."

He cocked his head at that.

She quickly explained. "Mrs. Southey told me my previous physician was going to try that method to see if I had any feeling left in my limbs."

Morgan looked incredulous, and then with a sly grin, reached over and squeezed her upper arm. She nodded in acknowledgment of the gentle pressure, which she'd obviously had no trouble feeling.

"Blasted doctors," he grumbled. "Always going about things backward."

He left his hand there, rubbing a tiny circle of comfort on the wool of her sleeve, and said, "It's going to be different now, Miranda."

"I hope so." She met his eyes and gave him a tight smile. It was winsome and appealing, and it wrung his heart.

Morgan felt a primal rush of protectiveness. The need to slay dragons or battle barbarians for her sake. It was something he'd never felt before for a female, not even for his bedridden aunt Bertha and certainly not for Kitty.

His hand unconsciously stroked down from her shoulder to her wrist, which he gripped tightly. "You're not alone any longer," he whispered gruffly.

"I know," she said.

Four days after sending his note to Edinburgh, Morgan received a lengthy reply. Dr. Ealing claimed to be deeply interested in spinal injuries and their treatment. It was his considered opinion, he wrote, that, based on the young lady's curious lack of true paralysis, a series of very hot baths followed by a vigorous manipulation of the limbs might restore strength to her muscles, if not effect a total cure. To that end, he'd sent along a series of diagrams demonstrating how the treatment was to be carried out. He further assured Morgan that his methods would in no way imperil the lady's general health.

Morgan felt a rush of excitement. One of the medical texts from London had also mentioned this treatment, but he'd had no idea of how to implement it.

The following day he reviewed the doctor's drawings and instructions with both Miranda and Mrs. Southey, who seemed elated by the chance to participate in her charge's recovery.

"I used to do something suchlike for me old mam," she said. "A heavy rubdown with hot liniment was best thing in the world for her arthritics." She looked at Morgan. "You can trust me to see to it, sir."

He was encouraged by her determination, especially since that part of Miranda's treatment would naturally have to remain outside his domain.

Miranda was less enthusiastic. She made a woeful face at Morgan. "Hot baths and manipulative massage? Am I to end up as a parboiled petticoat going through the laundry mangler?"

"Only if you do it correctly," he drawled. "Though it's not as radical as it sounds; Dr. Ealing writes that it's an ancient

Eastern treatment. He seems to be very forward-thinking—or perhaps, wisely backward-thinking—in his approach."

After Mrs. Southey went off to study the diagrams, Morgan touched Miranda's hand. "You don't seem very pleased over our new plan."

"Your Dr. Ealing sounds quite legitimate, but—oh, maybe I'm just being cautious. Or maybe I don't want to be boiled and pummeled and . . . twisted like a corkscrew."

"I thought you were joking just now, about the parboiled petticoat."

"I was only half joking. You've got your campaign, and now Mrs. Southey has one." She looked at him dead on. "But what is to be my campaign, Mr. Pearce? I am still just the rag doll who gets thrown about. I realize it is not very gracious of me to say that, after all the effort you've made. And I know my own focus should be on trying to recover. But beyond practicing my writing, what else can I actually do to help myself?"

"You won't always be so . . . powerless." He paused for a moment. This wasn't going at all as he'd planned. "But if you mislike this idea, there's no need to go forward with it."

Her mouth twisted into a testy grin. "Which is your odious way of suggesting I am being cowardly."

"Not a bit of it. It was something new, is all. Perhaps we can try the method another book recommended, suspending an iron bar over your bed, so that you can practice swinging your arms."

She nearly hooted. "After which, do I then become an attraction at Astley's Amphitheatre? Miranda the Magnificent and her Amazing Iron Bar."

Morgan harrumphed. "A few scant weeks ago, making jokes about your condition was well beyond you. I see all this levity as a positive sign."

"You think I'm mocking your plans, but I'm not. It's myself I am mocking."

He braced his arms on the table and leaned toward her. "I just wish you would tell me what you want. I wrack my brains every night, trying to come up with ideas."

"Perhaps," she said softly, "I am afraid to try for more than

I have right now. I've been battling circumstance for so long . . . and it always seems to win."

"I know. And it's a blasted unfair opponent, fierce and relentless, something even the bravest soldier shrinks from. But I will tell you this—I have yet to see a man in battle muster the amount of courage you've shown these past weeks. You threw off your shroud, as you said, and faced the world head-on."

"I rather think I had no choice in that."

"No," he said. "If you hadn't wanted this, hadn't welcomed it, you could have been rid of me that first day."

"*Now* he tells me," she muttered. "And how exactly could I have done that, Mr. Pricklebur?"

He couldn't prevent a swift grin. "You didn't have to engage me, Miranda. But you did. You baited me and belittled me. Surely you know enough of human nature to understand that it was a cry for attention."

"You make me sound as though I were a child indulging in a tantrum."

"Infants cry when they need looking after. That's not an instinct that necessarily fades as we grow older."

"And why did no one else perceive this need that was so obvious to you?"

"Mrs. Southey saw it every day. . . . You know that's true. Only she had no means to help you. Until now."

"Oh, very clever," Miranda said with a scowl. "You have neatly brought the conversation back to this new treatment, making me seem like an ungrateful wretch if I deprive Mrs. Southey of the chance to finally help me."

Morgan stood up abruptly and moved toward the opening in the railing. "I can't be with you when you are in this mood. It makes me want to shake you till your teeth rattle." He paused and gave her a long, considering look before he went down the steps. "Hardly what the doctor ordered."

Miranda cursed herself six ways till Sunday after he'd gone. Morgan Pearce was the only bright spot in her entire day, and here, she'd driven him off with her foul temper and pitiful attempts at humor.

Miranda the Magnificent, indeed. More like Miranda the Maladroit.

"Morgan!" she called, unaware that she had used his Christian name. *"Morgan!"*

He eventually came sauntering back along the path and stopped at the foot of the steps. "Is that you making such an unholy racket? You're driving off all the waterfowl."

She drew in a deep, unsteady breath. "I'm sorry. . . . I didn't mean to insult you. Please, I'll do whatever you think is best."

He crossed his arms on his chest. "Even be boiled and pummeled and twisted like a corkscrew?"

"Even that."

He returned to his chair and drew the pack of cards from his coat pocket. "Now, Miss Runyon," he said with a cryptic smile as he began to deal them out, "let us see if you can finally hold your own hand."

Miranda didn't see much improvement during the first week. The manipulation and stretching of her limbs was difficult for Mrs. Southey at the start, but she was a strong, dogged woman, and before long she was able to follow Dr. Ealing's instructions to the letter.

To prove to Morgan that she was receptive to *all* his ideas, Miranda asked him to install an iron bar above her bed, suspended by two ropes. It was days before she mastered her grip; once that was accomplished, she was able to lie flat and swing the bar above her head and down below her waist. Before long, the strength in her arms and shoulders began to increase noticeably. Mrs. Southey brought down a set of scarred Indian clubs from the attic, and Miranda began to exercise with them, as well.

Her legs were more problematic. Except for now being able to wiggle her toes, she didn't have any control over them. Mrs. Southey pummeled her regularly, and while Miranda was pleased that she could feel the therapeutic blows all along her nether limbs, she still hadn't regained her strength or coordination. She reminded herself that the thing you wanted most was often the hardest to achieve.

Several times a week, Morgan would confer with her on her

progress, jotting down any changes or setbacks on the gold-encased notepad he used for their rummy scores. It amused her that he needed to keep a log when she was living proof of everything he wrote down. He also noted any questions they had for Dr. Ealing, which she knew he would then send off to Scotland.

He read her every letter he got back, and she was charmed by the doctor's wry sense of humor and his no-nonsense manner in addressing their concerns.

All in all, Miranda was happy with her progress so far. She could write, hold a book, and was struggling to relearn the use of dining utensils. She purposely did not think ahead to the time when Morgan Pearce would be gone. He'd become a fixture in her life; the person she wanted most to please. And if she sometimes wondered if he ever thought of her as more than a project, she did not let herself dwell on such things for long.

Her body was improving daily; the last thing she needed was for her spirits to fall into a decline.

As the days and then weeks went by, Morgan's life also took on a fixed and steady meter.

Since he now had his mornings free, his sessions with Miss Runyon sometimes stretched to two hours. If they lingered longer than that, he feared someone inside the house would catch them in the pavilion. Even though Mrs. Southey assured him that the family rarely strolled the grounds until later in the day, it never hurt to be cautious.

He was especially careful about leaving the house each morning. Some days he would ride out early, and then tether his horse near the pavilion. Other times he would exit through the kitchen and cross the formal gardens at the back of the house, before making a circuitous path toward the lake. He always varied his route and had yet to meet up with any of the Palfrys once he was out-of-doors.

He'd also set up a small office in one of the disused rooms on the upper floor of the house, a remote location where the Palfrys were unlikely to stray. It was mostly a subterfuge, though he made sure that he spent at least an hour there each day. It gave him a place to review Miss Runyon's progress and see to his occasional correspondence with his men at Grambling House.

Oddly, the problems there that had once so obsessed him seemed to recede with each passing day. He still felt responsible for the firm, but now had the sense that his hand on the tiller was not necessary every minute. His uncle had hired able assistants and from the reports he was receiving, they were assisting . . . ably.

As for Lady Farley, well, he still had a few bad moments late at night, when his body cursed him for this enforced celibacy. A man didn't walk away from a woman like Lavinia without feeling the occasional gut-struck urge to just chuck everything and race panting back toward her. But his chief focus, at least by day, remained Miranda Runyon.

He and Sir Janus seemed to be rubbing along tolerably, and the memoir grew apace. As an editor, it wasn't Morgan's job to judge a writer's personal ethics. But the instant that constraint fell away, his condemnation of the General returned full-blown. He didn't care that he continued to mislead the man; his was a negligible sin beside the one Sir Janus had commit. Morgan's conscious was lily-white as far as he was concerned.

Miranda had brought up her cousin only that morning.

"I find it difficult to credit that Sir Janus still doesn't know about our meetings. He always prided himself on being beforehand with all his estate business."

Morgan tried to reassure her—even though he fretted over this same thing daily. "Mrs. Southey will never tell anyone—she's far too pleased by your progress. And Alice . . . well, Alice knows which side her bread it buttered on."

"The Pearce side, I gather."

He grinned. "The servants, most of them, are all for you, Miss Runyon. My valet, Hodges, reports to me that there is a general resentment over the way you've been treated. No, I don't envision any talebearers revealing our meetings to your family."

He then reminded her that they could avoid the whole issue if she would consider returning to Cornwall.

"No, it's out of the question. It still hurts too much to even speak of the place. At any rate, I'd be just as isolated in Nasrannah as I am here, with only myself and a few servants in a rambling old house." She hesitated noticeably, then blurted out, "Besides, you wouldn't be there to badger me. I'd grow lazy and idle again."

"I could come to Cornwall," he volunteered. And then wondered why it seemed in his mind to be a forgone conclusion.

"You wouldn't," she said in a sensible tone that did not allow for disappointment. "And I wouldn't ask it of you. I used to love living there, but it's truly the back of beyond."

"Please, just think about it. It's at least a solution to all this skulking about."

"I don't skulk," she pointed out with a grin. "You need workable legs to skulk."

"You'll be skulking in no time, Miss Runyon. And slinking and slithering. Now where did we leave off yesterday? Ah, yes . . . the letter G."

When Morgan went to his room to change for dinner that night, there was a letter from Lady Farley awaiting him, awash with the scent of gardenia.

Her husband *was* on his way to London, she wrote, but had been delayed by government business in Paris. She apologized for her behavior during their last meeting—she'd turned pettish when he told her about Windermere and had refused him her favors—and now hinted broadly that her bedroom door would be wide open to him if he cared to rush back to London.

He stood by the window, where he had gone to read the missive while Hodges fussed over his shaving gear, and looked out into the gloaming light that bathed the front lawn.

He tried to muster some elation over her invitation. Nothing. He tried for a mild simmer. Still nothing. He purposely recalled the last time he had made love to her, the lady naked and tangled in her gardenia-scented sheets doing something to him that was probably illegal in most English-speaking countries.

All he got for his efforts was the recollection that at the time he'd found the heavy scent of gardenias particularly cloying.

I've turned into a blasted monk, he thought wretchedly.

And he suspected he knew why. During his days at Oxford he'd wondered how the dons, who were mostly ancient, confirmed bachelors, managed to live for decades without the delights of the flesh. Now, after nearly three weeks of instructing Miss Runyon, he had an answer.

Apparently teaching took all the starch out of a fellow.

Hodges who, with the spooky intuition of servants, seemed to know exactly what the letter contained, paused in soaping up the shaving mug and asked guilelessly, "And will we be leaving for London anytime soon, sir?"

"Damn your eyes, we will not," Morgan snarled as he turned back into the room and cast the note onto the fire.

"Dr. Cheney is coming tomorrow to examine me," Miranda informed Morgan several days later. "I'd completely forgotten he was due."

"Do you want me to speak to him?"

She rolled her eyes. "Of course. Just blithely inform him that you've taken over my care. He'll go running to my cousin, whereupon, I will be confined to my room for all time, and you will likely be arrested for quackery."

Morgan grinned. "If lack of special schooling were a crime, half the physicians in England would end up clapped in irons. We both know that. But there's nothing I'd like more than to review your treatment with a doctor who has seen you. Dr. Ealing writes that we are progressing nicely, but it makes me uneasy to be doing this without firsthand guidance."

Miranda pivoted on the bench so he could see her wiggle the toes of her slippers.

"Whatever we're doing, it's working very well. I'm only wondering if I should demonstrate my new abilities to Dr. Cheney . . . or just lie there like a bag pudding as I normally do."

Morgan thought this over. If she showed signs of recovery to the doctor, the man would be bound to report it to the General. That would work to Miranda's benefit when it was time for Morgan to leave.

"Show him all you are able to do now . . . your writing, your exercises. You needn't bring me into it yet—in case he feels the urge to report my meddling to Sir Janus."

*   *   *

It was late the following afternoon when Mrs. Southey found him seated at his desk in the upper room. She didn't even knock, but came straight in, startling him.

"You must come to her room, sir," she cried, wringing her apron. "I know it's not proper, but she is that upset."

Morgan was on his feet in an instant. "What—?"

"That horrid, horrid doctor," she wailed softly. "Turned a blind eye, that one. Made light of all her improvements and forbade me to continue with the hot baths."

"The devil he did!" Morgan erupted, already heading for the doorway.

He found Miranda lying on her bed, eyes closed, arms limp at her sides, like a corpse. Her face was pale, but he saw the blotchy stains on her cheeks from recent tears. He stood there staring down at her, simmering.

"I'll kill him," he said. "The festering buffoon."

She gave a little hiccup and opened her eyes. "You shouldn't be in here," she said, and then started weeping again, silently, with heartrending restraint.

"Oh, bother all that, Miranda. What did he say?"

She shook her head. "It doesn't matter. All that matters is that he will not tell my cousin about my improvements. They are all in collusion against me."

Morgan dragged a wooden chair to her bedside and perched on it. "Now, no more crying. . . . You've had a shock is all. A rather nasty one, I admit."

"He said . . . he said it was all a fluke. That sometimes paralysis appears to be diminishing but that it inevitably comes back worse than before—"

Morgan's head reared up. "Of all the infernal codswallop. And you believed him?"

She stopped sobbing long enough to shoot him an irritated frown. "Of course I didn't. My wits haven't gone begging. But you know that is what he will tell the General. He also said the hot baths and manipulation were extremely harmful . . . and might even prove fatal."

She gave a stuttering sigh. "I was a fool to have told him anything, Morgan. I know enough of human nature to understand that you don't tread on a man's professional pride. He actually looked horror-struck when I showed him my writing samples. I see now that I caught him out in a faulty diagnosis—and proved him fallible. So he struck back."

Morgan stroked one hand along her sleeve, wishing he could do more to comfort her. "What does any of it matter? We shall continue on as we were, following Dr. Ealing's methods. And when Sir Janus at last learns of your progress, well, if Dr. Cheney is unwise enough to refute what any fool can see, just to salve his pride, we shall bring in a dozen new doctors who will call him a horse's behind."

Miranda chuckled, but then her face grew wistful. "I was so proud of myself, Morgan. So sure he would be pleased beyond anything. He's been one of the more benign doctors, you see, even if he did prescribe the porter."

"I bet he'll be imbibing something a lot stronger than porter when he gets home. But you can't drown the truth in brandy, and make no mistake, regardless of the nonsense he spewed here today, he *has* seen the truth."

Miranda touched his hand, where it lay on the mattress beside her. "You must wonder where your sharp-tongued shrew went. I am turned into a quivering, cowering mouse."

Morgan raised her hand, cupping it between his two palms. "Listen to me. I may have prodded you away from your old path, but you are the one who had the courage to reach for those changes. That effort alone was bound to wear you down. I . . . I don't think less of you for weeping."

"I hate weepers," she grumbled. "And I hate feeling so defeated."

"What happened here was not a defeat; it was a validation." He grinned slightly. "You scared the stuffing out of the good doctor. If that doesn't tell you that it's working . . ."

Mrs. Southey hissed from the doorway. "You'd better go, sir. It's nearly time for supper and the ladies are ringing for their maids."

Morgan stood up. He didn't want to leave, even though Miranda was calmer now. It still infuriated him that she had been put through this ordeal and it frightened him a little that the doctor could so ruthlessly turn away. Had the others also seen the potential there and likewise turned away?

He slipped past Mrs. Southey into the hall, wondering, as he made his way back to his bedroom, if the good doctor was still about. It was possible he was accustomed to sitting down to a meal with the family during his visit. Morgan prayed not.

Sir Janus might not approve of it if his captive editor leaped across the dinner table and throttled his tame physician.

Six weeks to the day that he'd arrived at Palfry Park, Morgan made his leisurely way around the lake, and then paused at the turning in the path where the pavilion came into sight. Mrs. Southey had warned him, but he still could not stop staring.

From this distance, the young lady sitting on the bench might have been mistaken for a society belle—the flowing sprigged gown and lacy white tucker, the short waves framing her face beneath a delicate, beribboned bonnet.

He hurried along the path now, eager to see this miracle up close.

She grimaced as he came up the stairs, and then grinned. "I feel like a china cat being displayed on a mantel."

"I . . . I don't know quite what to say," Morgan returned in a gruff voice, wondering where his usual polished address had gone.

"Something nice would be very helpful."

"No, I didn't mean . . . Good God . . . it's just such a difference."

He'd seen it that first day; he'd had an inkling that beauty lay dormant in her parched face. But suspecting it was not the same as seeing it fully realized.

She'd begun eating regular meals, he knew, and although he'd seen the changes in her face as it filled out, he'd still not actually noted the level of improvement. Until now. He'd not realized that beneath the heavy wool gowns her body had become increasingly—and enticingly—female. Until now.

He looked and marveled and still could not articulate what he felt.

"Mrs. Southey raided the attic," Miranda explained, trying to fill in the obvious gap. "The gown was my own, packed away up there. And the bonnet belonged to Leanne, the sister who moved to Chester. Anyway, I'm afraid the changes are all for show."

"Nonsense," he managed finally. "I think sometimes the bravado you can muster is all the difference between hope and heartache. If you appear more normal, you might very well end up feeling that way."

"That's the odd part, Mr. Pearce. I always felt normal . . . on the inside. The old Miranda Runyon trapped inside a failed body. It was what hurt the most, that everyone suddenly started behaving as though my brain had been affected. You heard the way Alice spoke to me. Even the doctors insisted on treating me like a half-witted child."

She slid her hand across the tabletop. "You, Mr. Pearce, were the only one who didn't talk down to me. Pity of it is, I'd gotten so used to being coddled that I was angry at you for not respecting my . . . delicate sensibilities."

"My dear girl, you have the sensibilities of a cod fisherman."

Miranda laughed at that. "I believe my father often made a similar observation."

"I was wondering about something, though," Morgan said. "They all knew you, Ronald and the Palfrys, in that other life, but I obviously can't ask them. So I have no clue as to what you were like . . . before. Who is it I am bringing back to the world, Miss Runyon?"

She wrinkled her nose. "I've been thinking about that a great deal lately. I thought I'd forfeited the best parts of my character in that accident. But the more I think on it, the more I see that I was nothing but a sanctimonious bit of fluff, rather full of myself because my parents encouraged everything I did, but untested in any way that mattered."

"A dilettante, then?"

"Oh, quite horribly a dilettante. Head stuffed with glorious nations of change and progress and no idea under heaven how to enact them."

"Sometimes it only takes an idea, you know. I believe it was Mr. John Adams who said that there are two creatures of worth on the planet—those with the commitment to an idea and those with the commitment to follow it. You were the former."

He paused a moment, not sure of how she would react to what he was going to say. "I've read several of your essays, you know," he admitted in a low voice.

"Oh, dear."

"They were in storage with your family's personal possessions, and your lawyer in Truro was kind enough to forward them to me. I wrote under the letterhead of Grambling House."

"So old Northam now fancies I am to be published, hmm?"

Morgan smiled. "It's not out of the question. You made an interesting argument in that piece on the admiralty and Seaman Jaynes—"

Her eyes flashed and her whole manner grew animated. "It was an infamous situation. Imagine casting a sailor's entire family into debtor's prison because they couldn't pay his medical bills after he died—bills that were incurred treating a lingering wound he'd received in battle."

"And how did you phrase your rebuttal?"

She put her head back and quoted, " 'The sovereign who calls a man to arms in defense of his nation dares not renege on his responsibility to that man when his usefulness has been compromised through enacting that same defense—' "

Morgan finished for her. " '—else he risks undermining forever the very stirrings that prompt good citizens to rise up against their enemies, for he has himself become one with them.' " He blew out a breath. "Strong words, Miss Runyon, if a bit republican in tone. I see that you are your father's daughter. I knew something of that case, by the way; it was a dark hour for the navy. Fortunately Poole heard of it and paid off the family's debt."

"Sir Robert Poole the cabinet minister?" she said, and then sighed. "Now there is a man after my own heart."

"A university friend was his secretary for one summer. . . . I got to meet him several times." He was amused by the awestruck expression on her face. He'd clearly possessed a trump card with her all along, had he known it. "He is just as you would imagine, enormously energetic, involved in a dozen critical causes at any given time, and yet, if you were to sit down with him, he'd become so composed, so focused, that you would swear your petty problem was all that mattered to him in the world. He is a rare combination, both statesman and gentleman. When you come to London, I will make sure to introduce you."

Her face sobered. "Whatever are you talking about?"

"I . . . I just thought that once you recovered enough to face the outside world, you might like to see London." He shifted toward her over the table. "I know that's where you were heading before the accident, but there's no reason you couldn't go there now. I have to leave Palfry Park by the middle of June and I don't like to think of you here alone. You've told me you won't return to Cornwall, so why not come to London?"

Miranda knew she had gone pale. This was beyond anything her wildest imaginings could have conjured up. Surely she must be misreading him.

She gave a nervous laugh. "Ah, but I don't know a soul in London."

"You mean besides me and Ronald?"

"That's not the point. I can imagine what sort of figure I should cut being pushed along the Serpentine in my Bath chair. No, I think not. I'm not nearly ready for such a thing."

He sat without speaking for a time, his fingers drumming on the table, and she watched as his expression changed from pensive to determined.

"Then how about starting with an excursion into Ambleside?"

She blinked at him several times in bewilderment.

"The General and his family have been invited to spend two nights in Grasmere," he explained. "At Lord Sayreville's house party. They're leaving in three days. I have, however, declined an offer to accompany them, pleading edits on a book sent up from Grambling House." He shot her a swift grin. "You see that I am become an unrepentant liar on your behalf, ma'am. Anyway, I can borrow the General's gig and drive us into Ambleside—"

"Where we will do exactly what?"

"Whatever you like. Take in the sights, stop for tea. You don't ever have to leave the carriage if you prefer."

Miranda wondered if this was a dream—first his praise of

her writing, then the invitation to London and now his offering her a chance to get away from Palfry Park.

"Do you think I am ready for such a thing?"

He tipped his head back and met her anxious gaze. "You won't know if you don't try."

"We will need to go cautiously. I recall my cousin has several friends in Ambleside. Perhaps I should wear—"

"Oh, no," he protested, "not the veil. I forbid it. Besides, who there would recognize you?"

"I'm not thinking clearly. I doubt the General's friends even know I exist. But what of the servants and the grooms? I hate to enlist them in yet another deceit."

Morgan nodded. "The simplest plan is for me to take the gig and meet you in the lower garden. The drover's lane there leads to the public road behind Palfry Park."

"Perfect," she said.

Chapter Ten

Miranda took special care with her appearance that morning, choosing a jonquil-striped muslin gown with a sheer tucker that formed a high ruffle at her throat. It was one of Leanne's and sadly out of date, but she knew the color suited her. Mrs. Southey fussed with her hair, coaxing the waves into tiny elflocks that framed her face, then topped it off with a chip-straw bonnet adorned with a spray of gentians, courtesy of an unknowing Ariadne.

When Mrs. Southey held up the mirror for Miranda, they were both grinning.

"Tell me I am not being rash," Miranda said. "I'm suddenly feeling a little frightened."

Mrs. Southey squeezed her hand. "Not a bit of it. Mr. Pearce will see to you properly. 'Tis less than six miles to Ambleside, so if you start to feel peaky, he'll have you home before the cat can lick her ear."

It seemed to Miranda that an inordinate number of servants were standing about in the hallway as Mrs. Southey wheeled her toward the kitchen. That room, likewise, seemed to be full of loiterers, even Jem the dairyman and two of the gardeners.

"This was supposed to be a discreet adventure," she complained under her breath to Mrs. Southey as they ran the gauntlet of watchers.

Still, some part of her was gratified. She'd known most of these people since childhood, from her visits to Palfry Park before the accident. She hadn't always been a sullen invalid to them, and she saw now that they wanted to witness her recovery.

Morgan was waiting at the bottom of the garden, seated in a shiny black gig with a placid-looking gray cob in the traces.

"Morning, Miss Runyon," he called out. "And well done, Mrs. Southey."

He saw Miranda settled on the padded seat, and then drew a light throw over her knees.

"We may stop for luncheon," he said to Miranda. "If you're up to it."

She assured him she was and added that she'd been eating like a field hand lately. When he smiled at that, her stomach did an odd little flip, and she wasn't so sure about food after all. She realized she was still caught halfway between excitement and trepidation.

They set off at an easy pace and were soon on the north-bound road that led to Ambleside. Lake Windermere, edged by scattered clumps of woodland, lay off to their left, a glistening expanse of alpine blue dotted with the occasional sailboat. Beyond the lake, a rich green bolster of hills rose up, where the numerous waterfalls and freshets caught the sun and twinkled like elusive stars.

Morgan seemed to be focused on his driving, so Miranda amused herself, once she'd had her fill of scenery, by watching his gloved hands, strong and sure, on the reins. Today he wore a biscuit-colored driving coat over his customary dark clothing and she couldn't help admiring the dramatic contrast it made with his black hair.

She wanted to tell him how much his appearance pleased her, had always pleased her, but it would be totally improper to say such a thing. Though she didn't know why that should stop her—her daily encounters with him were hardly high on propriety.

If she were a normal young lady, her behavior with him— spending hours alone together and, now, driving out beyond Palfry Park—would have been considered fast, if not down-right scandalous. It was an indicator of how far from the realm of normal she was that neither Mrs. Southey nor Mr. Pearce seemed in any way concerned over this. Who would care if her reputation were ruined? Reputations were chiefly of value if a woman planned to wed, which was certainly not ever going to be one of her options.

Miranda decided there might be a blessing in this, that she could be as daring with Morgan as she liked.

"You look very fine today," she said brightly, trying not to blush at her own boldness. "I've grown used to seeing you only in dark colors."

"The devil cloaked in darkness," he quipped. "And I am a cawker for not paying you the first compliment. I can only plead in my defense that the sight of you this morning was so delightful that I became hopelessly tongue-tied."

"Fustian," she retorted, getting some of her nerve back. "And besides, these are merely more borrowed feathers. Or purloined, I should say."

Morgan slowed the gig as he turned to her and said in a low, rasping voice, "It was not the feathers I was admiring."

Heat swept over Miranda. Not the blushing sort that skimmed up from her chest, but a truly sizzling heat, sweeping upward from deep inside her. If she'd ever doubted that her more delicate inner workings had survived the accident intact, this singularly intense sensation reassured her.

She was nearly breathless and a little fearful. He rarely came this close, rarely spoke in such an unguarded tone. Even when he was curt or angry with her, it was always from a detached observer's distance. But he was here now, virile and powerful, sitting beside her. No teasing tormenter, determined teacher or fledgling friend, but a man . . . in his rugged, very potent prime.

Francis Halliday, that callow youth, had sparked her and even kissed her and had never once smote her with the dark, unsettling sensations that Morgan Pearce's gruff words evoked.

He was still looking at her, his black eyes narrowed and probing, and when she met that unwavering gaze, she swore the landscape around them tilted dizzily for an instant.

By the time she recovered, he'd returned his attention to the cob, rattling the reins to set the gig in motion again.

They drove on in silence after that, both of them keeping their eyes fixed firmly on the road ahead.

Ambleside was a charming village, its high street a collection of magpie-fronted shops and granite-faced business establishments. Miranda recalled earlier excursions there with her young cousins, the five of them wandering contentedly through the various shops of the sleepy little town. That was in the years before the Lake District had become such a magnet for scenery seekers. Now, there were several new guest houses on the main thoroughfare, where groups of fashionable people strolled the sidewalks and overflowed into the street.

For this reason, Morgan kept the cob to a walk as they passed through the center of town. Elegant curricles swept past them, mindless of the pedestrians. Heavy draft wagons drawn by feather-legged shire horses edged around them.

Miranda saw a tea shop she recognized and was about to suggest they stop, when a man stepped off the pavement directly in front of the gig and grasped the cob's bridle. "Hold up there! I say, hold up."

As Morgan reined in his horse, the man moved up to the side of the gig. He was wiry and sallow-complected, with thinning hair slicked back beneath a dented beaver and dressed little better than a tinker, in a blue- and orange-checked waistcoat under a tattered frock coat in a poisonous shade of green. By the pungent scent of him, he'd been whiling away the morning in a tavern.

Miranda at once determined the man was no threat—he was hardly the sort of person whose acquaintance the General would have cultivated.

"Steady on," Morgan whispered to Miranda, and then said in a cool voice, "Can I be of assistance, sir?"

"Isn't that General Palfry's gray gelding?"

"I hardly see that it's—"

"That's Palfry's nag," the man insisted, "or I'm Jack Sprat. Ought to know. I sold the beast to him last August." The man winked at Morgan. "Run off with one of his daughters, have you?"

Morgan's voice could have now frozen steel. "The Palfrys and their daughters are well accounted for, I assure you."

"And who might you be?"

She saw Morgan's hands tighten on the reins. "I am a guest at Palfry Park."

"Not in the market for a horse, are you?" the man asked, shifting position to get a better view of Miranda. "Or perhaps the lady is," he added with a leer. "No? Well, can't blame a fellow for plying his trade. Don't let me keep you. I understand. Was young m'self once. Nothing like a carriage ride with a pretty lady at your—" His eyes suddenly widened. "Oh, I say, no offense meant, ma'am. Pity about your face." He touched the brim of his hat and staggered backward. "Really, quite a pity . . ."

Morgan unwittingly jerked on the reins; the cob reared up and whinnied before a snap of the whip set him in motion. Morgan kept the beast going at a brisk clip until they'd passed right through the town. At the edge of a cornfield, he pulled up and turned to Miranda.

"Gad, I never imagined . . ."

There were tears streaming down her face. His heart sank. "Please, dear girl . . . I feel wretched already. . . . Don't . . . *Ah*." His hands clenched and unclenched, and all he wanted was to put his arms around her.

"You *should* feel wretched," she sniffed.

"I don't know what to say. Sorry, certainly. I had no way of knowing some ruffian would recognize the General's horse and accost us in the street."

"I can't believe you let that oily little man embarrass you."

He shrank back. "Me?"

"Well, I wasn't the one who whipped up my horse to get away from him."

"I was trying to save you from more embarrassment."

"*More* embarrassment? What made you think he bothered me in the least?"

"I . . . I . . ." Morgan gaped at her. "Damn!"

After setting the brake with an abrupt tug, he leaped down from the gig and went marching off along the border of the cornfield, beating his hat against the flapping edge of his driving coat in time with his angry strides.

There was no getting away from the truth. He'd done it,

done exactly the same as the General—neatly removed Miranda from view the instant things became awkward.

When he was about ten yards from her, he swung around. "I am an idiot," he called out.

She said nothing.

He started back toward her. "I overreacted," he called out again, then added in a level voice as he approached the gig, "Because protecting you is the only thing I think about lately."

She still wouldn't look at him. "You hated it that he noticed my cheek."

"Not at all. I hated that he was ill-bred enough to point it out."

Her eyes flashed at him now. "Ill-bred people and old people and children . . . they all say what they see. I didn't expect any different. How is it that I, who have been so cloistered, know that, and you, who have been to war and back, do not?"

"You expected it?"

"People gawk, Morgan. I had steeled myself to that possibility. What I wasn't prepared for was you having a fit of temper over it . . . and in the middle of the street." She met his gaze and said curtly, "Or was it a fit of regret?"

He gripped the side of the gig. "Oh, that *is* unfair. Any gentleman would have reacted the same—with annoyance. How dare the fellow leer at you and then call attention to your cheek?"

"I'm telling you it was an honest reaction. At least the part about pitying me for my face."

He leaned in closer. "And you think the leering part was not honest?"

She chuffed once. "It's hardly likely, is it?"

"How typical of you, Miranda, to steel yourself for dismayed reactions from people and then act incredulous when a man ogles you."

"I believe he was foxed."

"Just for the record, not that it's any compliment considering the source, he *was* leering at you." He smiled with artificial sweetness. "Just so you know."

"Thank you," she said stiffly. "Consider me edified."

He lowered his head and laughed ruefully to himself. "This is a pretty mess. Nothing's turning out as I planned it."

"Perhaps we should just go home."

He went around to his side of the gig, and swung himself onto the seat. "Whatever you like." He released the brake, and then turned the gig around on the grassy verge.

Miranda was still struggling to understand what had happened. The oily man had done two things to her and they'd both stirred Morgan's temper. She only wished she knew which one bothered him most.

"Morgan," she said after a time, "do you think it's your responsibility to . . . to protect me from unpleasantness?"

"Yes."

"And do you truly spend time worrying about that?"

"Yes."

"And that makes you angry?"

"Yes . . . *No*. No, it doesn't make me angry. It makes me . . . frustrated."

She reached out tentatively and touched his sleeve. "Don't protect me, Morgan. That's what *they* think they've been doing. Let me take my own knocks, if you please. I think I've managed to survive a few more than most people."

He stole a glance at her. She appeared resolute, if a little pale.

"It's difficult to stop," he said frankly.

"No more coddling, isn't that what you said? You've brought me back to the world. Please let me deal with it in my own way."

He nodded slowly. "Very well. Now, shall I drive back to Ambleside and let you harangue that rude fellow in the street?"

She chuckled. "No, I think I'd rather you found an inn to stop at. It's been fully three hours since my breakfast and I am famished."

Morgan knew the perfect place. Hodges had told him of a small inn that catered to the Lake District's more well-heeled visitors. Since it was not yet noon, it should be nearly empty, and even if there were patrons in the dining parlor, they would likely be too well-bred to gawk at Miranda.

The Speckled Trout lay in a wooded grove, gabled and stuccoed in the Elizabethan style, and shaded from behind by a truly spectacular chestnut tree. A winding stream ran beside the property, its near bank shored up by a waist-high wall of hewed granite stones.

An ostler came running when they pulled up in the yard, and he held the cob steady while Morgan lifted Miranda from the gig. Since it was the first time he had performed this office, he raised her carefully. She was a featherweight in his arms—in spite of her renewed appetite—and she smelled of lavender and verbena, like a treasured object that had been carefully packed away inside a trunk.

The innkeeper, a broad-hipped, bright-eyed woman with a mass of reddish hair came out onto the porch to greet them, introducing herself as Mrs. Crandle. She held the door for Morgan as he went through into the hall. "Private parlor or dining room?" she inquired.

"Dining room," Morgan answered without hesitation. As ordered, he was going to cast Miss Runyon to the figurative wolves.

He followed the landlady into a dark-beamed room with a dozen tables, only four of which were in use. Two or three people looked up in idle curiosity as Morgan went past with Miranda in his arms, and one of them, a pinch-faced young woman, quickly spoke an aside to her companion.

If Miranda can stand it, he told himself, *then so can I.*

The landlady indicated a high-backed booth at the back of the room, which lay beneath a mullioned bay window .

"If you would fetch us a cushion or two," Morgan said as he set Miranda on the bench, "I would be very grateful."

The woman quickly returned with two flat pillows and arranged them behind Miranda.

"All comfy now, pet?"

Miranda smiled, turning her head to look up at her. "Yes, very, thank you."

The woman winced slightly when she noticed Miranda's damaged cheek—and Morgan held his breath—but she quickly recovered her poise and recited the day's bill of fare.

"The salmon's come direct from the lake this morning," she said. "You won't find fresher in all of Cumbria."

Morgan looked at Miranda, and she nodded. "That will suit us both very nicely," he said.

Once she was gone, he took an oblong package from his coat pocket and slid it across the table.

Miranda shook her head. "You and your mysterious packages," she chided. "I should tell you, in case you are trying to make up for it, that I did not lack for gifts as a child."

"Then you should know how to say thank you."

She fought off a grin. "Thank you. But perhaps I should open it first." She undid the twine, easily, he noted, and pulled apart the stiff paper. Three silver utensils lay there—fork, spoon and knife—each with an elongated handle wrapped with smooth, dark cork.

He watched with pleasure as her eyes widened. "Oh, this is rare. However did you—"

"I ordered them from a silversmith in Windermere. I added the cork to the handles myself. To make them easier to grip."

She lifted each one in turn, testing the balance. "You are . . . a genius," she said. "I suppose Mrs. Southey told you I still have some trouble maneuvering with food. I was going to warn you before the meal arrived."

"Don't fret. I have acquaintances in London who are afflicted the same way—and without your excuse. Old Romney Barkhurst invariably wears more of his meal than he swallows, and he can't keep a valet for more than a month running, they are that shamed by the distressing state of his waistcoats."

Miranda laughed. "There, you've put me very much at ease."

When their meal came, he watched her negotiate the thick slice of salmon and the blanched mix of vegetables with her new implements. Four weeks ago, a pencil had to be tied to her hand with a strip of cloth. Now, even though she gripped knife and fork with obvious effort, and her motions were not delicate or refined, she was neither clumsy nor tentative. Most importantly, the food got to her mouth in one piece.

"Stop staring at me," she grumbled amiably at one point without looking up from her plate. "I can feel you gloating from across the table."

"Yes, I am rather," he admitted. "It's quite remarkable."

"Do I get any of the credit?"

He leaned back against the high oak support and observed her judiciously. "Mmm, perhaps a little."

She set her empty fork on the table, tines up, and looked at him through her brows. "If I really tried," she said slyly, "I could probably spear your hand right where it's lying beside your plate."

He drew both hands out of range. "Touché, ma'am. I'll give you that point and avoid any bloodletting. Foolish of me to arm you when I know how easily you rile."

She jabbed the fork in the air. "Keep that in mind the next time you try to bully me."

Her eyes were still dancing as she returned to her meal, and Morgan was again struck by the vast difference between this Miss Runyon and the bitter, pallid creature he had first met in the garden. If he had any doubts that he was doing right by her—and he still harbored plenty—it was moments like these that reassured him.

After the serving girl cleared their plates, Mrs. Crandle reappeared and suggested they might want to view the flower garden behind the inn. "There's a table and several wicker seats . . . and a pretty view of the stream."

Since Morgan had several times caught Miranda gazing out the window toward that very spot, he said it sounded ideal.

He again carried Miranda through the inn, Mrs. Crandle following behind, a pillow in each hand.

"On the wall," Miranda said. "I want to feed the ducks."

Morgan hesitated. On the stream side, the wall rose almost six feet above the water and the ledge offered no support for her back, but Miranda assured him she was strong enough to sit upright.

He was still dubious, but Mrs. Crandle had already placed the pillows on the ledge.

"Got a mind of her own, that one," she remarked to him under her breath.

"You have no idea," Morgan responded.

"I heard that," Miranda said, poking him in the chest. Morgan merely tightened his hold on her. "Trying to suffocate me into submission?"

"Now there's a thought . . ."

Mrs. Crandle stepped back to allow Morgan access to the wall, then stood there beaming at them. "I'll fetch you some crusts to throw to the ducks. And if you like, sir, a glass of my special gooseberry cordial."

"We'd both like," Miranda said determinedly before he could object, and then, "No, Morgan. I want to sit *facing* the stream. What's the point if I am left staring at that enormous tree trunk?"

He rolled his eyes and shifted her around so that her lower legs were dangling off the wide ledge. "If you tumble in, I am not ruining my boots to rescue you."

She made a face at him. And then looked down over her knees to the stream, where two dozen ducks had already assembled in anticipation of rich pickings. "What sort of ducks are those, do you think?"

He braced his hands on the wall and peered over it. "Brown ones."

"Oh, I forget," she teased. "You never went in much for blasting away at waterfowl."

He tipped his head toward her. "I'm surprised you remember that. I wouldn't think you'd want to recall that particular encounter."

She turned and met his eyes. "It's fairly etched in my memory."

Again, as had happened in the gig, the instant their gazes locked, neither of them seemed able to look away. Morgan had never experienced anything like it before. It wasn't as though she were plying him with the seductive, sleepy, half-shuttered look that some women used to their advantage. No, her eyes were wide open, holding a hint of mischief.

Then the impishness faded from her face, and she said in a faint, whispery voice, "In fact, that is one of my favorite days . . . of all time."

His response was no less ragged; he uttered her name, "Ah . . . Miranda," but before he could say anything more, Mrs. Crandle came hurrying into the garden with a basket over one arm.

"Plenty of crusts from the kitchen," she announced, "though

the creatures are so fat from all the guests feeding them, I wonder they can float. The ducks, that is, not the guests. And there's a bottle of my cordial and two glasses . . . since the lady wants to sample a dram."

After Morgan took it from her, she lingered there beside them.

"If . . . if I may have a word alone with the young lady."

At a nod from Miranda, he took himself off, praying the innkeeper did or said nothing to dispel his companion's rare, lighthearted mood. He'd never seen Miranda so playful or so approachable. In spite of their awkward beginning in Ambleside, the day was turning out very well.

Miranda was trying desperately to keep a straight face when Morgan completed his turn about the small garden and strolled back to the stone wall.

"It was nothing of moment," she told him. "She's really quite kind. She gave me this jar of skin cream, a special recipe from her granny in Scotland, guaranteed to smooth away all burns and blemishes."

He took up the porcelain pot and opened it. "It smells of heather and honey. I don't suppose there's any harm in it." He paused. "You weren't . . . affronted . . . that she . . ."

She took the pot back from him and tucked it into her reticule. "Not a bit. As I said, she is kind. If a trifle nosy." She gave up fighting the amusement that was bubbling inside her and grinned at him wickedly. "You see, she also delicately hinted that if . . . if I was your . . . lady bird, then I could take it from her that I had found myself a right proper gentleman and no mistake."

Morgan sank back against the stone ledge and put his hands over his face. "Oh, Lord. That was definitely not expected. I'd thought that in these rural outposts, people would be a bit more relaxed about a man and woman dining together."

"My reputation is apparently in tatters," she said with a chuckle. "And I have to thank you, because that might be the most exciting thing that's happened to me in the last three years. Who could have ever imagined?"

She was surprised when Morgan's face turned serious. "You

were assuming, maybe we were both assuming, that you'd never be back in proper company again. But, Miranda, that is what awaits you if you continue to improve at such a rate. I was worse than an idiot to jeopardize your good name."

She held one finger up near her lips. "Shhh. I won't tell if you won't. And it really doesn't matter. I don't ever expect to marry."

"Don't you?"

"My part of Cornwall, if I ever do go back there, is seriously lacking in eligible men, if any of them would even have me. I'll most likely dwindle happily into eccentric old age and raise canaries or rat terriers or some such thing."

Morgan snorted. "That's a pretty picture."

"Don't be cross. I am having too fine a time today to worry about something so far in the future. Here, give me some bread. . . . Those ducks are preparing to scale the walls to get at the food."

He plucked the wine bottle and the glasses from the basket, then handed it to her. After pouring each of them a glass, he boosted himself onto the wall beside her, facing away from the stream. "You can't see the ducks," she protested.

"I can see exactly what I need to see," he answered cryptically as he handed her the glass. "Now go easy with this. These home brews tend to be—"

"Potent!" she gasped as she downed her first swallow. "Good heavens! My father sometimes gave me a glass of brandy after a winter ride, but brandy isn't a patch on this."

Morgan sipped at his own drink, then shut his eyes slowly, like a cat savoring a sunny windowsill. "This is not bad. Not bad at all. I'll have to see if she has any extra bottles laid by."

"Yes," Miranda said primly. "That will do my reputation the world of good . . . when we return home bearing a case of incendiary spirits."

"Feed your ducks," he ordered with a mock scowl.

Miranda broke the crusts into crouton-size bits before she tossed them, wanting to prolong this time with Morgan as much as she could. She should have known that teasing him about being his lady bird would make his conscience flare up, make him rethink this excursion. But he seemed to have settled down again; she could almost feel him beside her, relaxed, sipping his drink.

She knew his mission today was to entertain her; she had a mission of her own. It seemed that every conversation they shared revolved around her: her ailments, her restrictions, her past, her present, her future. It was long past time she found some things out about him.

"What is it like being back in England?" she asked idly, keeping her eyes on the stream below her. "I mean, after the Peninsula."

"A relief, to tell the truth."

"And even though you told me that war was a 'bloody business,' you stayed in Spain for all those years?"

"This is probably going to sound daft, but men grow to like being in a war. And don't ask me to explain it; it just is that way. Your instincts, your whole outlook, alters, and you find yourself adjusting to it quite quickly. And after that, it's what you do each day, just as if you were going to your club or driving out on morning calls."

"Only you are carrying a gun, and other people are shooting at you."

"Very little of the time, actually. It's mostly marching and camping, with indifferent rations and heat and dust and icy cold . . . and still you end up craving it."

She liked the way his face had grown earnest while he spoke; maybe this wasn't going to be so difficult after all.

"And yet you didn't mind coming home."

"My uncle Cyrus was ill; he needed me at Grambling House. He is far and away my favorite relation—aside from Kitty—and I was glad to take over running the place, a good thing, since it's likely to be my only inheritance. Besides, the war remade me, and I was eager to see how I would fare in civilian life."

She shifted to look at him—and was surprised that he had also turned toward her. Their faces were only inches apart. Miranda tipped back her head. "Remade you how?"

His eyes narrowed. "You are full of questions today."

"Humor me," she said. "You know excruciatingly personal

things about me. I merely want to know a few details of your life."

"War changes most men," he said. "I've seen carefree, youthful recruits turned into grim-faced warriors in the space of a few weeks."

"And was that how it affected you?"

"No, it had the opposite effect on me." He leaned back and gazed up at the canopy of thick chestnut leaves. "I enlisted as a grim-faced young man, at odds with my father and half the civilized world, determined to prove myself on the battlefield or die trying."

"Things were not good at home?" she asked cautiously.

"They were wretched, in plain language. My father couldn't accept that I wanted no part of a country gentleman's life. The night he discovered I preferred working with my uncle at Grambling House, his anger just erupted." He paused to refill his glass. "Are you sure you want to hear this? It's not—"

She gave him a mulish frown. "I told you about my entrails."

He chuckled and nodded. "So you did. Anyway, he told me I'd always had lowbred tendencies, just like all my mother's kin—she was originally from a family of printers. We argued— it's a wonder we didn't come to blows—and then he . . . he—"

"What?" she coaxed gently.

Morgan drew a deep breath. "He told me he was sorry I hadn't died at birth—"

Miranda gasped.

"The army was my only recourse after that—since I'd fully determined to die a hero's death." He added a trifle sheepishly, "You know how it is with young men, they go off half-cocked with some ill-formed idea rattling around in their heads. I thought to make my father regret his words. But something happened during those first few months, something to do with all the bravery I witnessed in battle. It's hard not to have faith in your fellow man when you see selflessness at every turn. Once I got that back, I no longer wanted to die."

"I understand now," she said wonderingly, "why you took so much care with me. You knew somehow that I felt the way you had, trapped, unable to live my own life, almost wanting to end it."

"You were also an outcast, as I was, cut off from home and family. I suppose I saw you as my chance to restore someone else's faith in humanity."

"And I resisted you for days and days," she said with a sigh. "You might have told me some of this, you know."

"And you'd have listened?"

She hung her head. "Probably not."

"Anyway, you know how much I relish a challenge, another trifle brought home from the war."

"And what of that other 'baroque' reason for helping me you spoke of weeks ago? I think it's time you shared it with me."

"It's not something I ever speak of. Though you rather tugged it out of me that first day."

Miranda thought a moment. "Is it something to do with the friend you mentioned, the one who lost one of his legs?"

He nodded. "It's still difficult for me to talk about him."

"Because his injury was so . . . distressing to you?"

His expression darkened. "I would hope you know me better than that by now."

She shifted her hand to cover his where it lay on the wall. "Then tell me, Morgan. If he is responsible for you helping me, I at least would like to know his name."

"His name is Phillip DeBurgh," Morgan said. "He was one of Wellington's dispatch riders. During a skirmish, he was thrown from his horse, and before he could remount, he was struck by a length of timber from an exploding munitions wagon."

She heard her own indrawn hiss of dismay. Morgan gripped her wrist. "Sorry. I feared this would stir up your own memories—"

"No, please. I want to hear."

His hand slid down to cradle her palm. "For six months afterward he lay in a hospital in Lisbon. I visited several times on leave, but he was in a black despair. About a year ago he was sent home to London. He refused any help from his family and took lodgings in Chelsea."

"You've seen him since you came home?"

"For what it was worth. He would not even rise from his bed. We've . . . I've hammered at him to take back his life, but it washed right over him."

"You said *we*. Who else was there?"

Morgan grimaced. "Phillip wasn't only my best friend. He was also my sister's intended husband."

Miranda winced. "And now she is marrying someone else." She'd spoken the words softly, but they'd sounded accusatory.

He turned her to face him, gripping her shoulders so she would not tumble off the wall. "Don't say it in such a way! Kitty is the most loyal creature in the world. He refused to see her, but for months she wrote to him, begged him to take up his old life. She swore he could overcome his infirmity—"

Miranda wriggled in his hold. "I'm not sure that was the best way—"

"It was the only way she could see to encourage him, to pry him out of his black moods. I bought him a Bath chair. He would not use it. I brought in a doctor to fit him with a wooden leg. He wanted none of it."

Miranda's jaw tightened. "And so your sister finally gave up."

"No," he said bleakly. "In February, Phillip wrote to both of us. He was done with us, he said, weary of our constant badgering and our meddling in his life."

"And you and your sister accepted that?"

"We had little choice. He was growing increasingly morose with each visit. He felt he had no prospects left and nothing we did could convince him of it. Kitty and I both determined to move on."

"I gather she, at least, had some success at it."

Morgan looked at her sharply. "My sister is ultimately too prudent to chase after lost causes. She'd waited faithfully—for nearly five years—for Phillip to come home from Spain. Viscount Waverly had been a friend to her that whole time and she rewarded him for *his* faithfulness by agreeing to become his wife."

"But you don't like it."

He pushed up from the wall, moving away from her toward the trunk of the great chestnut. "I hate all of it, Miranda. Every last part. Phillip only enlisted because I'd gone off in such a pelter that he thought I needed a steadying influence." He spun back. "If not for that, he'd most likely be sitting in Parliament right now happily wed to my sister and with a sprat or two toddling at his heels. Instead he's lying in a dark room, with a broken body and a broken spirit."

He ran a hand through his hair, then dropped it, clenched, against his thigh. "And that is why I could not leave you alone. I could do nothing to save Phillip from his own worst nature. I failed to convince him that he is dooming both himself and my sister to unhappiness. The man she is to wed knows of this situation . . . and I suppose he cares for her enough to overlook it. But Phillip will have no one to ease his pain. His family and friends have been driven away by his bitterness and his anger."

He took another step closer. "So you will understand that when I met you, I saw a second chance. I told myself I'd be damned if I would let another person shattered by circumstance pass through my life without at least trying to give her back her dignity—and a shot at a normal life."

He was trembling visibly, whether from anger or pain, she could not tell. She wanted to look away from him, there was that much grief in his voice and in his eyes. But he had taught her how a soldier faced his fears.

"Come here, Morgan," she whispered.

He came forward until he was nearly up against the wall. She touched his arm.

"Lean down."

When he did, she set her hand against his face, forcing the fingers to open flush against his warm skin. "Thank you . . . for telling me and most especially for not abandoning me."

He covered her hand with his own. "With all those things in my past conspiring against you, there was no chance I could have walked away from what I saw that day."

"Except that you did," she pointed out with a benign smile. "Left me among the reeds like a garden gnome."

He stood upright, still holding her hand, and smiled back at her, an odd, pursed smile. "Gad, I wish I could take you to London to meet Phillip. He'd like you. You keep me on my toes, exactly the way he used to do. And he'd see in you proof that a person can come back from even the blackest despair."

"Do you blame yourself . . . for his loss?"

"I did at first, but not any longer. I fancy he's not the first soldier who joined up to keep an eye on a friend. If anything, it's Providence I blame."

"Providence has a lot to answer for," she said softly. "Then again, it's Providence that leads us to blessings on occasion."

"It does," he said, "if we are wise enough to notice."

He released her hand, took up his glass again and refilled it. He stood there, sipping the cordial, gazing out at the stream and the trees beyond it.

"And how," she asked gently, "would you have reacted if you'd suffered a similar injury?"

"Actually, I've wondered the same thing myself. With anger, I'm sure, and most probably disbelief . . . for a month or two, maybe even longer. But then my anger would have changed to rebellion. I believe I would have fought back, Miranda. Fought and scratched my way back to some kind of dignity. A man on crutches in the street still has some dignity. A man lying useless in his bed is a crying waste."

"And what about a woman in a Bath chair? Is there any dignity to that?"

"Of course there is, if she is out and about, doing something useful with her life. But if she merely wears out a path from bedroom to garden and never goes any farther afield . . ."

"I take your meaning."

"I don't believe I was being obscure."

Morgan feared for an instant that she would take offense at his sarcasm, but she laughed.

"You never do give me any quarter. And look—here I am truly off the garden path, sitting beside a stream with all these hungry—" She'd swung her arm out in a sweeping motion as she spoke and nearly unseated herself. She gave a startled cry.

He flew forward and tugged her back. "Careful, sweetheart. Those hungry ducks would make short work of you."

She looked up at him and grimaced. "Still not enough meat on these bones to tempt them."

Morgan's arm tightened around her; there was plenty enough to tempt him.

He ought to release her, not stand there practically embracing her. But for all her slightness, she was a delight to hold, the sun-kissed skin, sun-warmed shoulders, the scent of wildflowers drifting up from her throat. He hitched himself onto the wall beside her, swung both legs over the ledge, then drew his left arm more firmly around her waist.

Hang impropriety. He needed something to hold on to right now just as much as she did.

He shouldn't have told her about Phillip. It still hurt like blazes, even if the failure had been eased by his success with Miranda. He wasn't a blasted miracle worker, after all. Why should he endlessly blame himself when Phillip's own family and the woman he loved had been unable to motivate him?

He sat quietly beside Miranda, watching her pitch bread to the ducks, listening to the chestnut leaves cascading in the breeze. The sun shifted and their perch became shadowed, the breeze growing cooler now. He raised his arm to shelter Miranda's shoulders and tugged her closer. Her bonnet came to just below his chin. He noticed that the basket in her lap was empty. The cordial bottle, a little ways beyond him on the ledge, was half empty. No wonder he'd rattled on to her in such a way. Spirits always loosened his tongue.

When he felt her relax back against his arm, something warm and sweet washed over him. He wanted to put a name to the feeling but could not. He'd felt desire for women—in the arms of Spanish whores and English ladies. He'd often felt a fond tenderness for his mother and his sister. Yet he had never before felt a roundelay of both, where one and then the other emotion tugged at him, until they commingled into something he could not grasp, a sort of yearning, burning contentment that was totally illogical.

Perhaps it was best if he blamed it on the gooseberry cordial.

"You must be getting tired," he said as Miranda's head nodded against his shoulder.

"Mmm, a bit. And the cordial's made my brain go a little muzzy. It feels nice." She looked up at him. "It was a good day, Morgan."

"Yes, it was. But I think it's time we headed home."

Before he moved away from her, he leaned his head down and whispered against her ear, "And for the record, Miranda, that first day by the lake . . . it's etched in my memory, too."

She gave him a sleepy smile. "I know."

As he carried her to the front of the inn, it hit him again, that jumble of feelings . . . nurturing . . . tender . . . *urgent*. That last he quickly squelched, pretending he didn't enjoy holding her flush against his body, didn't savor the warmth and the subtle energy that coursed through her. What the devil was happening to him?

He figured it out on the drive home, as Miranda drifted into sleep against him. It made him wonder exactly when his simple need to protect her had become something much more—and he smiled ruefully at the adjective his brain chose—"baroque."

Miranda decided this was as close as she would ever come to dancing on air, this heady, giddy feeling that kept intruding in all her thoughts. She was supposed to be practicing her penmanship, but every so often she'd open the small drawer in the table to gaze at the three silver utensils lying there. Her throat caught each time as she smiled down at them.

She and Morgan had passed so many milestones that afternoon, she'd lost count. For one thing, she'd learned that he came from a most unusual family—a gentleman father who'd married a printer's daughter, a publisher uncle whom he worshiped, a sister who would take a seriously injured man as her husband without hesitation. The normal societal boundaries that Miranda had grown accustomed to, even within her own unorthodox family, did not apply to the Pearces.

And because of these revelations, his and her own, the bond between them had altered. They were no longer uneasy allies or budding friends, but something much closer. She'd seen his eyes linger on her face any number of times today and what she'd read in them—puzzlement, delight, an undefined yearning, but never regret—had lifted her heart. Still, she promised she would not let herself form any deeper emotional attachment to him. There was no reason she couldn't simply *like* him and avoid all serious repercussions.

Chapter Eleven

Morgan was also a little dazed after their outing.

Sitting there above the stream, so close beside her, he'd wanted the day to go on and on. She had somehow coaxed him to speak openly of things he'd barely dared to touch on in his thoughts—Phillip and Kitty, his troubles with his father. It was as though his forcing Miss Runyon to lower her barriers over the past weeks had had a reciprocal effect on him. All he knew was that he felt more at peace than he had in months—except for a niggling suspicion that having cracked that door, it would not be easy to close it again. At least not to her.

He also saw that he needed to do something to ensure Miranda's future once he was back in London. Drat the girl for refusing to return to Cornwall, which would have been the sanest solution. Since she insisted on staying at Palfry Park, he had to find a way to make her family accept her.

Dr. Cheney's intervention had turned out to be a forlorn hope, but it made him wonder if he could prevail on Dr. Ealing to come down from Edinburgh to review her case. Surely the testimony of a specialist would help to convince the General.

Morgan knew he had to do something soon—the Palfry sisters were making him nervous.

Even though he found it harder and harder to play the genial and accommodating guest, he had forced himself to attend another dinner party at the squire's earlier in the week. In the drawing room afterward, Bettina had teased him about his disappearances each morning.

"If I didn't know better," she'd said with a coy look, "I'd think you were conducting an intrigue right under our noses."

Morgan had opted for humor as a defense. "I fear you have found me out, my dear," he said with a deep sigh. "I am quite smitten with Mrs. Partridge, the blacksmith's wife. We dally each morning while her husband plies his bellows all unawares."

Bettina giggled at the notion, since the lady in question weighed at least twenty stone and was known to have the tongue of a Tartar. "You are a brave man, Mr. Pearce, to risk the wrath of our local Hercules."

"Ah, but the lady is such an ample armful."

She left off teasing him, and he hoped he'd allayed her suspicions. But then Ariadne had attached herself to him and mentioned that she'd seen him from her bedroom window that morning walking toward the lake. "I am prodigious fond of boating," she said. "I wonder if I could prevail upon you to forsake your solitude some morning to row out with me."

Morgan assured her he would be happy to do just that thing, except that he feared the old rowboat was badly in need of caulking.

Yes, it was clear the Palfry sisters were beginning to grow pettish and perhaps even spiteful at his defection, as though he were a shiny new plaything that had been whisked from their grasp. He only wondered if they had said anything yet to their father.

Since Cornwall was not an option and since he couldn't reasonably take Miranda to London with him, he decided the best course, the one that would ensure her continued recovery, was to tell Sir Janus of their meetings. Surely when the General saw the incredible progress his cousin had made, he would welcome her back into the fold. It was one thing for a man to turn a blind eye because he was too frightened or distressed to see, and quite another to look away when the truth was laid out plainly before him.

And on the off chance that he would no longer be allowed to meet with Miranda after his revelation, Morgan determined to offer her one last day of pleasure.

The morning after the trip to Ambleside, Miranda found herself again being wheeled down to the drover's lane at the bot-

tom of the garden. Morgan was there, leaning against the trellised entranceway, holding the reins of a powerful bay gelding
that had been tacked with a sidesaddle and pair of saddlebags.

"It occurred to me that you must miss riding," he explained
simply.

She eyed the restive animal with some misgiving. "I'm not
sure I could manage."

"Nonsense," he said. "I'll see to the reins, and you'll get the
sense of being able to move about freely without that cursed
chair."

This notion certainly appealed to her, and since she'd been
a fearless rider once upon a time, she agreed to let Morgan lift
her onto the sidesaddle.

The horse nickered softly and shifted on his feet. Miranda
closed her eyes, suddenly transported back to Cornwall, to the
sea cliffs where she'd ridden her crossbred moor pony every
day. She swore she could smell the tang of the ocean, hear the
soothing swell of the surf.

"It's a pity you need to lead me like a child," she lamented
as Morgan set off down the farm track. "This is so tame."

He looked up at her, his eyes teasing. "Three minutes ago
you were afraid. Now you want to race?"

She shook her head. "No, you're right. But soon enough I'll
be riding on my own again. I'll . . . I'll go flying across the
fields just the way I used to. You'll see, Morgan."

His face tightened, but he said nothing.

They soon veered off the track, crossed a wide field and
moved onto a woodland trail she recognized; it led to a huddle
of hills with a small lake and a group of standing stones in their
midst.

They walked for nearly half an hour, with Morgan fallen
into a silent study. Miranda wondered if he felt a bit awkward
about yesterday, if he too sensed the change in their relation-
ship. Or perhaps there had been no change, and she was merely
being a paper wit.

On a wooded hillock that rose above the lake and the circle
of craggy neolithic stones, he tethered the horse and went to un-
strap the saddlebags.

"I thought you might be in the mood for a picnic," he said

as he drew out a cloth sack and a folded blanket. This he shook out, positioning it on the grass beside the trunk of a venerable oak. Then he lifted her down and set her on the blanket near the tree so she could use the trunk as a support. He stretched out on the opposite side, reclining on one elbow, the sack of food between them.

He still would not look at her.

"What's troubling you, Morgan? And no, don't scowl at me. You're all but wearing a placard that says 'man in deep thought.' "

"Am I that transparent?" He fiddled with the cord on the sack. "It's nothing really. Let's eat now and we can talk about it later."

She wrinkled her nose. "As if I could eat a single bite. You must tell me what's bothering you."

"Later," he said. "Let's not spoil the day."

"Oh, that's reassuring. Am I to be on tenterhooks then, until you decide the time is right?"

Her first panicked thought was that he was going back to London and was afraid to tell her. She knew he still resented the General for keeping him from his work there, but she'd hoped their time together had ameliorated some of his frustration. Nevertheless, she couldn't hold him here forever.

The day suddenly took on a fragile, precious quality, and she understood now why he'd wanted to wait to tell her his news. Maybe that *would* be best.

"I've decided to tell the General about our meetings," he said before she could stop him.

Miranda's heartbeat faltered. It wasn't as bad as she'd feared, but still something that meant more risk, more change. "Do you think that's wise?"

"I don't believe I have a choice. Bettina and Ariadne have started to press me about my daily disappearances. It's only a matter of time until one of them follows me. I think it would be better to explain things to Sir Janus, rather than being caught in the act, so to speak."

Miranda was having trouble hiding her anxiety, but Morgan was looking down toward the lake.

"I want to see you a part of this family before I leave for

London," he said. "The General will be back tonight, and we can talk to him then. Talk to him together." He turned to her. "You're not saying anything."

"I don't know what to say. What if he refuses to see me—"

Morgan's eyes flashed. "How can he? You live in the same house, for God's sake. If it comes to that, I'll park your chair in front of his study door, and then he'll have to deal with you. It's time the Palfrys saw the real Miranda Runyon instead of this monstrous chimera they've created in their heads."

"What if he's angry over your deception and forbids us to meet?"

"I don't doubt he will be angry. But I am hoping that when he sees the positive results, he will have enough sense to forgive me."

"He won't be pleased that you've been meeting me alone— I mean, without a chaperon."

"We haven't exactly been sneaking off to the woodshed together," he pointed out. "Everything's been out in the open. I made sure of that. And there won't be any impropriety from here on if one of your women sits with us. I did think of that at the start, but you were so difficult to reach, and I knew it would be easier if we could be private."

No, she realized, in spite of all the time she'd spent with Morgan, there had been no truly clandestine moments between them. Even yesterday's outing might not have offended the General who thought nothing of allowing his own daughters to drive to town with their beaux.

Miranda almost wished she and Morgan *had* shared a few improper encounters. Today was as close as she was likely to come to throwing caution to the wind. And yet what was this, after all, but a placid picnic a few miles from home? Hardly the stuff of heady remembrance.

Morgan had begun laying out the food from the sack, a wedge of cheese, a loaf of brown bread and a small crock of ale.

"I don't like you telling the General," she said after a time. "But it probably is our only course. You'll be needing to return to London soon, and that way Sir Janus can take over—"

"London has nothing to do with it," he said brusquely as he attacked the stout brown loaf with a kitchen knife, creating more crumbs than slices. "I'm not itching to be away, in case you haven't noticed."

She reached out toward him. "Morgan, stop. What is it? You're still upset."

"Shouldn't I be?" he asked, lowering the knife and finally meeting her eyes. He must have seen her wounded expression, because he quickly added, "Oh, not at you, my girl. Never that. I hate the situation we've been placed in, all these weeks of sneaking about. I wish to God I'd confronted Sir Janus the day I met you. Told him he was being a pigheaded old fool. I should have wheeled you into the drawing room that very night, let him—let them all—have a proper look at you."

"I would likely have swooned." .

"Then they'd have seen beauty in repose," he said.

Miranda thought she must have heard him wrong.

"They are not outright cruel," he went on. "Merely selfish and self-involved. Somehow I find that almost as intolerable. And now I am afraid . . . that the General's anger at me might spill onto you. I won't see you made a victim again, Miranda. I won't sit idly by if he tries to lash out at you."

Personally, she thought it was ludicrous that they should both feel like children caught out in some mischief. She was a woman grown, and Morgan was years past his majority, but it didn't matter. When General Palfry was upset, he had a gift for making people feel small and powerless.

Except for her father, she recalled. Jacob Runyon had never let his cousin intimidate him. "Old Bluster Britches," he called him. She smiled at the remembrance, and then determined she would be her father's daughter in this.

"He can't stop me," she said staunchly. "Even if I never recover completely, I vow I will take back my life. He's hardly going to lock me in my room like the heroine of some two-penny novel."

Morgan frowned and his whole body seemed to tense. "Why shouldn't you recover completely?"

She hitched one shoulder. "I don't know, just a feeling I get sometimes. That the things I need to learn are greater than merely recovering the ability to walk."

"I thought that was what you wanted." His voice grew

sharper. "What have we been working toward all this time? If you don't care whether you walk again, what have I been doing with you all these weeks?"

Her face tightened. "Is this how you coaxed Phillip to respond? With harsh, accusatory words? It's no wonder he's still abed."

He pushed to his feet and stood there glaring. "Yes, there were harsh words. And kind words, and jollying words. Christ, I used up the whole blasted dictionary trying to reach him."

Miranda leaned forward, bracing herself with her hands. "But did you ever tell him he was fine the way he was?"

His eyes blazed. "Of course I didn't. He wasn't fine. Isn't fine."

"I promise you, that is what he needs to hear."

"And how the devil would you know that?"

She smiled wistfully. "Because it was what I needed to hear." She looked down at her clenched fingers. "I still do."

Morgan threw himself onto his knees beside her, tugging at her hands. "What do you mean? I don't understand. Help me, Miranda. I did everything I could think of to reach Phillip. If there is something more—"

He was canted above her, his face troubled, his dark eyes intent. If he hadn't been gripping her hands so tightly, she would have stroked them along his cheeks to soothe him. "I can't tell you. You need to figure this one out for yourself."

He let go of her and shifted around abruptly, sitting down with his back against the tree trunk. They were nearly shoulder to shoulder.

"You're not going to edify me."

"No."

He rubbed at his face with one hand, muttering under his breath. "This doesn't have anything to do with some perishing Bible parable, does it?"

Miranda nearly chuckled. "No . . . at least I think not."

He meshed his fingers and set them on his bent knees, staring at the knot of flesh as if he could deduce the answer there. "Tell Phillip he is fine the way he is," he said. And again, "Tell Phillip he is fine the way he is."

"You sound like a schoolboy reciting his times tables. Good retention but no comprehension."

"Shut up, Miranda," he growled. "You've set me a puzzle and I intend to solve it."

Through the filigree of leaves overhead, she watched the plush white clouds float past, pure aerial fleece today. She liked them that way. Morgan's shoulder was now up against hers. She liked that, too.

"Perhaps you need to eat first," she suggested.

"No, unlike you, I think best when I'm peckish."

"I can give you a hint. . . . Think about your father."

"Oh, that is wonderful. All my past failures are coming to light now."

"And why were you a failure in his eyes?"

Morgan uttered a soft curse. "I should never have told you that, not that I could have changed any of it. I was just too different from him, eager to try new things with my life, not wanting to plod along the same tired traditional path he and all the other Pearces had followed for centuries."

"Some parents approve of such brashness."

"Not him. He could never accept that I was cut from a different cloth and nothing I did ever pleased—" He stopped and turned to her. "That's it, isn't it? Even though his idea of what was acceptable didn't jibe with mine, he never had the generosity of spirit to tell me that I was fine just as I was."

She smiled wanly. "It all comes down to acceptance, Morgan."

"And you're saying I refused to accept Phillip as he was, that I made him feel as though he had to become a person he was no longer capable of being in order to be accepted?"

"Something like that."

"Was it that simple?" he whispered, as if to himself. "Something so basic and none of us saw it?"

"I am not saying that he wouldn't eventually want to improve his situation. But I know from my own experience that all you really require, what you crave beyond anything, is for the people who love you to accept you just as you are. Without that first critical assurance, it's so hard to come back. The fear of failing, of disappointing them and yourself, is just too great."

"And now it's too late."

"Oh, pish. It's not ever too late. Look at me. Three years of solitude and self-pity, and you came along and jarred me right out of it."

"But why did it work with you and not with Phillip? I never pretended you were fine the way you were. Quite the opposite, in fact."

"But you did in a way," she said, touching his sleeve. "You treated me as though I was normal, just a run-of-the-mill cranky, self-pitying woman who needed a good shaking. You never tiptoed around my infirmities or offered me any quarter. It was invigorating."

"I'm still confused."

"Listen. It's true that you let me know how much you wanted me to improve. But here's the important part—you never made me feel that you would abandon me if I didn't. I learned from you that most of the victory is in the trying, not necessarily in the achieving."

He shifted toward her. "So let me get this straight. I am to tell Phillip that it's immaterial to me whether or not he ever rises from his bed, and that if he does try to better his lot, it won't matter to me whether or not he succeeds, I'll still be supporting him all the way."

"Precisely," she said with a grin.

"It's a good thing, Miss Runyon," he grumbled as he reached again for the bread, "that they never let women go to war. You've got your priorities all topsy-turvy."

"Amen to that," she said. "Though I fancy if women conducted wars, we'd all be home in time for tea."

He'd write to Phillip that very night, he decided as he portioned out their food onto linen napkins. Better yet, he'd enclose his letter in a note to Farthing, Phillip's valet. Good old Farthing would see to it that his master read Morgan's letter.

He still wasn't convinced that Miranda had the right of things, but he'd tried every other tactic imaginable, and so had Kitty. Maybe he should write to her first, let her convey this new message of unconditional acceptance to Phillip. What was it Miranda had said? That you want the people who love you to accept you just as you are. That was definitely more in Kitty's line. Furthermore, she was there in London; she could carry the message in person.

Of course, he'd momentarily forgotten her betrothal to Waverly. Hardly the done thing to visit a bachelor in his bedroom when you were plighted to another.

For the first time since he'd started meeting with Miranda, he wished himself back in London. If there was a chance of reuniting his sister and his friend, it had to be done before Kitty's wedding, which was a little over four weeks away.

He heard Miranda give a small grunt of impatience and saw that she was struggling gallantly with the crumbly cheese, which kept tumbling off her jagged slice of bread and onto her napkin. Her face had scrunched up into a comical frown, which did nothing to destroy the appeal of her fine-boned features. Perhaps she was not a paragon by London standards, but he increasingly found his recollections of the beautiful women he'd known there growing hazy, while, oddly, her gamine face remained firmly etched in his thoughts.

He didn't want to go anywhere, he realized with a start.

He'd write to Kitty and then wash his hands of the whole matter. She and Phillip would work things out or they would not. He couldn't save everyone. He wasn't even sure if he needed to save Miranda any longer. Five minutes ago, it was she who had saved him.

She caught him watching her and gave a rueful grin. "I've made a sorry mess."

"No matter," he said, retrieving the napkin from her lap and bundling it into a ball. He then leaned forward on his elbows, gazed up at her through his lashes and murmured, "I think you're fine just as you are."

He'd expected her to blush, but she gave a gurgle of laughter. "It's just as my mother warned me. How sad that a woman has to put the words in a man's mouth if she wants to be complimented."

"The thought may not be original," he said with a lazy smile, "but the sentiment is quite valid."

"Then tell me you won't mind it if I never walk."

Her words struck him like a shot. His glibness evaporated as he struggled to maintain a calm front. Her smoke-colored eyes never wavered from his face as she waited for a response.

What the devil could he say? In truth, the notion infuriated him. If she never walked, if she never danced or rode or stamped her foot in anger or hugged herself in delight, if none of those things ever came to pass then she would always be an outsider and—

And what? Why should it bother him if she remained outside society? Society had clearly meant little to her before the accident. Did he want her to fit in because that world still had some meaning for him, because he enjoyed moving among amusing, attractive people? If she ever came to London, would he put his dignity at risk by keeping company with her?

Can you credit it—Mad Morgan Pearce has taken up with a lady in a Bath chair!

He could just hear the tabbies whispering behind their infernal fans. Lavinia Farley would laugh herself into an apoplexy.

And there was something more, a matter he had not dared to dwell on, even if his thoughts, to be honest, had strayed there more than once. They came pushing forward now and would not be stayed. If she never left that blasted chair, would she ever be bedded by a man? Would she ever know the joys of giving and taking pleasure in a lover's embrace?

She was fair of face and body, and from the start he'd never doubted that there was a great, untapped well of passion for all of life inside her. Would some man see beyond her infirmities and reach for that passion, feeding it and nurturing it until it blazed into carnal desire? Could any man muster the patience and control to school a partner who would virtually be—and he used her own word intentionally—a rag doll in his arms?

Could he?

"I see," she said softly, "that you have borrowed my habit of drawing in on myself."

He cast her a look of appeal. "I wish I could say it wouldn't matter if you never walked, Miranda. But how could you endure the thought of being forever dependent on others to get around? Worse perhaps, for how long could you dwell in the wings of life, always watching the other players but never joining in? Year in, year out? You'd soon grow to hate it."

She *tsked.* "I wasn't asking how *I* would feel, Morgan. I was asking how *you* would feel."

As if he didn't know that.

He closed his eyes for an instant and forced himself to speak his own fears. "I . . . I don't think I could tolerate it."

Her breath drew in sharply. "Honest," she said, "and a bit hurtful."

"Damn . . . I didn't . . . that's not what . . . I only meant that . . ."

Her hand flashed up—he took an instant to feel proud of that swift reflex—and she said, "No! Don't try to smooth it over. I am strong enough to hear the truth. Besides, you'll be long gone from my life before it ever becomes a question."

Morgan felt his blood begin to pound. "Is that what you think? That I will abandon you because you might not live up to my expectations? Am I to suffer that icy glare—and let me tell you, ma'am, you excel at that look—merely because I want more for you than you want for yourself?"

Her jaw set. "Has nothing of what I said earlier filtered into that brick wall of a brain? I didn't say I wouldn't try to walk. I only said I had an uncanny feeling it might not ever happen. You have to accept that, just as you have to accept that Phillip might never rise from his bed or that your father may never understand you."

He leaned toward her and said earnestly, "I'd take the lesser victories with them, Miranda. Truly I would. A smile of welcome from Phillip, a simple handclasp from my father. It's only for you that I want it all."

"And why is that?"

He gave her a sly, ghost of a smile as he tossed her own words back at her. "I can't tell you that. You need to figure it out for yourself."

He heard her low grumble of complaint as he shifted back to his side of the blanket and stretched out on his belly, resting his chin upon his crossed arms. "And to allow you to do so uninterrupted, I am going to have a nap."

Morgan made a pretense of sleep, while his thoughts churned and tumbled. After a few minutes of cogitation the only thing reasonably clear to him was that he'd gotten in deeper with Miranda Runyon than he'd ever intended. Far, far deeper.

It was no use pretending she was merely his friend. Yesterday they had strayed into some place wholly foreign to him, a place, however, that did not have "friendship" posted on any of the road signs. Today they seemed to have returned to the combativeness of their earliest encounters. He wasn't sure which state made him more uncomfortable.

He heard her moving away from the tree—it pained him to think of her dragging herself across the blanket. Was he turning into his father, unable to tolerate those who were different? Throughout his childhood, he'd watched his father increasingly distance himself from his mother simply because she was of a different class.

It had been a notorious mésalliance, the wealthy sprig of a fine old Surrey family wedding with the daughter of a printer from Cheapside. They had met in Vauxhall Gardens, his mother separated from her friends during the fireworks, his father on the prowl, a little drunk, but not so jugbit that he couldn't see that Maria Grambling was the most beautiful girl he'd ever stumbled across.

Courting and marrying her had been the great folly of his father's life, one he'd come to regret before many years had passed. When Maria invited her rough-and-tumble family to visit Roselinden—cousins in the printing trade, a brother with aspirations of becoming a publisher—his father had been appalled by their loud laughter and bawdy humor. He quickly banished them from the place. But it was too late. His ill-advised marriage had already made him the butt of numerous jokes among his well-bred London friends. Now he watched as his fellow landowners in Surrey gradually excluded him from their sporting pursuits.

Morgan knew his father's withdrawal of affection had broken his mother's spirit, chiefly because she'd never understood it. Not until the day she died. She was neither unschooled nor unpolished. Her rough-hewn family had had the means to educate her as a proper young lady, but none of it mattered to Elliott Pearce in the long run. She was ultimately different from his own kind. . . . She was *low*.

Morgan wondered if that was how he viewed Miranda. Different, set apart by her infirmities and therefore low in society's eyes. Could he, like his father, feel contempt for a woman he had taken under his protective wing, a woman he truly cared about? Miranda deserved someone decent and generous, not a man who set such store by appearances, who could rescue her from everything except his own need for perfection.

When Morgan tried to picture this man of sterling qualities who would make Miranda the ideal mate, his brain grew fuzzy and he was overcome by a sort of black rage.

Plague take my father and society both! It was what *he* thought of her that mattered. Nothing else.

And what exactly did he think of her? How could he find some of her qualities so appealing, so utterly compelling, while others made him wince. He really *had* been mortified yesterday in Ambleside, furious at the drunken lout, but more furious at himself for his own reaction. If only the world was made up exclusively of people like Mrs. Crandle, who did not gawk or gape or make rude remarks.

I am the one who is crippled, he thought wretchedly. *I cannot accept that she might never be more than she is right now. That is why I failed Phillip and will never truly be there for Miranda, because I want to turn back time and make them what they once were . . . whole and upright and . . .*

He must have dozed off for a time. Something had awakened him, brought him back to an awareness of the sun on his back, the slight breeze on his cheek . . . and a light, feathery touch on his hair.

Miranda was sitting close beside him, he didn't need to open his eyes to know that. She was stroking his hair, lightly, as a mother soothes a fretful child, her hand moving over his crown, then down until her fingers brushed the bared skin of his neck.

A sensation of awareness shot through him instantly, alerting every nerve in his body.

All his sour musings faded away at that touch. This tactile reassurance was exactly what he needed at this moment, to be reminded that the bond between them was all that mattered, that his pleasure in her company made insignificant any squeamishness he might feel. Surely if Kitty were so afflicted he would not balk at being seen with her or ever question his allegiance to her.

That was what he would do, he decided, think of Miranda as a beloved sister or a cherished cousin.

When her fingers drifted to the sensitive skin behind his ear, he couldn't stop himself from groaning softly in pleasure. All benign, brotherly thoughts fled instantly away as his whole body flexed involuntarily. He felt lust stir and then come wide-awake, predatory and sharp-set.

He pressed his forehead into his crossed arms, willing the sensations to cease. The last thing he needed was that hot lick of desire to confuse his already jumbled emotions.

He gave up the pretense of sleep then, and opened his eyes, yawning a little. Miranda was looking down at him with an odd, curling smile.

"Sorry if I woke you. There was a wasp flying above your head."

Five or six at least, he thought wryly, based on the number of times she'd touched him. He saw that she'd packed up the sack with the remains of their lunch, as though she were anxious to return home. In light of their forthcoming interview with the General, he realized this might be the last time they were alone together. He was a complete sapskull for spending it fighting with her and then falling asleep.

It couldn't end like this—he needed to recapture the sweet intimacy of yesterday.

He stood up, gauging from a distance the proportions of his horse, who stood idly lipping a tree branch. "I have an idea—"

"Oh, no," she said warily. "Your ideas invariably mean I have to do something disagreeable."

"Coward," he teased.

"Bully," she countered.

"How would you like a proper ride? Not being led about like a child."

Her eyes lit up. "You shouldn't even have to ask. I am Cornish bred and we ride before we even toddle."

He stashed their gear in the saddlebag, settled her in the saddle, and then untethered the horse. He managed to boost himself up behind her with some grace, and reached around her for the reins.

"Lean back, Miranda," he said, sliding his left arm around her waist. "I am going to show you how we cavalry officers did it in Spain."

He set the horse at a slow, controlled canter down the slope of the hill, and when they reached the flatland, he asked for a bit more speed. The gelding lengthened his stride and Morgan felt Miranda ease into the fluid, rocking motion. She was warm against his chest, relaxed and supple. His arm tightened around her, feeling the spring of her ribs, sensing the rise and fall of her breast.

He approached the standing stones, a dozen granite menhirs forming a large irregular circle, and skillfully wove the horse in and out of the narrow spaces that separated them—until Miranda was crowing with pleasure.

After one circuit, he moved to the perimeter and began to circle it at a loose canter. "Faster, Morgan," she called out, fisting her fingers in the horse's mane. "I want to fly."

He urged the horse into a gallop then, the mighty hooves sending up clods of reddish dirt and spidery tangles of grass. He leaned forward, curling himself around Miranda as his calves gripped the beast's flanks. His father might have belittled him for his lack of interest in field or stream, but he was a natural and gifted horseman.

He felt her head press into his shoulder, felt her body arch away from him and knew if she could, she'd have flung her arms wide, relishing the whipping wind and ground-eating motion of the gelding, whose every hoofbeat pounded out *freedom, freedom.* . . .

When Morgan pulled up at last, Miranda's bonnet was tipped over one shoulder and her sunny brown elflocks were in scrambled disarray. She shifted her head around to beam up at him, her face flushed, her eyes bright and vividly blue.

Morgan couldn't have looked away if his sanity depended on it.

If Miranda thought their wild ride had stolen all her breath,

the ardent, burning expression in Morgan's eyes proved her
wrong. It hit her like a hard thump to the belly.

"Happy now?" he asked gruffly.

"Yes . . . Thank you," Miranda gasped out, and before she
could stop herself she leaned up boldly and kissed his cheek.

Next instant he shifted his head so that their mouths met—
full on.

It was no accident on his part; the heat she tasted was immediate. His hands rose to her face, tipping it up while he deep-
ened the kiss. Nothing had ever felt like this . . . shaking her,
rousing her, raking through her insides until she felt she might
expire from pleasure. She strained up toward him, needing to
match his intensity, and she heard him groan as her tongue
danced against his.

"God help me, you're madder than I am," he muttered
against her mouth. "Mad and wild and . . . God, do that again—"
She took another savoring, tugging bite of his nether lip and felt
his arm clasp her waist in a grip of iron, possessive and primal.

She sensed the remains of his restraint falling away then,
swore she could feel the blood pounding through him, drumming in time to her own thundering heartbeats. His name was
on her lips, a soft, shuddering cry, as he tore at the strings of her
bonnet and cast it roughly away, just before his mouth seared a
path along her throat.

He somehow managed to get both of them off the horse,
which had drifted back inside the circle, lifting her from the
horned saddle, sliding down first, then cushioning her with his
body as they tumbled to the turf. He never stopped kissing her,
fierce, frantic kisses blazed against her lips as they fell, entwined and—for the first time since they met—completely of
one mind.

Miranda was truly flying now, soaring airborne, no longer
earthbound, chair bound. Their galloping ride had exhilarated
her spirit, but this heady combination of urgent, open mouths,
tangled limbs and arcing bodies set something new free inside
her, something earthy and stunningly potent. Heart and soul and
every muscle and fiber were bent on connection.

This is passion. . . . This is utter joy, she marveled, breathless with the discovery.

Morgan was watching her between kisses, his eyes narrowed, full of a dark, dangerous light. But she refused to be afraid, too enthralled by his mastery, his lithe body and the stark, haunting beauty of his face.

He must have seen something disturbing in the fearless wonder that shone from her eyes. He drew back slightly with a frown, removed the heavenly pressure on her chest and belly.

"Don't stop, Morgan."

"I never took you for a fool, Miss Runyon." His voice was hoarse, almost cross.

"I never took you for a quitter, Mr. Pearce."

"If I don't quit now, we'll both play the fool." He shifted off her completely and sat up.

She was too weak, too shaky, to push herself upright, so she lay there, sprawled on her back on the grass and watched him turn away from her.

A tiny crevice formed in her heart.

So this was how men behaved after a heated encounter. She'd always wondered. Francis had kissed her those few times, but never with such open passion, and he'd always laughed afterward, as though the exercise were a frolic.

This was no frolic.

She toyed with the idea of apologizing, but decided it would make her look ridiculous. It wasn't as if *she* had assaulted him.

"Should I be mortified?" she asked at last. "Because, let me tell you, this is very awkward."

He swiveled back to her at once, concern creasing his brow. "No, of course not."

"But I was the one who kissed you first—"

"No, that was not what you offered me; it is what I took. And would take again . . . if we had not lost the moment."

She dwelled on this for a heartbeat or two. It had possibilities. "And how exactly did we lose the moment?"

"Because I came to my senses." He cursed under his breath when she winced at his harsh tone. "And stop looking at me like that. Christ, you're only four years my junior and yet you are still such a blasted innocent. Don't you understand . . . about men, about what kissing leads to. My sister already knew those things when she was rising thirteen."

Miranda forced herself to sit up, not caring that she looked ungainly doing it. She had to meet this challenge face-to-face.

"I understand plenty," she said hotly. "About kissing, about what it leads to. I had a thorough education, for your information, and can probably name more parts of the reproductive system than Dr. Cheney. What I *don't* understand is how you could be crooning my name and kissing me one minute, and then the instant you stop, you just thrust away from me, as if I were a . . . a gorgon."

He slid closer, his eyes now bright with some secret humor. "Your thorough education obviously didn't stray into male physiognomy and the physical results of kissing. I was merely removing myself until I . . . got matters a bit more under control."

Miranda blushed, furiously, she was sure, if the blast of heat rising up from her bodice was any indication.

She understood; he'd been saving her from maidenly embarrassment, maybe saving himself as well, from being . . . found wanting. She nearly chuckled at her own pun, easier in spirit now that he'd explained his abrupt behavior.

She drowsed in the sun, shifting onto her side so she could look at Morgan. He faced her in a similar pose, two feet away. Close enough to touch, if she really put her mind to it.

The circle of stones seemed to protect them, forming a visual barrier from the outside world. But there were gaps in the stones, just as there had been gaps in the defenses she'd spent three years erecting around herself. Morgan had found those gaps, almost every one of them.

"There was a circle of standing stones near Nasrannah," she said, still gazing up at the nearest of them, a towering, lichen-laced monolith. "Older than the pyramids, my father told me. As a child I used to fancy witches lighting balefires in their center on Beltane and Halloween."

"That didn't frighten you?"

She gave a low, fond laugh. "Not a bit. You see, I also fancied that my parents were part of the ritual. They were intrigued by magic . . . though I learned as I grew older, it wasn't that sort of magic."

Morgan scuttled closer. "Now here's a tale."

And so she told him of the mystique of Cornwall that had intrigued both her parents at an early age, an interest that had ultimately brought them together. She described the sprawling redbrick house with its diamond-bright mullions numbering in the hundreds, its odd but evocative decor and its two secret passages. She relayed the rich history of Nasrannah, including its occupancy by a number of smuggling gentlemen and at least one French pirate.

"There was a small sea cave at the bottom of the cliffs," she said in a dreamy voice. "Enough above the high-water mark that it remained dry except during neap. Every September, on my birthday, my parents would bring me down to the cave to see what gifts the sea gods had cast up in my honor. Wonderful things . . . hand-colored picture books of exotic animals or faraway places, complex automatons that would have delighted a bored sultan. A telescope for viewing the stars, a microscope for studying the universe of flowers and insects." Her voice had lowered to a lulling whisper, like the night voice of the sea. "Those were the gifts I found in Prospero's cave."

Morgan was watching her with a curiously intent expression on his face, and she grinned sheepishly. "I never wanted to admit, even as I grew older, that it wasn't the gods, but my mother and father who had placed the gifts there."

"I think they *did* believe in magic," Morgan said, his voice rasping slightly. "The magic of people who truly understand another's needs and desires." He reached out—no great task for him—and trailed his hand along her arm, from wrist to shoulder. "That was their best gift to you, Miranda, there in Prospero's cave. The one you couldn't leave behind."

She nodded and felt tears gather. They were not tears of grief, however, but only the first tokens of a long-awaited release. She rubbed at her nose and her eyes, feeling an overwash of great peace settle upon her.

"Thank you," she said, and it was a testimonial to how far they had come together that he did not ask her for what.

Instead, he raised his hand to her face, stroking his fingers along her damaged cheek, then cupping them at the angle of her jaw. "I'm sorry I didn't handle things better just now. If I was curt with you, it was because *I* didn't want to stop."

Her mouth quivered. "I didn't want you to. I've never felt like that before."

"I got that general idea."

She puffed up a bit. "And it's not as though I've never been kissed before. I had a beau back in Cornwall."

He grinned. "Obviously a cawker."

"*He* didn't think so."

"They never do," he whispered as he leaned in to her and gently set his mouth over hers.

This time it wasn't an assault, more of a sidling in, sweet and honeyed.

She sighed as he coaxed her back onto the grass, wishing he would rest his full weight on her again; she was strong now, fit and sturdy. But he kept his body raised above hers, supported on one elbow, while he explored her face with his lips, drifting them over her brow, her eyes, down her nose, across her temple. She nearly cried out in aching relief when his mouth caressed her injured cheek, tracing over the scars. She felt the warmth of his breath, the cool moisture of his feathery kisses. These sensations were miraculous—because it was Morgan and because she could feel him there in that once-deadened place.

He had just reached the hollow of her throat when their horse, which had wandered off to graze, threw its head up and startled them both with a loud, trilling neigh of greeting. From the hill above them, several other horses responded in kind.

Morgan sat bolt upright with a muffled curse.

"What is it?" Miranda cried, trying to sit up, wishing she could see beyond his shoulder.

"Riders," he said, climbing to his feet.

Morgan cursed again. Three people on horseback, a man and two women, were rapidly disappearing over the rise of the hill. One distinctive dapple-gray rump was all he had time to make out clearly before they vanished. It was enough. The horse most certainly belonged to Bettina Palfry.

He folded himself back onto the grass beside Miranda, wondering if he should tell her what he'd seen. He looked down at her, flushed and starry-eyed, but with a tight line of apprehension forming around her mouth.

No, he decided. Let her keep her illusions a while longer. If the fat was in the fire now, it wouldn't serve any purpose to ruin the rest of her day.

He gave her a look of reassurance. "Just some visitors taking in the lake vistas, I expect."

"You don't think it was someone from the house?"

"How could it be? They're away at Lord Sayreville's till tonight."

"And when they return, are we still going to speak to Sir Janus? Together?"

He feared the General would be all too eager for an interview now and swore he'd do everything in his power to keep Miranda out of it.

"Mmm," he said. "But I think I should meet with him first. Just to get the lay of the land."

Before she could protest this new plan, he scooped her up and carried her to the horse.

"It will all work out. . . . You'll see. No fretting now."

Chapter Twelve

Morgan was quiet as he led the horse homeward, even quieter than he had been on the trip out. She watched the back of his sleek head and the swinging cadence of his strides, and she felt the pain of loss already begin to grip her.

He was not a very good liar. Someone from the house had seen them tangled on the grass, she was sure of it. All their honorable intentions to confess to the General tonight would be anticipated by someone carrying spiteful and overwrought accusations.

Not that she was sorry he'd kissed her. Could a person be sorry for the sun and the sky and the very air they breathed? But it had complicated things terribly. Sir Janus might even think she was compromised. And if that were the case, he would take this delicate thing that was budding between her and Morgan and trample it.

Morgan would either be forced to ask for her hand or risk disgrace by riding away from her. Neither solution held any hope of accord. They required time, not ultimatums.

She recalled what he'd said to her earlier, that he would find it intolerable if she never walked. She would need to meet him as an equal, then, face-to-face, toe-to-toe, and feared it might be years before she was capable of such a thing. Would he wait for her? What if he found another woman who pleased him in that span of time? Was it fair to bind him now?

He had given her so much already; she didn't have the right to ask him to wait. Not that she had any reason to think he would comply with such a request—except, perhaps, for the way he gazed at her lately, with a yearning, unarticulated question in his dark eyes and the way he had behaved yesterday, intimate and protective. There was also the fact that he'd just kissed her into mindless bliss, not once, but twice.

Convincing enough, maybe, but without an actual declaration from Morgan, she was chasing after moonbeams.

When they reached the grove where Mrs. Southey sat with her knitting, Morgan lifted her down and settled her in the Bath chair himself. He crouched before her, his face schooled into reassuring lines.

"I'll send Mrs. Southey a message tonight when it's time for you to come into the General's study."

"If you think that's best," she said, biting back the choke of tears. There would be no message, not if her suspicions were correct.

There was one way out for both of them, a solution that would require her to be very brave. If she left Palfry Park, left today for Cornwall, then Morgan would not have to meet with Sir Janus. Furthermore, there would be no point in her cousin forcing a confrontation. Morgan didn't deserve a single recrimination for helping her—or for kissing her. And whatever her cousin ripped up at him for, the deceit or the dallying, Morgan was bound to weather a great deal of unpleasantness.

The solution was within her grasp, and yet she hesitated. The thought of going home still filled her with a numbing fear. It was one thing to reminisce in a meadow, to stir up the pleasanter memories, and quite another to return to the house where those memories had been born. Every brick, every nail, every foolish painting of knights and wizards, would remind her of her parents and ultimately rend her heart.

Another thought occurred to her. If she went to Cornwall, Morgan would be free to court her openly. If he wanted to, that was. If not, she would find herself alone in the remotest, most barren part of England. Alone without him. That might rend her heart beyond repair.

"I'm sorry, Morgan," she murmured, emerging from her long silence. "I wish there was more I could do to ease matters."

If he had any clue as to what she meant, he did not let on. "Don't worry; it's on my shoulders now," he said.

But when he met her eyes, something communicated itself to her. He *did* know, somehow, the thing she'd just grappled with. And he understood.

It seemed, for an instant, that he wanted to say more, but then he stood up and turned away, catching at the horse's bridle.

She watched with hungry eyes as he led the beast away from her, storing up the memory of every line and motion. As she hadn't known to do with her parents.

"It's very bad," she whispered to Mrs. Southey in a faint, faraway voice.

"I thought the family wasn't due back till evening." Morgan was lingering in the barn after bringing in the gelding, trying to steel himself for the inevitable.

The groom he was questioning scratched his cheek. "They came back early, a bit before noon. In high alt they were, because Miss Bettina has got herself betrothed to Lord Sayreville's son. The lad traveled here with them, and then went out riding with the young lady and Miss Ariadne. But not long after, they all came pelting back here, Miss Bettina looking that upset."

Morgan could just imagine.

When he entered the house, he barely noted the butler's hissed instructions that Sir Janus wished to see him posthaste. He was already heading for the study, trying to tamp down his alarm. He doubted Bettina had recognized her cousin; the worst the General could do was rail at him for conducting his amours in such a public place.

Morgan found Sir Janus pacing the floor, his expression fixed into severe lines. He waited until Morgan had closed the door before he spoke, and when he did, his voice throbbed with barely contained anger.

"Tell me, sir, have I been harboring a scoundrel in my home?"

Morgan kept his hands relaxed before him. "Certainly not."

"What else would you call a man who attacks a poor crippled invalid?"

Morgan nearly reeled back. This was going to be worse than he'd feared.

"What you have done is monstrous . . . foul . . . detestable."

Forcing himself to stay calm, Morgan said evenly, "You do not have all the facts, Sir Janus. I know this seems—"

"Seems!" he snarled. "My daughter said she saw you forcing your attentions on her cousin . . . rolling about in the grass like a damned Gypsy. They all saw, God help them. My two daughters and young Sayreville. He was to marry Bettina, but she is now convinced that he will cry off. My wife is upstairs trying to calm the girl, but all hell's broken loose here. You've never heard such a caterwauling."

Morgan felt a small prick of spiteful pleasure.

"I understand your daughter has not seen her cousin in three years," Morgan pointed out, then drawled, "Surprising that she was able to make such a thorough identification."

The General's chin shot up. "Are you denying it?"

Morgan shook his head. "I was with Miranda Runyon, but as for forcing myself—"

"Ronald vouched for you," Sir Janus muttered in a bitter undertone. "He said I need not fear for the virtue of my daughters. But I have friends in London, Pearce. I've heard about your liaison with Lady Farley. I should have known better than to trust a libertine with any of the women in my house."

"I promise you, Miranda is not compromised in any way."

The General's gaze burned through him. "So you say. That would be a fitting punishment, eh? Make you marry the chit. Though how you could fancy such a wretched creature—your appetites must be sullied beyond all belief."

Morgan had to end this now. It was turning into the worst sort of melodrama. He moved forward and fixed the man in his gaze.

"For God's sake, will you stop passing judgment for two seconds and listen to the truth?"

Sir Janus drew back from him with a searing glare.

Morgan again moved forward. "I was going to come to you tonight with Miss Runyon. We were going to explain that we have been meeting in the pavilion."

The General's brows gathered over storm-dark eyes. "Then this *is* a liaison—"

"God, no," Morgan burst out. "I swear on my mother's memory that there is nothing illicit between us. I've merely been helping her . . . to recover the use of her hands, to practice her writing. It's more than you ever did."

"I did plenty!" he cried. "Two servants, any numbers of physicians, a special chair fitted with a hood. I'd even thought of placing her in one of those places that caters to such unfortunates, just haven't got around to it yet."

Morgan took a moment to thank Providence for that small mercy.

"Damn it, that is not at all what I meant," he said. "Why haven't you helped her to make some recovery? You surely must know of paralyzed soldiers who regained some mobility. But it takes the assistance of others and time . . . and, confound it, Palfry, you have given her neither."

The General stiffened. "We were told she would never improve, that the damage to her spine was irreversible. The doctors have assured me that she is completely helpless."

"They are the ones who are helpless. Helpless to make a decent diagnosis. After little over a month in my care, she's learned to write and hold a fork and—"

"And to fornicate in a field?" Sir Janus purred. "Is that also what you've been teaching my cousin?"

Only sheer willpower held Morgan back from striking the man. His advanced age, his rank and title, none of them would have stayed Morgan's hand. Sir Janus saw his anger boil up and quickly shifted to a wide-legged stance.

"Relax," Morgan muttered. "I'm not going to fight you. But you will not say such things about Miranda. Ever. Yes, it's true that I kissed her." He tugged at his neckcloth. "Because she . . . she was just so happy, and I was carried away by the moment. It was as innocent as such a thing can be, as innocent as she is. Don't, I beg you, don't sully it with your foul-minded accusations."

The General was unmoved. "If she is so innocent, then why did she agree to meet with you in secret? Hardly virtuous behavior."

"It was only because I feared, we both feared, that you would forbid it. And it was clear to me that she needed someone, anyone, to pay her some attention."

The General waved away this notion. "She has serving women for that."

"Did you honestly think two ignorant servants would be stimulating company for a woman of Miranda's intelligence?"

"The girl's never complained to me."

Morgan again had the urge to knock him down. "And how, pray, was she to do that? You've not troubled yourself to see her in three years."

Sir Janus had the grace to look abashed. But then he drew himself up. "She is a gently bred young lady who suffered a grievous injury. I had no wish to embarrass her with my presence."

"That is pure rationalization. And inhumane on top of it."

Some of the General's arrogance leeched away. "Don't judge me," he said in a low, thready voice. "I drove down to the vicarage in Warfield when she was first injured. I have seen men horribly wounded in battle, yet I never saw anything that so affected me as the sight of that wretched, broken creature."

"So you had to stay away," Morgan said a bit more gently.

He lowered his head. "Yes, I had to stay away. My cousin and his wife were great favorites of mine. And his girl, she was so different from my own daughters, clever and bookish. And determined. She went her own way that one, went seeking after things no female has any business wanting—"

Morgan's mouth opened in shock. "Surely you don't blame Miranda for the accident."

Sir Janus met his eyes now. "The girl was going to London to speak before a havey-cavey collection of literary rabble. If she'd minded her embroidery instead of her damned copybook, the Runyons would be alive today."

So this was the answer, Morgan saw at last, the thing he'd not been able to fathom. The General's neglect stemmed not just from his aversion to imperfection, but from a misguided sense of outrage.

"I don't suppose you shared that little insight with her."

He shook his head. "I'm sure she is aware of the burden of guilt she bears."

Morgan thanked God that this particular twist of logic had never occurred to Miranda.

"And so you don't care that she is alone and unhappy?"

"If she is so blasted unhappy," he shot back, "why the devil didn't she get word to me through her servants or her physicians?"

"Oh, you mean the physicians who've been conveniently lying to you about her condition all these years? Your Dr. Cheney attended her but a week ago and refused to tell you of the great improvements he saw. How much extra do you pay them to keep quiet about her?"

"Your damned insolence won't convince me of anything," the General warned him. "I've had any number of doctors here and not one word of encouragement have I heard. Not one."

"Then they are blind . . . or you are deaf." He gave a humorless laugh. "Miss Runyon, for all her infirmities, may be the fittest person in this sorry house."

"Sorry or not, I want you to leave here. Immediately."

Morgan should have seen it coming the instant he let his temper get away from him. "No, I can't. I at least need to say good-bye to your cousin."

"It's out of the question."

"Sir Janus, I cannot leave without any word to her. She trusts me. It would be unimaginably cruel."

"No, I forbid it. You will have no contact with Miranda Runyon. And I want your word on it before you leave this room. Swear it, on your mother's memory. I will set two footmen to guard you, if you do not."

So here again was the unbending steel in the General's makeup.

Morgan paused, his brain leaping ahead to calculate how he could circumvent this new edict. "Very well. I promise not to speak with her or send her a message before I leave."

He went to the door, halting at the threshold. "I need to say one more thing before I go."

The General grunted his assent.

"I've made a good start with Miranda, but she needs to continue with her treatments and more than anything, she needs to be with people. Just think about it . . . please. Miranda was dying on the inside, like a neglected flower. A little attention from me and she began to flourish. Don't abandon her again, sir. That is all I ask. Don't take your anger at me out on her."

"Why? Isn't she as guilty of deceit as you are?"

Morgan's cheek twisted. "Then call her in here and rail at her. You'll see exactly how helpless she is."

Sir Janus frowned as he settled himself at his desk. "I think you must be mad in truth, to have fabricated this tale. The lame do not walk, the broken do not mend. Unless you are some sort of blasted miracle worker, which I take leave to doubt. Now, I believe I've made my decision clear. My cousin shall remain in the care of her serving women and apart from my family . . . and you will leave my home."

Morgan came swiftly across the rug. "And thus you keep every minute detail of your life under your control!" he raged. "Every last thing ordered neatly and in its place. Your docile wife and dutiful daughters falling in with your every whim. Your cousin Miranda held captive. Even Ronald, poor timid Ronald, ordered off, shivering in his boots, to fight a war—"

"A boy needs war to season him," the General growled, and then added with an arrogant leer, "And as for timid, well, my son was brave enough to save *you* from a sniper's bullet."

Morgan nearly spat out the truth, but he couldn't. As angry as he was, he couldn't take that last cheap shot at Ronald.

He drew a long, steadying breath. "I am not a madman, Sir Janus. There is nothing wrong with your cousin. Nothing. I understand that when you first saw Miranda, her appearance distressed you. But, good God, man, that was three years ago!" He made a soothing motion with his hands, more to calm himself than the man opposite him. "Please . . . please, all I ask is that you meet with her now. To see the truth. A minute is all it will take."

The General's eyes narrowed to pinpricks. "If she is so recovered," he said evenly, "then why don't we ask her to come into the study." Morgan breathed a silent prayer of thanks, until he added, "Or should I say, ask her to *walk* into the study."

Morgan's fist crashed down on the desk. "I never said she could walk!"

The General cocked his head. "And her face, has it healed? No more ragged scars, no shattered cheekbone?"

Morgan wanted to throw himself across the desk and strangle the man. Instead he drew all that anger inside himself.

"All right," he said in a reedy, ominous voice. "Have it your way. She is still not recovered, still not worthy of your precious attention. But when the truth is seen, and I swear it will be seen, you, Sir Janus, shall have a stain upon your soul that cannot be eradicated in a dozen lifetimes."

The General raised one white brow. "Piffle," was all he said.

Morgan turned to go, then paused at the door. "And as for your memoir . . . " he said musingly, as if he were offering an idle afterthought, instead of a parting salvo. "That precious legacy you so earnestly wanted to hone for future soldiers? You know, you really didn't need to drag me up from London to help you. Not when there was a gifted writer living right under this roof." He gave a muted laugh. "Not you, you self-serving, pigheaded old fool. I was referring to Miranda Runyon."

Morgan had the satisfaction of hearing the fireplace poker— or something equally heavy and lethal—come crashing against the door as he quickly shut it.

Morgan packed his own valise, sending Hodges belowstairs to make some sort of contingency plan with Daisy. He feared Mrs. Southey would not survive the General's misplaced wrath, and Morgan knew he would need an ally inside the house.

When Hodges returned, Morgan gave him a note addressed to Mrs. Southey and some hurried instructions. He brushed off his valet's expressions of regret and with tight-lipped efficiency, buckled the straps of his valise.

He had one more obligation before he left Palfry Park, and he paused a moment, gripping tight to the bedpost, trying to compose himself before he faced it. He had a feeling it was going to break him in a way that the General's harsh words and hotheaded accusations had not.

*   *   *

"It is bad," Mrs. Southey said as she came into Miranda's room.

Miranda was sitting on the bed; she'd given up on trying to nap away her anxiety.

"How bad?" she asked.

The woman held up a single sheet of paper. "Mr. Hodges just brought this to me. He and Mr. Pearce are leaving—at the General's orders."

Miranda felt her vision dim as she reached for the letter.

"No," Mrs. Southey said, whisking it out of range. "I must read it to you. Those were Mr. Hodges's strict instructions."

She settled beside Miranda and began to read in a halting voice.

> Our world has come undone, my dear Miss Runyon. As I believe you suspected, your young cousin did see us by the lake, and she reported what she saw to her father. I tried to explain to him that my attentions toward you were harmless high spirits, but his anger at my duplicity in keeping our meetings secret overrode his fair judgment. I have been asked to remove myself from the house immediately.
>
> I am more sorry than words can say, mainly because I fear he will not make any attempts to continue with your recovery. He insists that you are beyond help and refused to even meet with you to see the proof of my claims. You must go forward alone from here on, although I will make it my mission to prevail upon Ronald to return home and act as your advocate. I would also remind you that Cornwall might be your best sanctuary in the days to come.
>
> Earlier, I felt a righteous anger over your cousin's irrational behavior, but now all I can feel is a great regret that I let you down—and worse, perhaps, that I brought you to some critical juncture in your life and find myself forced to abandon you before you can work your way past it.
>
> Even sending this letter is flying in the face of the promise your cousin elicited from me, that I not speak

with you or send any message to you. I have got around that nonsense by addressing this note to Mrs. Southey. (You see I am still practicing a certain duplicity on your behalf.) I could not depart Palfry Park, however, without letting you know that our time together was most special to me. I teased you once about the frailty of women . . . yet you turn all those glibly spoken calumnies to dust. Be strong, dear Miranda, and stay determined. Any day I expect you'll be ready to give up that Bath chair, and then the world shall see something. Life has got a good grip on you now; don't you ever dare shake it off.

I hold you in my thoughts and remain your most devoted friend and admirer, though sadly now at a distance.
M. Pearce

Neither woman spoke for a time afterward. Mrs. Southey took up Miranda's hand and held it between her careworn palms.

"How dare he!" Miranda exclaimed at last with an angry shake of her head. "How dare my cousin issue edicts to my friends, as though he has any say in what I do or with whom I spend my time. He is not my guardian."

"He is master here," Mrs. Southey said simply. "He's used to everyone doing his bidding."

"And so Mr. Pearce folded his tent and slipped away."

"Not quite," the woman said. "From what I hear, your Mr. Pearce put up a considerable fight for your sake. And he's not gone away, not just yet."

Miranda's heart jolted. "He's still here?"

Mrs. Southey reached for her. "Come . . . let me take you to the window."

"But—"

"Hush," she said as she settled Miranda in the armchair. Then, reaching past her, she pulled the window closed and latched it. "Just wait here, miss."

Mrs. Southey touched her hair once, and then went from the room. Miranda didn't have to wait long. From the shadows of the high hedge, a darker shadow emerged into daylight.

Morgan Pearce moved forward a few feet but did not approach the window. He was dressed for travel, his biscuit-colored driving coat sweeping his ankles, a low-crowned beaver held in his left hand. His face was fixed and stony, and— Oh, she wished she could see him smile just once more. One of them had to, there had been too much good between them for them to part in such a grim fashion. She tried to force a smile and knew it came out pained and mournful.

He nodded in acknowledgment of her attempt, then set his right hand over his heart and bowed. She was trembling as she raised her hand and pressed the palm flat against the window. Such a thing would have been impossible before she met him. Everything had seemed impossible before she met Morgan Pearce. And now he was leaving, and it felt as though he was taking all her possibilities with him.

"Morgan," she said aloud, though she knew he could not hear her. She realized now why Mrs. Southey had shut the window; he'd promised the General that he would not speak to her.

She had promised nothing.

"Morgan," she said again, nearly sobbing his name in a low, urgent voice. He took another halting step toward her, hands fisted at his sides now, his dark eyes fierce, his cheeks taut with regret.

She couldn't bear to watch him, to see the pain in her heart so clearly reflected in his face. She leaned her forehead against her raised hand, clenching her eyes, fighting back the tears.

When her vision cleared, he was gone.

Miranda waited until she was in bed that night before she allowed herself to deal with the blow of Morgan's departure. Nevertheless, the wound had been seeping inside her since that last glimpse of him, and now, when she finally examined it, she saw that it was a fearful thing.

This was a different grief than the loss of her parents. There was a level of acceptance when people died that forced you to let go of them, however hard it might seem at first. But to lose someone from your daily existence, and to know that they were now part of another existence, that they lived and breathed and shared the same geography, but were no longer in your particular orbit . . . it seemed almost incomprehensible to her.

She'd never dared admit to herself that she loved him. Now it made no sense to deny it. She needn't worry any longer about humiliating herself in front of him with lingering glances or sudden blushes. Ironically, in his absence, her feelings could now flourish.

It didn't surprise her that she had come to feel this way. She could recall a hundred moments that sealed her connection to him—all the times he'd drawn her out, the way he'd tried to make her come to terms with her past, his gentleness whenever he touched her—that he touched her at all. She thought of his tenacity in the beginning, the brisk efficiency with which he'd organized her recovery, his patience, which always encouraged her and his impatience, which often amused her.

She lay there with tears streaming down her face, finally reaching for the handkerchief beneath her pillow to blot them away. When she realized what she'd just done, she sobbed even harder. It was another simple action that would have been beyond her without the intercession of Morgan Pearce.

But then, along with her misery at losing him, she felt an iota of anger flare up, hot and red, like a nugget of ore in a crucible. The heat it generated eventually evaporated her tears, and she lay there hiccuping softly, trying to think clearly.

Surely, she reflected, he could have done something to prevent this separation. She wanted to imagine his emotions running away with him, prompting him to acts of great defiance. He was Mad Morgan Pearce, fearless, dauntless.

It was a stirring image, but she suspected his feelings did not go that deep. He had not ever been courting her, no matter how much she might have wished it. So what if he had kissed her, and they had shared that oddly intimate moment beside the stream in Ambleside. Typical of her gender, she had put far too much stock in those attentions.

His coming here had been like a miracle, someone finally realizing what it would take to shake her out of her despair. The irony of it was that with his leaving, a greater despair was already hovering close by.

He'd made her long for normalcy, made her believe it was within her grasp, but in the end, he had not treated her as a normal woman. True, he had engaged her and entertained her. It was even safe to say he had befriended her. Nonetheless, that was as far as he'd let it go—even though there were times she suspected he'd also wished for more. But there could be no more, because she was not like other women. If she were, she knew in her heart, that Morgan Pearce would have loved her.

And he'd have never left without her.

She awoke at dawn, still grieving but with a resolve to fight back. If there was one thing Morgan had taught her it was that circumstance was not invincible. The words he'd spoken yesterday afternoon came echoing back to her. *I'll park your chair in front of his study door, and then he'll have to deal with you.*

Mrs. Southey would do it, if Miranda asked it of her, wheel her out of the dark, hidden recesses of the house and right into the middle of the Palfrys' lives. Let them take a good look at her and decide then who was the monster.

And for insurance, in case the General still refused to acknowledge her, she would seek help beyond the walls of Palfry Park. She took her pencil and pad from the night table, and squinting over the page in the faint morning light, she laboriously wrote out a letter to Mr. Northam in Truro.

When Alice came in at eight, Miranda asked for Mrs. Southey to attend her.

"She's gone," Alice said as she poured a ewer of hot water into the bowl on the dressing table.

Miranda gaped at her. "What do you mean, 'gone'?"

Alice hitched one shoulder. "Dismissed last night on the General's orders. For helping you meet with Mr. Pearce in secret. She left for Windermere this morning on the milk wagon."

Miranda forced herself to keep breathing even though there was a fearful weight on her chest. "Why?" she gasped. "The whole staff knew about it. How could he single out one person to blame?"

"Because I told him it was all Mrs. Southey's doing." Alice looked across to Miranda, her mouth shaped into a prim smile. "I also told him my brother's wife from the village could take over the lifting work. She'll be here directly after luncheon."

Miranda was nearly inarticulate. She'd lost the only ally she had in the house. There would be no trip to the General's study, no letter sent to her lawyer.

"He had no right," she cried, pushing up from her pillow with a mighty shove. "*I* paid her wages—" She added darkly, "Though I will no longer pay yours or those of your brother's wife."

"No matter. Sir Janus will see to us. He warned me that you will need a deal more watching, especially now that Miss Bettina's young lord is staying here. Which means no more trips into the garden or to the lake. A pity," she said with the semblance of regret. "But what's the point now, without your handsome major there, pretending to show an interest in you?"

Alice went to the door and lingered there. "Oh, one more thing. The General also asked me how you were getting on. Mr. Pearce must have made a good case for you, that his nibs would ask such a thing of a servant."

"What did you tell him?" Miranda asked dully. She already knew the answer.

Alice's face lit up. "Why, miss, I told him that you were making fine progress, that you only drooled a little now when I fed you and that there were times when your face did not make me ill with disgust."

Miranda clutched at the bedpost, pulling herself nearly off the mattress in her distress. "Why do you dislike me so much, Alice?"

The girl took her time responding, as if reasons had never occurred to her. "I reckon, miss, it's because if I was in your situation, I'd not be given servants to wait on me or a fine house to live in. I'd likely be left in a ditch to die. And yet all those comforts you had never once made you agreeable . . . to me or to anyone."

Once she had gone, Miranda collapsed back on the bed with a strangled groan.

She'd properly reaped the whirlwind now.

Chapter Thirteen

Morgan went to see Phillip de Burgh the same night he arrived back in London. His friend's valet met him at the door and would not let him enter.

"He's not been himself these past days," Farthing said in an undertone. "This is not a good time."

"Phillip!" Morgan called out, trying to dodge around the hovering human obstruction. "For God's sake let me speak with you."

Farthing, who was tall and burly and therefore more than a match for Morgan, again placed himself firmly in his path. "Please, sir. Don't distress him. These are difficult days for my master as you must understand."

Morgan set his hand on the man's sleeve. "Tell him that it doesn't matter."

Farthing cocked his head.

"His injury . . ." Morgan said hoarsely. "Tell him I have no expectations of him . . . that he is fine just as he is."

The valet still appeared perplexed.

"Tell him exactly as I've said it," Morgan muttered. "Exactly."

Phillip DeBurgh ought to have been agitated by his friend's noisy incursion earlier that evening. The fact was, he lay quite restfully in his bed. The dram or two of laudanum he'd swallowed before retiring might have had something to do with his ease.

He was relaxed, but nowhere near asleep. There were too many dreams for him to risk that. And since his days were hardly taxing, he saw no reason why he had to spend his nights in slumber. Better to gaze out the window at the gossamer nets of fog rising up from the great river or to watch as the shadows on the bedroom wall shifted slightly and became all manner of amusing, phantasmagoric creatures. He spotted a horned hedgehog and a giraffe with a curlicue for a neck and then a misshapen troll . . . rising up from behind the dresser, looming over him, closer . . . *closer* . . .

A shiver coursed through him. Dear God, had he taken too much of the drug tonight?

He watched in horror as the shadow creatures begin to circle and dance maniacally. He heard the cacophonous music from a demonic carousel, which then dissolved into the endless screams of the infirmary tent . . . and there was blood, everywhere . . . and he knew he was no longer within the safe, shadowed walls of his bedroom.

Focus, man! he told himself, trying to keep hold of his place on the planet. *Focus on something pleasant, something lovely—*

Her face appeared before him, as he'd seen it the first time, the face that lived in his heart—Morgan Pearce's willful little sister. The petulant chin and deep-set eyes should have diminished her attractions; the narrow shoulders and tiny-boned frame should have made her too frail for his taste. Yet once he'd beheld the untamed mass of blue-black hair, the alluring sparks in her bright blue eyes and the perfect, heartrending swell of her upper lip, all those minor imperfections disappeared.

Kitty Pearce was the most striking girl he'd ever seen. Bar none.

And since he happened to be a young man brimming with intelligence, he counted himself lucky that his pocket Venus was also clever and full of sauce. He couldn't imagine giving his heart to a dullard, no matter how lovely.

From that first encounter, Phillip knew he would try to move worlds for her. A pity the lone task she had set before him proved impossible. He had been unable to stop Morgan in his headlong dash toward destruction, so he'd determined to follow him, to place his own life on the line beside his friend. Kitty had been furious when he told her and they'd had a nasty scene.

The morning he was to leave for Portsmouth, she had appeared at his doorway, her cheeks flushed, eyes fever bright. "I could not let you go with things so awkward between us."

"I left you a note," he said. "I would have called, but I wasn't sure you would receive me."

"Phillip—" The word came out like a watery hiccup.

There was so much misery in that lone word. Maybe he hadn't been imagining that she cared for him. "I cannot say when I'll be back. . . . Just tell me, Kit, will you wait?"

She gave him a crooked smile. "Don't be a clunch. I've waited this long, haven't I?"

Relief flooded over him. "I never said anything. I thought . . . you were so young and not even out yet and—"

"Hush," she said, setting her palm against his cheek. "You never had to say a word. I knew from that moment in the lane."

He lowered his head. "I fear I let my tongue run away with me, but God's truth you were the rarest thing I'd ever seen. I've spent the last two years trying to find the courage to tell you again—"

"Tell me now," she urged, up on tiptoes. "Before you go."

"Ah, Kitty," he murmured as his arms slid around her. "There are no words . . . only this."

He'd kissed her then, with all the hunger and longing inside him, a man clinging to paradise before he marched into hell.

He knew now he'd been a fool to tell her what was in his heart, to bind her to him when his future was so uncertain. But it had been worth it, even if their kisses had been bittersweet—dark, urgent and heated. He'd hoped that something indelible had been imprinted on her soul, a man's hunger, surely, but also his pledge of faith.

He had sailed away with the memory of that kiss still fresh in his heart. When he had finally run his friend to ground in Lisbon, it was a Morgan he barely recognized—drunk, unkempt and surly, sprawled in a tavern with a slatternly serving girl on one knee.

Morgan was furious that Phillip had enlisted to keep an eye on him. Morgan told him to take his good intentions and go to hell. When Phillip explained his promise to Kitty, Morgan wished her to the same destination. That was when Phillip hit him. They'd ended up laying waste to the small cantina and had barely spoken a civil word to each other after that. Phillip was eventually reassigned to Wellington's staff where he often heard of Morgan's exploits; it appeared his friend had a talent for soldiering.

Phillip knew he had failed in his promise to Kitty, but maybe Providence had come to his aid in the end. A good officer would not place his men in harm's way unnecessarily and, as such, Phillip determined that, barring the ill will of the French, Morgan was likely to return to his sister unscathed.

A pity he couldn't say the same for himself.

He lay there now, damning the impulse that had made him enlist. He'd been doing Kitty's bidding and had not stopped to think what repercussions *he* might suffer. He looked down at the rumpled blanket that covered him, trying to come to terms with the oddly flattened place on one side of the narrow bed. The sight of that . . . *nothingness* . . . still chilled him to the core.

No, he'd had no idea how radically his life would change when he set out after Morgan Pearce.

Morgan was beginning to wonder if he'd alienated everyone close to him. Kitty would hardly say two words to him; Phillip had his door guarded by the barrel-chested Farthing; Ronald, whom he most needed to speak with, had been successfully giving him the slip. He hadn't answered any of Morgan's urgently worded notes and managed to be away from home whenever Morgan called at his rooms. The young man who once dogged his footsteps had vanished, replaced by a canny will-o'-the-wisp.

On his forth night in London, Morgan finally tracked Ronald to a gaming hell in Knightsbridge. He stalked across the card room and yanked him out of his seat.

"Excuse us, gentlemen," he said urbanely to the startled players just before he dragged a protesting Ronald into the hall. He strong-armed his friend into a private card room, kicked a chair away from the table with his boot and threw him into it.

"You've doubtless heard from your father," he said as he leaned back against the door, blocking the exit with his body.

"Yes," Ronald grunted, glaring up at him.

"You think me a blackguard of the worst sort?"

"Yes."

"Well I think you are a weak-willed knave who dances to his father's tune without bothering to get any of the facts straight. Then again, that seems to be something at which you excel, Palfry, scrambling up the facts into a muddle of misinformation."

Ronald crossed his arm and looked away. "I'm not going to talk to you."

"You didn't save my life, for one thing," Morgan went on, pleased to see Ronald's head snap around. "The blasted Frog in the blasted tree was a deserter, not a sniper. He had no shot, no powder and his carbine was so fouled that if he'd ever attempted to fire it, he would have blown his blasted French head all the way to Paris."

Ronald's mouth opened and closed several times, but he was unable to make any articulate retort.

"For another thing, you and your family have been dancing around the truth concerning Miranda Runyon. Lying to her, lying to each other about her. For three years she has been neglected and overlooked, and all because your sainted father doesn't want his wife and daughters disturbed by any unpleasantness. And don't think you are off the hook there. You might not have been free to comfort her while you were on the Peninsula, but by my reckoning you have been back in England for over seven months, and she still thinks you are in Spain."

"My father thought it best—"

"Best to do what? Lie to her, deceive her? Make her think her favorite cousin was heroically off serving his country, instead of acting the craven in London, too afraid of what he might see to venture home."

"I *was* home. Over Christmas."

Morgan sneered. "Oh, then tell me, what holiday cheer did you share with Miranda? Anything, Ronald? No, damn it, you just rolled over and let your father call the shots. Again."

Ronald put his head back. "See here, Morgan, I'm not without feeling. My father wrote to me shortly after the Runyons' accident—a few months before I joined your regiment it was.

He told me how shocked he was when he saw her. I . . . I was devastated. Miranda and I had been very close. I wanted to come home, but my father forbade it. He said it would serve no purpose." Ronald blinked up at him. "I believe he was just trying to protect me, Morgan."

"And who the bloody hell was trying to protect Miranda? Protect her from self-loathing and boredom and from the terrible grief she felt for her parents. Who, Ronald? Certainly not you or your father. Not your mother or your sisters. I'll tell you who. It was me. I was the only person in three long years who gave a tinker's damn about your cousin's welfare.

"And what was my reward? I was cast out of your father's house in disgrace, like a lackey caught pilfering the silverware. Not to mention I was forced to endure a tongue-lashing that all but put a furrow in my skull. No one in Spain, not even Wellington himself, ever spoke to me in such a manner."

"I'm sorry that it came to such a thing."

Morgan leaned forward. "So here is what you are going to do. Tomorrow you will post up to Windermere and confront your father, tell him it's time Miranda was allowed a normal life—"

"But she's an invalid, crippled and malformed—"

"Shut up, Ronald. You haven't a clue what you're talking about."

"Are you saying the General has been lying to me?"

"Lying to you and to himself. So that he doesn't have to feel a crumb of guilt."

"Surely you don't expect *me* to feel guilty. Papa said the accident was the hand of God."

"And the sorry aftermath was all in your family's hands."

Ronald pressed his fists to his temples, as though he were beset by demons. Then his expression eased, and he held up one hand. "Wait a minute. If Miranda was beginning to recover, why are you the only person to have noticed? The Miranda I knew would have shouted the house down if she wasn't being treated fairly."

Morgan had spent some time asking himself that very thing. "I believe she no longer cared. She'd fallen into a sort of passive half-life when I found her. Even if she had cried out for help, I suspect at least one of her servants would have drugged her. With your father's blessing. He explained to me that the Palfry sensibilities were too refined to withstand any reminders of the family monster."

Ronald nodded grimly. "That's what Papa called her in his letter, monstrous."

"And what will you believe, what your father told you or what I saw with my own eyes?"

"And how about what my sister saw?" Ronald shot back. "Is that another falsehood?"

Morgan's mouth tightened. "No, I did kiss her. More than once. But I promise you, I had no designs on her virtue."

Morgan knew he was himself skirting the edge of truthfulness. He'd had no intention that day of tumbling Miranda in a meadow, but that hadn't stopped his body from clamoring for more. He wasn't sure if the need had subsided one whit since then.

Ronald gave a drawn-out sigh. "I suppose I believe you. A fellow need only look at Lavinia Farley to understand that you'd have to be truly desperate to set your sights on my cousin."

"That was most gentlemanly, Ronald," Morgan drawled. "Well said."

He blushed. "Damn it all, you know what I mean. What man would take a crippled invalid to his bed when he could have an acknowledged beauty?"

"Oh, that was much better." Morgan was glad six feet separated them, or he'd have been sorely tempted to clout Ronald on the head.

"Look, I am trying to say that I know you are not a hardened libertine, even if women do tend to fall at your feet. And I'd be happy to write my father and tell him that."

"You can tell him in person—"

"I'm *not* going to Windermere," Ronald exclaimed, half rising from his chair for emphasis. "The Appletons' masquerade ball is next week, and then I'm promised to dine with—"

"Sweet bleeding Jesus!" Morgan cried as he slammed fist and arm sideways into the silk-covered wall. A dusting of plaster fell from the ceiling as he crossed swiftly over to Ronald.

"How did that wretched girl ever get saddled with such a family of cowards, laggards and excuse-making pifflers." He grasped Ronald by the throat and shook him. "Now, listen to me, you sniveling little whelp. Your cousin can move her legs and her arms, she can sit upright without support, she can hold a pen, a book and a fork. I have every reason to think she will someday walk and ride and even dance. Now, you say you feel no guilt over her situation. How then will you feel, knowing what I just told you, if someday through sheer neglect she lapses into permanent immobility . . . and all because you did not care to miss the Appletons' ball?"

He gave him another shake. "Now, I don't care if you are dining with the Archbishop of Canterbury and all the heavenly host, you are going to Palfry Park or else—"

"Or else what?" Ronald croaked, struggling to get free.

Morgan's hands dropped away as his eyes lit up devilishly. "Or else," he said with slow relish, "I will tell all of London about that time outside Barcelona, when you were chased by a wild boar . . . and it turned out that you'd run screaming from a very large, very hairy rabbit."

"It had tusks, Morgan. I swear it did."

"This is no time for your foolishness, Ronald. A woman's well-being and maybe even her sanity are at stake. You've got to stand up to your father . . . for once in your miserable life."

"The General don't approve of discord; I gather you've already figured that out."

"Then it's time someone rattled the complacency of Palfry Park. And who better than the son of the house?"

"You should know," said Ronald under his breath. "You did a fine job of that with your own father."

Morgan shook his head slowly. "It was quite the other way 'round, if you must know. Not that it's any of your business."

Ronald's voice rose an octave. "And yet you insist on thrusting your nose into *my* family's business."

"You made your family my business when you forced me to go to Palfry Park. Didn't you worry I would meet up with your cousin while I was there? Though I thank God or Providence that I did meet her in time. You see, Ronald, I truly believe your cousin was . . . looking for a way to end her solitude."

Ronald pushed up from his chair, stood gazing around the room with a blank, bewildered expression on his face. He finally met Morgan's eyes. "I don't know what to say."

"Say you will go to Windermere."

"I'm not sure I can stand to see her. She was like a beam of sunlight in the old days, strong and bright and warm. I don't think I could bear to see her crippled and scarred."

"I got over it in about ten seconds."

"What of her humiliation if she guesses my reaction?"

"She'll deal with it. She's a lot stronger than any of you give her credit for."

Ronald went to the door, then turned at the threshold, his face pale and resolute. "Just tell me one thing before I go. Was it true what you said, that the sniper I disarmed was really a harmless deserter?"

"Sergeant O'Meara trussed him up; he'll vouch for me."

"Then why did you let me make such a cake of myself with you afterward?"

Morgan smiled wanly. "The last man who tried to protect me, I sent to Jericho. And spent a long time regretting it. I suppose I liked it that you wanted to protect me."

"I will protect Miranda now, Morgan."

"I know you will."

There was a half-filled brandy decanter on the table and two dirty glasses. Morgan dashed the contents of one into the fireplace, then refilled it to the brim. He sprawled back in the chair, set his chin on his hand and sipped at the brandy, trying not to fret.

It was going to be all right now, he told himself. Miranda had her advocate. Perhaps not so much a tower of strength as a burr under the saddle, but Ronald would do what was required to guarantee her treatments would continue. Perhaps even more important, in Ronald, Miranda would again have a friend at her side. Someone to make up for Morgan's defection.

He could focus on Grambling House now, immerse himself in his obligations there. Hard work was a great panacea for loss; he'd learned that in the army. And look how it had brought Miranda back to life.

He drained his glass and refilled it, sorting through his own life, the things he was proud of and those he wished undone. He had a feeling his days at Palfry Park would become a shining moment, one he might be able to tolerate looking back on when he was an old man.

He wasn't old yet, however. And Lady Farley's husband might still be in Paris. She was the perfect person get him past his fixation on the woman in Windermere. Even in her prime, he doubted Miranda could have held a candle to Lavinia Farley.

But then Miranda Runyon did not need candles. Once she'd put off her shroud, he had watched her become the person Ronald had described—a beam of sunlight, strong and bright and warm.

And it was dark in London, he realized bleakly, just before his head sank down onto his folded arms. Dark and so very cold.

Chapter Fourteen

For a whole week Morgan was was able to immerse himself in his backlog of work at Grambling House. On the eighth day, a letter from Ronald appeared in the afternoon post and as Morgan scanned it, his pulse began to pound.

> *Things have got beyond my control here, Morgan. You must believe I did everything in my power to address the situation—I broached my father within an hour of my arrival, but he refused to discuss the matter. I stood firm, I swear I did. But he grew increasingly angry. He would not even allow me to speak with Miranda.*

Morgan silently cursed his friend for bothering to ask for permission.

> *I left his study feeling very much like a whipped cur, but still determined to discover how my cousin was faring. Sadly, I learned from the servants that Miranda's benevolent caretaker, Mrs. Southey had been dismissed the day you left, and that my cousin was in the hands of a dour serving girl named Alice. I also learned that Miranda is no longer taken from her bedroom . . . and there are whispers she might even be drugged. A certain maid, Daisy, spoke to my valet, vouching for every word you said, that Miranda was much improved in both appearance and abilities. Of course, I cannot force a servant to say these things directly to my father, more's the pity.*

I became determined to see my cousin at all costs, but my father had set a footman to watching me—in my own home, Morgan!—and the wretch caught me just before I reached Miranda's room. Papa actually went so far as to have me banished from the place for daring to disobey him. Mama tried to intercede, but my father was deaf to her pleas. I was flung out of the house, while my mother and sisters watched, weeping, from the windows.

I have since taken up residence in the Dog and Kettle in Windermere and await word from you as to what my next move should be. And please, tell me, Morgan—is it wrong to wish ones own father at Jericho?

Poor Ronald, he thought. It was never pleasant for a child, even an adult child, to discover a parent's failings after years of unquestioning admiration.

And poor, poor Miranda.

He'd known about Mrs. Southey's dismissal; Daisy had sent him word of that. It was why he had wasted no time in getting Ronald up there. But Daisy had said nothing about Miranda being kept prisoner in her room or possible drugging.

Ronald might only be exercising his penchant for melodrama, but Morgan wasn't taking any chances. He left the publishing house and went four doors down Clarges Street to his uncle's home.

Cyrus Grambling rose from his chair by the fire as Morgan came striding through the door.

Morgan winged the letter at his uncle and announced, "More grand farce at Palfry Park."

After he'd read it, Cyrus looked up over his half glasses. "I wasn't sure Ronald Palfry was the right man for the job."

"You might have shared that with me. At any rate, I failed; now Ronald's failed. Who else is there?"

His uncle gave him the sort of challenging look that had been spurring him into trouble since he was breeched. "You didn't fail, Morgan. You gave up."

Morgan threw himself into a wing chair, nearly tipping it back on two legs. "Do you know," he said, glaring across at him, "that having you for an uncle is akin to having the devil for a confessor? You seem to encourage me to do things that will ultimately land me in the suds."

"If you are referring to the time I purchased you a commission in the army, I hardly think that was a disaster. You came to me agitated, defiant and determined to take the king's shilling. You'd have lasted all of ten minutes as a foot soldier before your temper earned you a flogging. Consider I saved your back, if not your whole hide."

"You might have talked me out of it."

His uncle smiled sagely. Morgan knew that smile; it was usually the precursor to a lecture. Odd, how he could withstand such things from his supposedly lowbred uncle, but writhed and boiled under his own father's tongue-lashings.

"You needed the army, Morgan. It taught you the things you refused to learn from me—or from your father. Lord, you were more fretful and nervy than a blooded horse back then. I know you wanted to come here and work for me. But I tell you now, I wouldn't have had you."

Morgan shifted forward in his chair, newly attentive. He'd always assumed the door to Grambling House would be open to him.

"You required seasoning, lad. A few lessons in controlling that uncertain temper for one thing, and in following through on a task. I recall the year you turned twelve, when you confided to me, in sequence, that you wanted to become a sailor, a carpenter, an inventor, an explorer of distant lands . . . and a highwayman."

"I was a child."

"No matter. The day you left for Lisbon, you still hadn't lighted on anything that held your interest for more than a month."

His words reminded Morgan of Palfry Park, that succulent plant he'd lighted on that had held him fast. But in truth it wasn't the place that held him; it was the plight of another unwitting victim.

"Unlike your father," Cyrus continued, "I knew I had to let you go. So that you could come back to me knowing who you were."

"And what is that, pray?" he grumbled, a trifle testy at being under the magnifying glass.

Cyrus smiled slowly. "I didn't even need to see you to know. I only had to read the letter you wrote me before you left Spain. You said were returning home—leaving a life that I knew had come to mean a great deal to you—because I needed you."

Morgan shrugged. "Is that such a wonder? Besides, the war was nearly over."

"That's as may be, but the point is, you came at once. After that it couldn't possibly matter to me what you chose to do with your life—butcher, baker . . . or highwayman—because underneath it all I saw a man with a great capacity for caring, one with the strength and willingness to shoulder his responsibilities. Beyond that, Morgan, little else matters. I . . . I was so proud of you. I still am."

There it was, Morgan saw with a shiver of recognition. Exactly what Miranda had spoken of. The unconditional acceptance that made a person feel as though they could conquer worlds. The one thing his father had always denied him.

"I never thanked you for buying me that commission," Morgan said, trying to ignore the lump in his throat. "I told Miss Runyon the army was the making of me. I never told her that you began the process a great many years before that."

His uncle waved the notion away. "Blame it on my need to tweak your father. Though I am sorry the breech between you has not been mended." He paused and stroked his chin. "And yet sometimes I sense there is a rhyme to things that we cannot see."

"If there is a rhyme, it's a sour one," Morgan muttered. "Phillip lies defeated in his bed, while Kitty marries out of anger and frustration. Then there's myself and Ronald, both of us forbidden to see Miss Runyon."

"The lady certainly benefitted from meeting you."

"All I gave her was false hope," Morgan said. "She's back under Palfry's thumb now, a virtual prisoner. If only I'd never meddled, if I'd left her alone—"

"She'd still be thinking herself a helpless monster," Cyrus reminded him bluntly. "Please, lad, spare me your self-recriminations. You did what you thought necessary. I just wonder if you didn't carry things far enough."

Morgan's mouth curled into a rueful grin. "And here is where I land in the suds."

"You and Ronald were both soldiers, yet I am amazed at how quickly you abandoned the siege of Palfry Park. Especially since you have at least one ally behind its walls." He removed his glasses and leaned forward. "In my day . . . we were a bit more impetuous when it came to the fair sex. You may have forgotten, but I whisked your aunt Dorrie right out from under her family's nose."

"Papa was always furious whenever Mama brought that up. He said it proved your low breeding."

Cyrus shrugged. "If anything, it proved I wasn't a hidebound prig when it came to displays of emotion. Not like some I could name."

"You mean me—"

"I was referring to your father. I never understood how my sister came to marry him—except that he was handsome as sin and possessed a decent income. Still, a very hard nut to crack. But back to Miss Runyon. Do I gather, then, that you've washed your hands of her?"

Morgan's eyes burned black as he rose from his chair. "You rattle on about my caring and sense of responsibility, and then make an accusation like that?"

"Then what are you going to do about it?"

Morgan went to the door, tugged it open and held on to it till his fingers cramped, wracking his brain for an answer that would appease both Cyrus and his own nagging guilt.

He finally turned back to his uncle and sputtered out forcefully, *"Something!"*

Morgan left his uncle's study, skirted the front parlor, where Kitty was cooing over some furbelow, and went out to the street. He walked steadily toward the river, his brain shifting this way and that as he grappled with the problem. Miranda, he suspected, was rapidly heading downhill into despair, and Ronald, his only hope in Windermere, had been banished.

Wellington had once confided to Morgan that a clever officer focused on the things he could alter and left the rest to Providence, which then often made up the balance. Morgan pondered which of the factors that kept him from aiding Miranda he had the best chance of altering. He soon found himself forced to agree with his uncle.

Palfry Park had a chink in its defenses and Morgan was going to capitalize on it.

Chapter Fifteen

Miranda couldn't sleep, she could barely breathe for excitement.

Tonight she had been put to bed by Alice as usual, but later Daisy had slipped into her room and helped her on with a long-sleeve carriage gown. "I don't know the particulars," the maid had whispered. "Only that I am to leave the back door unbolted after Cook goes to sleep."

Miranda gripped the girl's slim hand as tightly as she could. "There are no words, Daisy. First, smuggling the letter to my solicitor out of the house, and now this. If you suffer for helping me, you must find me in London and I will—"

"Not a bit of it," Daisy assured her. "If his nibs lets me go, 'twill be all the sooner that Mr. Hodges and m'self can set up our own little pub."

Miranda smiled; she'd had a feeling for some time that the wind was blowing in that direction.

Daisy went out, closing the door softly behind her. Miranda finally managed to doze a little, and when she awoke to the chiming of the mantel clock, she realized it was midnight. Had they forgotten her? Had Daisy gotten the day wrong?

But then she heard a faint scrabbling at her window. A dark, shadowed face appeared there, a hand motioning her forward.

"Miranda!" Morgan's urgent, low-pitched cry was muffled against the glass.

She dragged herself to the edge of the bed and virtually heaved herself to the floor. The tumbling fall winded her, but she fought off her breathlessness. *He needs to be let in!* was all she could think. She had to get there somehow and release the catch.

She heard a dull thud and after it the crisp tinkle of broken glass. By the time she'd managed to shift around toward the window, someone was already climbing through it. A caped figure came across the floor toward her.

"Dearest idiot," Morgan said just before he swooped down and lifted her from the floor.

"I was trying to get to you," she said in her own defense.

"I know. But I was only trying to warn you that we were out there, not asking you to let us in."

His arm tightened around her, drawing her up against his chest. It felt like heaven to be engulfed again in his warmth, held safe in those strong arms. He sighed out her name and lowered his head until his lips were a whisper away from her mouth . . . and she was holding her breath, needing his kiss, needing that final, delicious reassurance, when Ronald scrambled over the sill behind them with a loud *"Ooph!"*

Morgan muttered something under his breath, then set her on the bed and lit the candle on her night table.

She watched as Ronald came forward hesitantly, then stood looking at her in the soft light. His hair was in straggles and his face was flushed. He looked about ten—and much of her anger melted away.

She grinned up at him. "Hullo, Ronald."

"Cousin," he said with a catch in his voice, reaching for her hand. "Forgive me. I . . . didn't know. I truly didn't know. Then I came here to talk some sense into my father but—"

"I know you did," she said. "It's all behind us now."

"Not quite," Morgan said. "We've still got to get you away from here. And I fear something's gone amiss. Daisy was to leave the kitchen door unlocked, but it was still bolted."

Miranda frowned. "She came to dress me *after* she'd unlocked it. Someone must have come into the kitchen and seen it unbolted."

He turned to Ronald. "Go and check if anyone's still about out there."

When Ronald opened his mouth to protest, Morgan added,

"At least they can't have *you* thrown into prison for creeping about your own home."

The instant he was gone, Miranda reached for Morgan's hand. She needed to touch him, to trace her hands over all the lovely planes and angles of his face. She was certain he'd been about to kiss her earlier, but now his expression was composed, nearly remote.

He squeezed her hand once, and then released it. "Where are your things?"

"The valise is under the bed. Daisy packed it this afternoon. Just a few gowns and my books from home." And every precious gift he'd given her.

He retrieved the case and set it beside her.

"Where are you taking me?" she asked. "I mean, I don't mind if you leave me under a hedgerow at this point. Life with tinkers or Gypsies would be better than remaining at Palfry Park, but—"

He laid his hand over her mouth. It was easy for her to imagine that it was more of a caress than a curtailment. "Easy," he whispered, "it's all been arranged." Then he added with a bemused drawl, "Besides, I have more sympathy for tinkers and Gypsies than to foist you on them unawares, little shrew."

"Psst!" Ronald's fair head had appeared at the door. "All clear."

As Morgan moved toward the Bath chair, Miranda called out, "No. Leave it. It's too cumbersome. I can always get another."

He hesitated. If they left the chair behind, he would be required to carry her all the way to the end of the garden. Of course, he could always delegate to Ronald.

"Not a chance," he muttered to himself as he raised her from the bed. "Get the valise," he hissed to Ronald, just before he swept from the room with Miranda again clasped in his arms.

"Get the valise," Ronald mimicked in a high-pitched voice. "Dashed, high-handed, overbearing . . ."

They moved in relative silence across the kitchen. The hearth fire, banked for the night, gave off enough light for them to weave their way around tables and benches until they reached the recessed rear entrance. Ronald ducked in front of

Morgan and undid the bolt. It made a loud, rasping noise at it slid free.

"Who's there?" a voice called out.

All three of them froze as their eyes darted toward the voice.

A stout woman stood in a doorway on the opposite side of the room. She wore a night rail beneath a woven shawl and carried a candlestick in one hand. The wavering light barely penetrated into the large chamber.

"The cook," Ronald mouthed beside Morgan's ear.

Morgan swore he could feel Miranda's heart pounding right through their layers of clothing. Or maybe it was his own heart—if they were discovered now and an alarm raised, it was unlikely they'd be able to get Miranda away.

The cook took a step forward and raised her candle. Her eyes widened slightly at the tableau across from her—the two caped men, one of them carrying a woman dressed for travel—and Morgan was sure she looked right at him.

"Must be rats," she muttered as she turned back into her room. "I'll have to see about bringing in the barn cat tomorrow."

The instant her door closed, Ronald grappled with the latch. Within seconds they were outside, hurrying along beside the brick wall of the kitchen garden.

Ronald had suggested leaving their coach in the drover's lane at the bottom of the garden, where it would be screened by high lilac bushes. He swore the night watchman rarely wandered that far from the house on his rounds.

It appeared he'd miscalculated.

They heard muffled voices as they neared the end of the garden, and Morgan quickly set Miranda down on a stone bench. He'd almost said, "Wait here," as though she might leap up and run back to the house.

"Looks like two men," Morgan said as he joined Ronald behind a wide-trunked pear tree. "Sniffing around the coach like a pair of bloodhounds."

Ronald blew out a breath. "Just our bad luck that the watchman's son is making rounds with him tonight."

"We've got to do something before one of them goes up to the house and alerts the General. We need a diversion."

"We could cosh them on the head," Ronald suggested, bending down to pluck up a fallen branch.

"I don't like to manhandle servants who are merely doing their job. Now, let's think a minute and perhaps—"

A staccato cry split the night from somewhere behind them.

The two watchmen, drawn by the sound, came running into the garden, bypassing the tree where Morgan and Ronald hid.

"Please!" Miranda panted as the men approached her. "Help me. Two housebreakers carried me from my room. They . . . they went toward the stable."

The watchman sent his son off in the direction she'd indicated. "I'll stay here with you, miss. See that you come to no harm."

"I need my chair," she sobbed. "Please, fetch my Bath chair and my serving woman to take me back to my room."

He wavered for a few seconds.

"My chair," she uttered weakly. "Before I swoon—"

The man pelted away.

Morgan prodded Ronald forward toward the coach, and then turned back to retrieve Miranda. She was grinning smugly.

"You are a baggage," he said as he hefted her into his arms.

She was still smiling five miles down the road. Ronald was handling the ribbons over this stretch of terrain that was familiar to him, and Morgan was seated beside her inside the small coach. He'd propped her in a corner and was using his body to keep her upright as the coach lurched along the pitted country lane.

"Things should even out once we reach the post road," he told her as she was jounced nearly off the seat.

"I'm fine," she said. "In fact, I can't recall the last time I enjoyed myself more."

They pulled into a small inn on the outskirts of Kendal, where Morgan had earlier booked rooms. It was far enough from Palfry Park that the General wouldn't be likely to trace them, and Morgan had ensured the landlord's cooperation with a healthy application of gold coin.

Mrs. Southey was there, awaiting Miranda in a small bedroom. Miranda hugged her, nearly in tears, and blessed Morgan for thinking of this, for thinking of everything.

At a nod from him, Mrs. Southey murmured that she'd best be off to the kitchen to make up a pot of tea. Miranda had seen the subtle signal pass between them, and her heart began to beat a little faster. But once they were alone, Morgan didn't say anything, just stood there watching her from across the room, his eyes hooded. She was shocked at how haggard his face appeared.

"I'm . . . sorry," he said finally, "for not doing this sooner."

She tipped her head against the chair back, and said wistfully, "I had a faint hope that you would come back for me the night you left. I told myself that Mad Morgan Pearce would not let the General intimidate him."

He came a step closer. "I only left because I honestly thought Ronald would have a better chance at swaying him." He shot her a rueful grin. "He badgers me ruthlessly, you know."

Steeling herself, she spoke the question that had been gnawing at her since he'd climbed through her bedroom window. "And what do you intend for me now, Morgan?"

She looked at him expectantly, praying there would be some openness between them at last. He had, in truth, carried her off, and she assumed he hadn't done it out of caprice.

He shrugged lightly. "Now the world is yours for the taking, Miss Runyon."

She tried not to frown at this glib response. He was not going to reveal himself to her, that much was clear. He was forcing her to prod him, drat the man.

"The world is safe from me at present," she said, matching his light tone. "I was thinking in less general terms. For instance, what is to become of you . . . and me?"

His jaw tightened. "I was hoping we could go on as we have been."

She nodded and said in a strained, brittle voice, "Oh . . . yes, I see."

He narrowed the gap between them by another two steps. "That doesn't please you?"

She fought off the anxiety that was coiling in her belly.

"Pleased or not, you do have a knack for giving me honest answers that prick like a knifepoint."

"That was not my intent."

"Then perhaps you need to be more specific. When you say we shall go on as before, do you mean as teacher and pupil?"

He seemed to draw back from her, even though he did not move a muscle. "If that is what you prefer. Though I was thinking of something more in the nature of . . . friends."

Her anxiety curdled into irritation. "I only wonder," she mused, "that mere friendship brought you racing back to Windermere. Ronald surely could have rescued me; you had only to ask him. You didn't need to come all the way up here, take time away from your busy life in London."

He moved forward again, until he was directly in front of her.

"Did you think my feelings of responsibility toward you would just disappear?" he asked brusquely. "Oh, I know you told me once to stop protecting you, to let you take your own knocks. But I couldn't stand knowing you were trapped up here. I needed to see with my own eyes that you were safe." His voice lowered. "I cursed myself the whole way back to London for not taking you with me. But it was not an option. You'd have been ruined."

She nearly rolled her eyes. "Only normal women can be ruined, Morgan, not social pariahs. I thought you knew that."

He rubbed hard at the back of his neck. "Don't start that again. You lost any chance of being a pariah weeks ago. And as for being a normal women, well, I think I am better qualified than any man living to vouch for you there."

Her mouth opened wide. "How dare you bring that up? Especially since you insist on sidestepping the whole matter."

"Sidestepping?" he echoed blankly. "On the contrary, I am trying to speak plainly."

"And making a total shambles of it," she muttered to herself.

He went down on one knee and set his hand on the arm of her chair. "But before we can decide how we shall go on, there's something you need to consider. A matter to which I've given a great deal of thought." He added dryly, "Endless carriage journeys seem to foster such things. Now, listen . . . for weeks on end, I was your sole link with the outside world, the person who encouraged you and supported you. You depended on me and so it was natural that you should come to feel some . . . affection for me." He drew in a breath. "But I suspect these heightened emotions are merely the aftermath of your long solitude."

As the meaning of his words filtered into her brain, she began to shake, the tiny tremors emanating from deep inside her. He doubted her, and in doubting seemed to be turning away. What could she say to reassure him? Dear God, what could she say?

And what if it was true, that she cared for him because he was the only personable man she'd been near in three years. The words of that other Miranda came to her, eerily appropriate. *Nor have I seen more that I may call men than you, good friend.*

She too had been in exile and had fallen in love with the first man to cross her path. But that didn't necessarily make those feelings wrong or . . . artificial.

"Miranda?"

She shook herself back to reality, felt her resolve return. "You must truly think me a willow in the wind, that my deeper feelings could be so easily engaged."

His fingers clenched on the chair arm beside her. "So they weren't . . . engaged?"

She nearly growled at this exhibition of sheer denseness. "Not as a result of solitude."

"You still can't know that for certain, Miranda. And maybe I am to blame. I did nothing to discourage those feelings. I even took advantage of them the one time."

Miranda's eyes flashed dangerously. "Maybe *I* took advantage of you."

That earned her a swift grin. "Maybe you did."

She thrust herself forward. "But now I understand why you came back. I misread you. Just as I misread you all these past months. It wasn't because you had a care for me—"

"Of course I do, but—"

"You came back for me because I wasn't mended yet. And

you couldn't tolerate that, could you? Morgan Pearce doesn't leave any unfinished business behind him."

He reeled back. "That is damned unfair!"

"You're as bad as Sir Janus, thinking you can control everything. But you can't control people's emotions." She put her chin up and added, "Mine or your own."

"What is that supposed to mean?"

"It means you are not a very good liar. Or perhaps you really have convinced yourself that nothing of moment occurred between us. Whatever it is, you've once again fallen into that wretched habit of telling me how *I* should feel, how *I* should react, instead of speaking your own feelings."

He ran his knuckles over his chin, watching her with wary, narrowed eyes. "What do you want me to say?"

Miranda understood then. He was not going to come right out and tell her how he felt. He'd been turned away before, by his father, by Phillip, and he was not going to risk another dismissal. She couldn't really blame him. She hadn't exactly been forthcoming, had never once told him what was in her own heart. Who was she to cast stones, when her own deepest feelings remained unspoken?

She met his troubled gaze and said boldly, "I missed you dreadfully, Morgan. Every particle of you. And not out of some ridiculous sense of dependence or misguided affection. If I had a hundred men bent on rescuing me, it would be you I'd turn to. Always. So maybe what I want, what I was hoping you would want, is for us to remember what occurred . . . that day by the standing stones. It's still there between us, unspoken, unresolved."

She reached out and pressed her hand against his chest, never taking her eyes from his face. He closed his own eyes for an instant and drew in a sharp, shuddering breath.

"Don't," he warned her.

"See?" she said, refusing to back down. "Still there."

His hands went to her upper arms, gripping hard. "Be sure, Miranda," he whispered harshly. "Sure it's what you want."

"Yes." It was no more than a sigh.

He rose abruptly and her eyes widened as he effortlessly carried her with him, right up from the chair. "Yes, it's still there," he said, gravel-voiced. "Though why it should be baffles me. You are the most trying, the most vexing—"

He tugged her roughly against his body and kissed her, open mouthed and still testy.

This wasn't what she'd been asking for precisely; she'd merely wanted him to tell her how he felt. Still, this was not a bad alternative. And then the force of his hunger crashed into her and she was lost to all logic. It was as though everything he'd held in check since the moment they were interrupted in the meadow came rushing forward, carrying them both into a maelstrom.

She kissed him back, better than the last time now that she understood the pattern of the dance. She angled her head to mesh with his mouth, tasting him, feinting delicately with her tongue, feeling him smile against her lips before he parried boldly with his own tongue—and she wondered how such a simple touch could scorch her down to her toes.

He was holding her upright, easily it seemed, with one arm, and he now slid the other between their bodies and began to caress her—a warm whisper along her collarbone, a fleeting stroke across her breast that made her gasp into his mouth. He increased the pressure there, muffling his own groan in the hollow of her throat. She thought she might die from the sound of his pleasure.

She tasted his skin—heated, salty, heady. She nuzzled the slight stubble an his cheek, and sighed over the unexpected tenderness of the skin below his right ear.

She was making her way toward his left ear with tiny, biting kisses and had stopped to linger on his lips when his hand caught her chin. He tore his mouth from hers and stared down at her his eyes like twin obsidian stars. "I promised myself this wasn't going to happen," he panted. "But I can't turn away. This . . . this is what I came back for."

Before she could think of a response, he was kissing her again. Slower now, sipping, delving lightly with his tongue, making her strain up against him, reaching for more contact, more heat.

And then she had the oddest notion, rising above the multitude of sensations flickering through her, that her feet were on the floor and that maybe, just maybe, her legs were supporting her.

Her heart contracted once, but before she could say a word to Morgan, he'd raised her off her feet, up and into the curve of his body. And as he began running his free hand over her back with a dazzling pressure from shoulder to thigh and up again, she forgot everything. She could feel him, muscle and sinew and bone, everywhere, in all those places she'd once feared she had no sensation left.

Oh, why had she ever doubted? She could feel Morgan right through to her own bones.

Finally he drew back from her, collapsed down into the chair, and settled her, splayed, across his lap.

"It's never been like this," he murmured against her hair. "Not ever, Miranda. You shatter all my self-control."

She reached up to stroke his mouth, wondering at how something so soft could also be so commanding. "Only fair. You shattered my whole world."

"For the better, I hope."

"For the best, Morgan. As if you didn't know."

He sighed, and then grinned. "It appears I don't know much."

They sat there for a time in silence, still entwined, Miranda toying with a strand of his hair, the silky threads jet-black against her pale fingers. She knew it the instant he became restless.

"I should let you sleep," he said. "It's very late, and I need to be away at dawn."

He edged out from beneath her, then raised her up and carried her to the bed. She didn't want to let go of him when he laid her on the counterpane. It would have been easy to tell him, "Stay."

She yawned and then grumbled amiably, "I gather that means I have to be up at dawn, as well."

"No, you get to sleep in. I'm off to London, so I suppose this is good-bye for now."

She heard the word "good-bye" as from a great distance and managed to squeak out, "You aren't traveling with us?"

"No, I'm going down on horseback. I need to reach the city

before Kitty's wedding. You and Ronald will be taking the coach to Cornwall."

Miranda thought she must have heard him wrong.

"Cornwall?" she echoed, pushing herself up onto her elbows.

He nodded serenely unaware that she was instantly primed for battle. "Ronald's written to your solicitor there, instructing him to buy out your tenant's lease. Nasrannah should be empty by mid-July. I thought you could take rooms in Truro until—"

"Morgan," she said ominously, "I don't wish to go to Cornwall."

She saw his hands fist at his sides. "I don't mean to be peremptory, but Ronald and I have this all sorted out. Now it's late and—"

She plucked up a china pug from the bedside table and heaved it at his feet, where it exploded into tiny shards. "You've sorted it out? *You've sorted it out!*"

"Well, we could hardly confer with you about it."

"We can confer *now*," she cried. "Although Ronald seems to have disappeared. He's probably skulking down in the taproom."

"I'm not sure I blame him," Morgan muttered.

"Just go," she said. "I have nothing more to say to you." She drew in a mighty breath. "Except this. I thought you were done trying to control my life. Rescuing me doesn't mean you suddenly own me."

He cast about, snatched up a small vase, then sent it crashing to the floor. "Who'd want to own you? A badder bargain I've yet to—"

There was a soft, tentative rapping at the door.

"Go away!" Morgan barked. Then his voice softened. "Lord, why are we fighting like this, Miranda? Why are you so angry?"

"You order my life without consulting me, arrange to send me to a place I have dreaded returning to for three years, you rescue me and then abandon me again—"

"I am not abandoning you," he snapped. "I need to be in London for my sister's wedding. She is practically the only family I have left. Can you not understand that?"

"Then let us follow you in the coach."

"No," he said. "London would be far too taxing for you."

Was this really how he felt or was he making excuses to keep her away from his family and his friends? Even the mere suspicion of it crushed her.

"Please go," she said. "I am not letting you order my life any longer."

He sighed. "Miranda, have a little pity. I am half dead with fatigue; I rode practically straight through from London. And now I must get back to Kitty. She needs me there. But I swear to you," he growled intently, "the instant this wedding is over, I am done with meddling in other people's lives. It's too exhausting."

"I am very sorry if I have contributed to that."

His eyes sparked dangerously and Miranda knew she had again roused his temper. But then she watched as he mastered it. He'd always been better at that than she was.

"Miranda, don't do this," he pleaded. "Maybe I was wrong to *order* you to Cornwall. Chalk it up to old habits. I was only thinking that the place is remote enough that you would be safe there."

"Yes," she said, "Cornwall is conveniently distant from London."

His brow creased. "I meant remote from Palfry Park. The General isn't likely to swoop down there and carry you back to Windermere."

She sniffed. "There's even less likelihood he would come to London after me. But it's clear you don't have enough faith in me to let me test my wings there."

"Faith has nothing to do with it. London is not some rare, mythical place. It is a dangerous city that teems with crime and wickedness."

She *tsked* softly. "I wonder you allow your sister to live there."

"We are not going to waltz this around again." He leaned in closer and took her face between his hands. "Look, I would bring you there if I could. But I cannot. It's just not something I can deal with. You'll have to get used to that."

She thrashed out of his hold, as the pain cut through her.

"You *are* ashamed of me!" she cried. "Oh, it's fine for you to spark me in private, up here in the wilds of Windermere, but not among your peers. Never among your peers. I see now that wanting to kiss me isn't the same as wanting to keep me."

He stood upright and backed away, his eyes wide and disbelieving. "Good God, is this what all your temper's been about? I can't believe you're throwing something back in my face that I spoke in an unguarded moment. I am not going to discuss it with you. I'm so . . . befuddled right now that I might say something I'll regret later."

"That's a convenient evasion," she said under her breath.

"You're not going to bait me into another argument. I need to be a bit more rational before I go near that subject. You can't expect a man to have his wits about him when he's just come away from kissing you."

She raised one brow. "*My* wits seem to be just fine."

He nodded curtly. "Then I congratulate you."

She glared at him for an instant before she turned her head and thrust her face into the pillow. She heard him moving toward the door; she wanted, as she had a dozen times in the past whenever they fought, to call him back, to apologize. She was thinking how best to do this when she heard the snick of the chamber door closing.

Morgan lingered in the hall outside her bedroom, unable to walk away, unwilling to go back inside and face her icy disdain. It was his own fault she'd ended the night in such a sour, antagonistic mood. She'd been doing so well before he left Palfry Park, before she was placed into the sole care of the unfeeling Alice. Now her playfulness had all but vanished, along with her trust.

And how had he tried to reassure her? By issuing edicts and kissing her like a man possessed. No, he reminded himself, she had been the one who'd prompted that encounter. It only felt as though he'd engineered it because he'd been aching to kiss her since he climbed through her bedroom window. The instant he'd lifted her from the floor, he'd had to fight the urge to crush her against his chest. He hadn't been expecting that much of a reaction, hadn't factored in the joy, the overwhelming relief, of holding her again.

How could she imagine that he was ashamed of her, especially after the way he'd practically devoured her in there just now? Her accusation still stung, still rankled. He cursed himself for ever admitting that he'd find it intolerable if she never walked. It hadn't been true for weeks. He'd take her to London in an instant—Cyrus and Dorrie would gladly open their home to her. But unless he could focus all his attention on Miranda, the city would be too risky for her. Not to mention, the preparations for Kitty's wedding had turned his uncle's house into a place of near lunacy.

Once the wedding was over and his obligations to his sister were fulfilled, he would sort things out with Miranda.

He cracked the door and looked inside, needing a last glimpse of her. The sight of her sprawled in relaxed disarray on the counterpane drew him unresisting to the side of her bed. Her cheeks were flushed, soft rose against ivory, and her hair was a scattering of golden-brown sheaves upon the pillow. Beauty in repose, as he'd once told her.

He eased himself down beside her, sliding one arm beneath her head. She shifted slightly, relaxing into his embrace as her hands curled on his chest. The familiar fragrance of lavender and verbena washed over him, mixed now with some new scent that he could not quite place, something beguiling. It was all Miranda, that scent—brave, stubborn and stunningly passionate.

She made an inarticulate noise and burrowed her face deeper into his throat. His little shrew, he thought fondly, tamed for the nonce. Tomorrow, it was anybody's guess. But he wouldn't be here tomorrow. Ronald would have to be the one to jolly her out of her peevish moods. Morgan wondered if he was up to the job.

As he felt his own head begin to nod, he drew away from her and stood up. She reached for something in her sleep, her fingers flexing slightly; he leaned down and kissed them, each in turn. Blessed fingers, so delicate, and now, finally, so deft.

He left her room with the memory of that victory—and the hope of all the ones still to come—to spur him on to London.

Two weeks ago Miranda had given him the possible means to reach Phillip and he was damned well going to try . . . again.

Ronald and Mrs. Southey were waiting at a table in the deserted taproom, sharing the pot of tea intended for Miranda.

"The pyrotechnics over now?" Ronald inquired. "Mrs. Southey said it sounded as though the two of you were reenacting Trafalgar in there."

"Your cousin was not happy about Cornwall, but I think I convinced her. You can go up to her now, Mrs. Southey. She's sleeping."

Ronald's eyebrows shot up in feigned shock, but before he could make any comment, Morgan raised one hand. "Don't say a word. I am for my bed, before I keel over. If you're thinking of calling me out or anything, for God's sake, do it in the morning."

Chapter Sixteen

Miranda knew the instant she awoke that Morgan was gone. It hadn't been a bad dream after all. This wasn't the way it happened in her picture books. The knights did not rescue the damsels and then ride blithely away. Or maybe they did, she realized. Her books never went much past the rescuing part.

It was typical that she and Morgan had ended their time together fighting. No wonder he was growing weary of her. She'd been a thorn in his side since the middle of April, first resisting him and then, as he'd pointed out, depending on him completely for companionship and encouragement. She needed to prove to him that she could take care of herself, and maybe even that she could occasionally take care of him. Wasn't that what normal women did?

She also had to find some way to repay him. Morgan had done her a very great service and he needed to discover that he wasn't the only one who honored his debts. She might even be able to combine both those goals, repay him and prove her mettle, in one fell swoop. But the scenario that began to form in her head would not be possible in Cornwall.

Now, London, on the other hand . . .

When Mrs. Southey came in to tend her, Miranda asked for some writing paper. She spent the next hour composing a letter, with Ronald banging on the door every so often, reminding her that "Cornwall isn't exactly around the corner" and that they needed to be off. He barely rattled her concentration—after years of writing essays about the foibles of the government or the sorry state of society, she realized this might be the most important piece she'd ever attempted. The happiness of real people, not just the faceless masses, was at stake here.

Finally Miranda was satisfied with her efforts and recopied the scratched-out and blotted letter onto a clean page.

> *Dear Mr. DeBurgh—I am taking the liberty of writing on behalf of a friend. For his sake, I am opening my heart to you, that you might consider opening your heart to another.*
>
> *You will wonder at my presumption and grumble that I could not possibly understand the drastic alterations in your life that made you turn away from Kitty Pearce. You would be wrong. I too lost some vital part of myself in an accident—my parents, for one thing. I also lost the use of my limbs and, for some time, my will to thrive. We do not ever, even in our wildest imaginings, envision a life lived entirely in a chair or a bed—such things are incomprehensible. When circumstance betrays us, however, the incomprehensible becomes our daily lot.*
>
> *What joy, then, if someone is willing to share that burden? I fear I may never have that solace, but it has already been offered to you. What I most wish for is already within your grasp, and against all common wisdom, you refuse to reach for it. And why? Because your body is no longer as it once was. Yet our spirits are no more bound by our sedentary bodies than they were when we were whole and upright. And isn't that what those who love us truly value, our inner spirit and the unique workings of our minds? Our impairments cannot tarnish the light of true devotion any more than the natural encroachments of old age.*
>
> *Still, you have determined that turning away from Kitty Pearce is the kindest course. And thus you cavalierly dismiss her own determinations, this woman who has weighed her options and chosen the difficult path. I say the difficult path, but in my heart I believe the path you have now thrust her upon will be many times more difficult.*

Here is what I know: If you suffer humiliation, love will bolster you. If you rail against circumstance, love will ease you. If you languish, love will vitalize you. Most important, if you doubt your worth, love will validate you.

Morgan Pearce taught me those things and so much more. I was not a willing student by any means, but Morgan is, as you know, a man who does not shrink from battle. I imagine Kitty is no different and that like him, she rushes forward to face the challenges in life. Unfortunately that often gets in the way of clear thinking, that need to always be fixing things and never just letting them be. It doesn't mean they don't accept you as you are; it's simply their nature to always push for more.

In the end, I ask you to take what I cannot. Take love, sir, and live your life among the blessed. While it's true that love itself is not a solution, it offers the possibility of many solutions. Beyond that, there is only the feeble nobility of false pride—surely a paltry companion and a hollow compensation.

Miranda set down her pen and put her hands over her face. Whom had she really written this letter to? Herself? Morgan? Phillip DeBurgh seemed to encompass both their worst traits—her stubborn pride and Morgan's inability to deal with any sort of failure. It was to be hoped that Mr. DeBurgh would choose to behave more wisely than either of them.

She sealed up the letter, then realized she had no idea where to send it. Ronald would probably know, but she doubted he would abet her in this. As it was, she was going to have her hands full, convincing him that she needed to go to London.

Once she was there, she was sure she could find a way to locate Mr. DeBurgh. She'd carry the letter to him in person if need be. It was only six days until Kitty's wedding, six days to accomplish the one thing that would repay Morgan Pearce for saving her—and prove to him that she was no longer a helpless burden.

*   *   *

London was a wondrous blend of sights and smells and noises. Not even the unpleasant things she saw, not the noisome odor of the great river or the raucous din that assaulted her ears on the busier streets could blight Miranda's pleasure. The "magic of place" rose right up from the pavement and wafted down from every stately building and each quaint shop front to welcome her.

She'd insisted on keeping the coach windows open once they reached town, in spite of Ronald's protests. He should have known it was useless to argue with her. She'd been besting him in most things since they were five, when she'd managed to trick him out of a particularly ripe peach by beating him at riddles. Life itself was a riddle to Ronald back then, so even the simplest of them perplexed him.

During the earliest stage of their journey, he'd still been in a snit over being coerced into bringing her here. She knew he was afraid of Morgan's reaction. She'd tried to convince him that Morgan needn't know, that it was really none of his business where she chose to go. Ronald insisted crossly that he'd been given a commission and not lived up to it. She retaliated by pointing out that if *anyone* had a grievance against anyone, hers surely outweighed his.

This reminder of how he'd shunned her for four years, struck home. As a result he'd sat on his seat in affronted silence for an entire day.

By nightfall she could stand it no longer and apologized for hurting his feelings. She knew, as Morgan had obviously learned, that it was nigh impossible to resist the heartrendingly soulful looks Ronald mustered whenever he felt badly used.

He then instantly metamorphized into a merry companion, regaling her for the rest of the trip with stories of Spain, fortunately the more amusing ones. He also coaxed her into reminiscing about Nasrannah, pointing out that it was a part of *his* past, as well, and that it wasn't fair to expect him to jettison all his fond memories of the place at her whim.

She would go back there someday, she knew. Ever since she'd spoken about the house to Morgan, Nasrannah had begun to weave its spell around her again, and thoughts of home became increasingly less painful. For now, though, she had work to do in London—and the hourglass had nearly run out.

They had suffered several unlooked-for delays at the tail end of their journey; first a lame wheeler, and then twenty-odd miles of ground fog in Oxfordshire had made them lose valuable time. It was late afternoon, the day before Kitty's wedding, when they finally reached the capital.

Miranda insisted they detour past the Chelsea Pensioner's Hospital, pointing out that it would be a likely place to locate a secondhand Bath chair. After Ronald went inside, she sent Mrs. Southey to ask after the location of Phillip DeBurgh. The woman returned shortly with a boy of twelve or so in tow.

"Mr. DeBurgh lives but five minutes away," she announced. "Young Jones, here, will carry your letter to him directly."

The boy had scurried off just as Ronald appeared with two men, one of them pushing a rather beat-up chair. Her cousin supervised the lashing of it to the back of their coach as though he were overseeing the preparations for an expedition to Timbuktu.

Miranda realized how much she'd missed his entertaining company.

She changed her mind when, after they'd arrived at his rooms on South Audley Street, he adamantly refused to take her to the Gramblings' home.

"Not a good idea," he said. "Kitty's wedding is tomorrow—"

"I know the date, Ronald. But are you sure it's still on?"

He goggled at her. "Well, why wouldn't it be? My valet was telling me not ten minutes ago that half the city is turning out to see the beautiful Miss Pearce marry her lord."

"And he'd have heard if it was called off?"

"What nonsense is this, Miranda? Of course the wedding is going forward."

Miranda nodded briskly. "Then that is precisely why I have to go there tonight. I need to see Kitty Pearce *before* she is wed."

"Well, let me tell you, that is the last place you want to go. Things will be completely at sixes and sevens. Plus, Morgan's liable to be there. Though if he has any sense at all, he will stay in his own rooms until the last possible minute."

"I will chance running into Morgan. Please, Ronald. Mrs. Southey is strong enough for simple lifting, but will I need you to carry me."

"All the way to Clarges Street? I should say not."

"Down the stairs to the coach," she said with a look of long suffering. "I told the driver to have some supper and return here at seven."

"I hired that coach and driver," he complained. "And I'm not fronting you the money to go careering all over London in it."

She tried to stay calm and not panic. "Listen, Ronald. I believe I can prevent this ill-starred marriage. But I can't manage it alone."

He grumbled a great deal at first, but finally agreed to it when she told him she *would* see Kitty Pearce—even if she had to hang out the window and shout up a carter from the street to aid her.

Once the coach returned, the Bath chair still lashed to its boot, Ronald saw Miranda settled inside beside Mrs. Southey. He was about to climb in himself, when Miranda leaned forward and handed him a piece of paper. He looked at the name on it and scowled. "No—"

"Yes," she said. "It's the only thing I can think of. I've written down the instructions."

He scanned it quickly and his expression grew more and more fretful.

"B-but . . . you didn't say anything about this earlier! You're going to give me palpitations, Miranda, just see if you don't."

"Ronald—" It was the stern, implacable voice she'd used to intimidate him when they were children.

"Then again," he added with a toothy grin, "I always thought Kitty was making a terrible mistake."

"So you'll do it? And no tarrying? We haven't much time."

He nodded. "But if this works, Morgan is really going to owe me. You have no idea."

Miranda sat watching anxiously out the window until the coach reached Clarges Street, which proved to be a pleasant, tree-lined thoroughfare. The driver leaped down to untie the

Bath chair and wrestle it to the pavement. It looked even shabbier than before.

Miranda instructed him to knock on the door to Number Fifteen and ask for Miss Pearce.

"I'm thinking you've caught the meddling disease from a certain major," Mrs. Southey noted as she settled Miranda in the chair.

Miranda grinned up at her. "You'd be thinking correctly."

The driver spoke to the Gramblings' maid—Miranda saw him pointing to her down on the pavement—who then disappeared back into the house. It took nearly five minutes for that door to open again, and Miranda sweated out every one of them.

She was convinced now that hers was the worst plan ever hatched. She'd rarely been duplicitous as a girl and feared she had no talent for intrigue. Arranging people like figures on a chessboard was more in Morgan's line. He'd pulled the wool over the eyes of the entire Palfry clan for nearly six weeks, while she'd been incapable of even sending a letter for help to her lawyer in Truro. Then again, Morgan wasn't impeded as she was. Which was the chief point of her being here—to prove to him that she could accomplish things like any normal person.

Any normal, calculating, manipulative person, that was.

When Kitty Pearce stepped out onto the porch, Miranda's head snapped up. Even though it was early dusk and the flat light was diffused by the trees overhead, Miranda could make out enough of her features to be struck by how much she resembled her brother. Her blue-black hair had been gathered into a chignon, with a few tendrils left to drift around her heart-shaped face. Her dinner gown was a frothy confection of tulle and lace over satin.

Miranda felt pure female envy rise up inside her. First thing tomorrow, she decided, she was going to find a decent dressmaker.

Kitty Pearce hurried down the steps, but then approached the chair cautiously.

"Miss Runyon," she said. "I . . . I am so happy to meet you. My brother has spoken of you with the highest regard. Though

I admit I must have misunderstood him. I thought you were traveling to Cornwall."

"There was a change of plans," Miranda said. "I know this is very awkward, calling on you with no forewarning, but I needed to speak to you away from your family."

Kitty nodded. "I can only give you a minute or two, I'm afraid. You must know that I am to be wed tomorrow."

Miranda clutched the arms of the chair; she had to find some way to keep her out here. Then she remembered something Morgan had said, that Kitty always rose to the bait whenever he impugned the female sex.

"First I must wish you happy," Miranda said. "And congratulate you on your choice of husband. A very old and titled Midlands family, I understand. I wager most women would be in high alt to have snared such a promising catch."

Kitty drew back and her face grew a little hard. "Yes . . . well, that hardly enters into things. Lord Waverly and I have been acquainted for any number of years, and we are quite fond of each other."

"And you perforce grew weary of waiting for your other beau."

Kitty gasped. "Miss Runyon, I don't wish to be rude, but—"

"But you gave up on Phillip DeBurgh, so you could marry a lord."

"Please, you do not understand the first thing about—"

"That is how I see it, Miss Pearce. I expect that is how most people in your acquaintance see it. Not that they would condemn you for such a thing. After all, who would expect a woman to spend her life fetching and carrying for an invalid, when there are balls and parties to attend on the arm of a healthy young peer?"

Kitty leaned forward, so she could make direct eye contact with her. Miranda nearly grinned; it was a posture Morgan had quickly mastered.

"You have no right to come here the night before my wedding and call my behavior into question," she said. "I know how highly Morgan thinks of you, Miss Runyon, and I know something of your unfortunate past, but that does not excuse your presumption or your plain bad manners."

She turned to go, but Miranda caught her hand in a firm grip. Kitty looked down in surprise, as though she expected Miranda's grasp to be feeble.

"You haven't told him," Miranda whispered fiercely.

"Told him what?" Kitty cried softly with no pretense of misunderstanding. "That I loved him, that I would do anything to help speed his recovery? I wrote him all those things over and over till my fingers bled."

"But you never told him that it didn't matter whether he improved or not," Miranda said evenly. "That you loved him enough to take him as he was."

Kitty stuck out her chin. "Morgan wrote me something of that . . . of what you just said. It made no sense to me. What man wants to be loved for being less than he could be?"

"A frail, broken, uncertain man," Miranda responded. "You see, I believe there's a sort of loving acceptance that must come first, before the healing can begin."

Mindless of her pristine gown, Kitty crouched down beside the chair and urgently tugged on Miranda's hand. "How can you know this? Is that how my brother helped you to recover? Is that why you sound so very certain now? Because Morgan offered you that same loving acceptance and it gave you the encouragement you needed to mend?"

Now it was Miranda's turn to squirm. Oh, it was love that had begun to mend her, all right, though not Morgan's love for her, but rather her love for him. That, however, was not what Miss Pearce had asked.

Miranda shook her head. "Your brother offered me a challenge after everyone else had given up on me. But for three very long years I ached for someone to accept me, just as I was. I can't imagine it's much different for your Mr. DeBurgh."

Kitty pushed upright and went pacing along the street, the back of one hand pressed to her mouth. "It's too late," she said in a wavering voice as she swung around. "Too late to try. It would hurt too many people . . . and besides, there's no hope in heaven that he would even see me."

Miranda heard a vehicle approaching from behind her and prayed that it was Ronald. When a closed carriage pulled up in font of her coach, she beamed up at Kitty and said, "There's always hope in heaven, Miss Pearce."

Ronald climbed out of the carriage and motioned Kitty toward him. "I've got someone here who wishes to speak with you, Kit. I'll . . . I'll just wait outside with my cousin."

He went stalking over to Miranda. "Is this more of that West Country magic you used to threaten me with? Because he was just preparing to leave London. He even had that carriage standing by, since he apparently had no wish to be in the city tomorrow morning."

Miranda merely looked up at him serenely.

Circumstance, it appeared, was beginning to smile on her again.

It was surprisingly dark inside the carriage, but Kitty had no trouble identifying the lone passenger. She would have known him in the blackest reaches of space.

She perched on the seat opposite him, trying to make out his features in the gloom. It was six years since she'd last seen him. Six endless, unendurable years.

Her senses surged forward, needing to reacquaint themselves with form and substance, with texture and scent. She understood, of course, the odd absence on the floor of the carriage across from her. A carriage rug lay across his lap and its fringed edge—lit by a diffused patch of light from the street—dangled above his solitary left boot.

"Phillip," she managed at last, and added feebly, "I hope you are well."

"Well enough." His voice was a harsh whisper.

"You . . . you wanted to see me?"

He made a curt, chuffing noise. "No. It was Palfry's idea. Or rather his cousin put him up to it."

"You mean Miss Runyon?" Kitty motioned toward the window. "She's out there, on the pavement."

"That's surprising. I had rather gotten the impression she was an invalid."

"Not for some time now. Ronald's father was keeping her hidden away in his home. . . . Morgan rescued her."

"Well, good for Morgan," he drawled. "He needs his little victories."

Kitty leaned forward. "If you are going to be hateful, Phillip, I won't stay."

"It doesn't matter. I'm on my way out of London. I was just about to depart when young Palfry came calling."

"Very well," she huffed. "I won't keep you, then."

She began to grapple with the door latch. A hand snaked out of the darkness and gripped her wrist.

"No, don't go," he said as he released her. "I did come here to see you. D'you think that Palfry whelp could make me do something against my will when you and your brother were unable to budge me all those months? Have a little sense, Kit."

"Well, if I budged you today," she said, "it's likely to be the first time."

"It was partly Morgan's doing. He sent me the direction of a doctor in Edinburgh who is working with men who have . . . lost their limbs. I wrote to the fellow and he's willing to see me."

"And you weren't going to tell me?"

"Where was the point? I am out of your life now. I suppose I came here because I wanted to wish you happy. Because I always had a care for you, Kitty."

"So you aren't making this trip to appease Morgan or to please me?"

"Let's just say I couldn't stand the boredom of my own company for one more minute. And that I didn't much like it that laudanum had become my best friend." He laughed softly in the darkness. "My own fault for driving off all the other ones."

Kitty screwed together her courage and shifted across the carriage to sit beside him. "What if I were to tell you that you don't have to go to Scotland and put yourself through new tortures? What if I said it doesn't matter to me whether you ever improve? I know I badgered you time and again to make some effort, but I was wrong. Who you are right now, this minute, is the man I want."

There was a long silence in the carriage, and then he said stiffly, "I fear it's a trifle late for that, Kit, even though I needed to hear you to say it. God, you have no idea how much."

She reeled back from the finality of his words. How could she have known that such a simple omission would keep them apart forever?

"Is it really too late?" she asked, her voice trembling.

"You've other obligations now."

"And whose fault is that, Phillip?" she cried, reaching out to find his hands and then clinging to them fiercely. "You are the one who spurned me. Maybe you had a right to blame me for saying all the wrong things, or not saying the right things, but I only ever had your good at heart. Fault the words, but not the love behind them. If Morgan and I were misguided it was only because neither of us had any concept of what you were going through."

"No, I realize that now. Morgan's Miss Runyon did, however. And she made a rather good case for you. A pity she waited so long to write to me."

"She was being held at Palfry Park, as I told you. I assume she only arrived in London today."

"Worlds have turned on such unfortunate delays," he muttered.

"But you are here now; you came knowing about those other obligations. Why would you do that, if it were really too late for us?"

"Because I am a fool. And because I . . . I needed to see you one last time before you were bound to another man."

Kitty began to cry, softly but audibly.

Phillip drew his hands away. "You'd better go now."

"You haven't," she sniffed. "You haven't seen me. It's black as pitch in here. And, please, I want to see you."

"I don't think that's wise."

"Please . . ."

With a muffled curse, Phillip pulled a tinderbox from his coat pocket and lit the hanging lantern beside him. Soft light bloomed in the interior.

She sat there gazing at him, wondering at how little he had changed. His face was thinner than she remembered, his complexion paler. But his hair still shone with a ruddy gleam and his eyes were still a bright, crystalline blue. He was muffled in a driving coat, but his form appeared robust. All those months in bed had not diminished the width of his shoulders or the span of his chest. He still conveyed an aura of capable masculine strength.

He was going to need all of it.

She stroked her fingers lightly across his cheek and then over his mouth. He stifled a gasp, and she renewed her onslaught, tracing her hand down the starched front of his shirt.

"Kitty—"

"Hush, Phillip. I am proving a point. That there is nothing that could ever cause me to turn from you. Nothing."

She flicked away the carriage rug, letting her eyes grow accustomed to the sight of his damaged leg, which had been severed just above the joint. The leg of his buckskins had been neatly turned back, and there was a coyness in that attention to detail that jarred her.

She reached out to touch him there and he uttered a cautious, "Don't! Please . . ."

"Very well; we can leave that for later. Does it still pain you?"

He put his head back against the squabs and closed his eyes. "Less and less," he murmured. Then he asked in a strained voice, "Can you truly bear it, Kit? Looking at what I am become?"

She made a noise of disparagement. "It's no hardship, I promise you. Much worse for you, I imagine." She tickled him gently along his rib cage. "Morgan always said you were a vain fellow."

He opened his eyes. "You're joking about this?"

She held his gaze. "You'd rather I fell upon your manly breast with weeping? I am not a weeper, Phillip. Oh, well, I know I was crying just now. But that was before I knew you'd come back to me, after all."

"I haven't," he said with a scowl. "Come back to you. Not precisely." He drew in a long breath and said haltingly, "What I really came here for was to ask you . . . to ask if you wouldn't wait for me—"

She gave a sharp cry of relief.

"—since I can't very well expect you to take me as I am."

"But I can. I will. Oh, Phillip!" She launched herself at him, clinging to his lapels as she gazed up at his beautiful, beloved face. "Didn't you hear what I said before? You are the man I want, just as you are." She reached down and stroked one hand lightly over the tops of his thighs; he drew a sharp, inward breath.

It had not been an expression of pain.

"See how wrong you were?" she crooned, tracing her fingers along his tensed jaw. "You kept me at bay for all these months . . . fearing if I saw you, I would flee away. Could you possibly know that little about me, Phillip?"

"It never occurred to me that you wouldn't flee," he uttered. "Not until I received Miss Runyon's letter. She reminded how much the Pearces love a challenge . . . and that they don't shrink from battle."

She settled herself in his lap and wrapped her arms around his neck. "Then you are forewarned," she teased. She looked up at him through her lashes and murmured, "Anything else you want to fight about, now that you've got me in a combative mood?"

"Not a blasted thing," he said as he lowered his mouth and took hers.

Kitty emerged from the carriage ten minutes later, looking rather shaky at the knees.

"We're going to Scotland," she announced breathlessly as she approached Miranda and Ronald.

"You're running off to Gretna?" Ronald asked with an incipient frown.

"No, silly," she said. "I'm not that lost to propriety. I convinced Phillip to wait a few days. We'll be married by special license in London and honeymoon in Edinburgh, where there's a doctor who wants to see Phillip."

Dr. Ealing, Miranda thought jubilantly. And she knew that it was Morgan's doing. He hadn't given up on Phillip, not even after all the discord between them. It somehow encouraged her that he would not give up on her either.

Kitty stopped beside Miranda and leaned down to kiss her cheek. "I'm not sure how you accomplished it, my dear Miss

Runyon, but thank you. That is one very stubborn man in there."

Miranda's mouth quirked. "I believe I have him beat by a mile."

"But what of Waverly?" Ronald muttered.

Kitty paused, trying to muster a look of regret in the face of great happiness. "I will write to him, of course. And do you know, I think he might actually be relieved. He's known my heart hasn't been in it for weeks now. I suspect he was only going along with everything because he couldn't cry off himself." She sighed. "A pity I have to put him through this; he's really the dearest fellow, though not very bright."

She went tripping up the stairs, her feet barely touching the flags.

"He'll be a laughingstock," Ronald whispered darkly to Miranda. "For a time, anyway. Too bad we can't find him a brainless miss who's hanging out for a titled husband."

The thought struck the cousins at the same instant, and they both crowed, "Ariadne!"

"That's just the ticket," said Ronald. "I shall befriend Waverly and invite him up to Palfry Park. Get him away from the scandalmongers *and* restore myself to Papa's good graces. Nothing like showing up with a tame lord in tow when one has unmarried sisters."

Then his face fell. "We forgot, Miranda. Tomorrow morning there's going to be a church full of people expecting a wedding. Who's going to tell *them?*"

Miranda winced. This was where things got really awkward. "Morgan will figure something out," she said with more certainty than she felt. "It's just the sort of challenge he loves."

Kitty stuck her head out the door, still wearing a dreamy expression. "I forgot . . . Phillip would like to speak to you, Miss Runyon. And please, come inside when you are through. My aunt and uncle want to meet you."

Ronald waved away Mrs. Southey and dutifully raised Miranda from the chair, muttering, "Bless me if I'm not going to be quite wasp-waisted after all this carrying about."

*   *   *

She and Phillip DeBurgh didn't speak at first, but studied each other assessingly and with a certain measure of kinship.

She was taken by the beauty of his countenance, his imposing size, and the intelligence and awareness that shone in his eyes. She thought of what Morgan had said on that fateful first day. *The waging of war is bloody business.* More so, it seemed to her, when it struck down one so fair and full of promise.

"You've led the Pearces a merry dance," Miranda said at last. "Impressive for a man in your situation."

Phillip's mouth twisted. "How refreshing that all I seem to be meeting tonight are women who can joke about my impairment."

"Ah, but can *you* joke, Mr. DeBurgh? Are you able to brush away all traces of self-pity and have a good laugh at yourself?"

He shook his head. "Nevertheless, I am getting there. And sharing a carriage with a pretty woman is bound to raise a man's spirits."

"Yes, Miss Pearce is quite beautiful."

He cocked his head. "I was referring to you, Miss Runyon."

She blushed, and then laughed. "You know, it's the most wretched thing. I can weather the gawking and odd looks from people, but still cannot handle a simple compliment."

"Then Morgan is not doing a proper job of things. You should be quite used to them by now."

Her eyes widened. "I'm afraid you are mistaken. There is nothing between Mr. Pearce and myself, save . . . friendship."

Phillip DeBurgh inclined his head forward. "Yet you implied in your letter that he had taught you a great deal about what it meant to love someone."

This time, thank heavens, she did not blush. "I was simply trying to make a point."

"And you did a very good job of it. Which is why I wanted to meet you . . . to offer my deepest thanks. And to ask you how you came to be so wise. Especially since I understand you were virtually a prisoner at Palfry Park for a number of years."

"For one thing, I had very wise parents. And Morgan taught me a great deal about moving forward and letting go of the past, about trusting someone enough to let him help you. I don't think I'll ever have a better friend." She leaned toward him. "I believe every word I wrote in that letter, and I'm so pleased that you saw the truth in them in time to act."

He frowned slightly and looked down at his knotted fingers. "Kitty seems to think that everything will be easy now, that it will all fall into place."

"They can't ever really know what people like us face, Mr. DeBurgh, even though they try. We have to be patient with them."

He grinned again. "You may have noticed that the Pearces are not patient by nature. Morgan was hammering at me again only last night, trying to shake some sense into me. Fairly effectively this time, I might add."

Miranda hadn't known about that. Was that the real reason Phillip had come here tonight? She decided it didn't matter which of them had effected the reunion.

"Morgan used different tactics with me," she said. "He was patience personified and eventually wore down all my defenses."

"I am amazed. But grateful, in the end, that your capitulation resulted happily in my own."

He reached for her hand and she nearly blushed again as he raised it to his mouth. "It's been a true pleasure meeting you, ma'am. You are . . . pluck to the backbone." He squeezed her hand encouragingly before he released it. "And in light of that, I think your *friend* Morgan Pearce is a blind fool."

She offered him a slow, rueful smile. "For what it's worth, I believe he already knows that."

Chapter Seventeen

Morgan stalked into Ronald's parlor at eight the next morning, wearing a fine black dress coat and gleaming Hessians—and a thundercloud upon his brow.

After she'd returned from Clarges Street—and her brief visit with the Gramblings, who'd both been rather dazed by the sudden turn of events—Miranda had spent the night in her chair, wondering when the reckoning would come. Ronald had finally wandered off to bed, promising to rouse himself if Morgan got violent. She wondered now if she should call out to him.

Morgan stopped in the middle of the floor and gazed about theatrically, pivoting his upper body around, one way and then the other.

"That's odd," he mused. "This doesn't *look* like Cornwall. But it must be . . . because you are in Cornwall at this moment, are you not, Miss Runyon?"

"There was a change of plans."

"Now, *there's* an understatement. Care to explain what you've been up to lately . . . say, in the past day or so?"

"I am taking hold of my life, as you once recommended I do."

"It seems more *my* life you've taken hold of, Miranda. Mine and my sister's."

She made a noise of vexation. "I thought you'd be pleased. Isn't this what you wanted, getting Phillip out of his bed and back together with Kitty? I did it to repay you for all your kindness and care . . . because it was the only thing I could think of that you really wanted." She put her chin up. "*Someone* had to have a happy ending."

"Yes, it appears you did the impossible."

"You don't sound very pleased."

"Perhaps I wanted to do it myself." He added dryly, "Considering I was the only one of us actually *acquainted* with the two parties concerned."

"You *did* do part of it, Morgan. Phillip told me that your visit this week finally stirred him. I only furnished the coup de grâce by reminding him of how miserable Kitty would be with the wrong man."

"Hard to believe you used *guilt* to tweak him."

She hitched one shoulder. "You found it very effective with me. Anyway, the thing is, we did this together. Is that concept so distasteful to you that you can't even acknowledge it?"

"All right, I am glad of it, even though I never expected you to help me."

"No, you expected me to go away," she said hotly. "Off to the back of beyond, where you wouldn't have to trouble yourself over me any longer."

He moved closer and leaned toward her, his brows meshed. "Have I missed something? Because the last I recall, we were rather fond of each other, you and I. If that's changed, Miranda, I'd rather you let me know straight off."

"Fond?" she parroted, wishing she could read his expression more clearly. It was such an odd mix of icy reserve and barely restrained annoyance . . . and yet there was something skittering in his eyes that looked very much like fear.

"For lack of a better word," he said.

She spread her hands across her lap, to keep her fingers from clenching, and nodded once. "Yes, I do believe you are fond of me. The way one is fond of a well-trained retriever or a performing monkey."

His face hardened as he turned away from her, moving to the bow window beyond her chair. He stood there gazing out, a muscle working in his jaw. When he spoke at last, his voice was hollow. "That might be the cruelest thing you've ever said to me."

He sliced a glance toward her, then quickly looked away. "How is it you were able to offer so much compassion to Phillip and have so little to spare for me?"

Miranda was shaking now; she felt the tremors rising right up from her toes, for once unhappy with this evidence of her body's recovery. Something was happening here, something they had both lost control of.

Her throat grew parched, her vision fuzzy and her ragged, plunging heartbeat seemed to be stealing all her breath.

"Morgan," she said in a faint, strangled voice, "I thought I was the one with the grievance and . . . and if you don't fight back as I am used to . . . and if you don't stop looking at me as though you've lost your soul . . . why, I think I'm going to fall to pieces."

"I don't want to fight," he said in a dull, dead voice. "You think that's the only way to solve anything."

Tell him! a plaintive voice inside her cried. *Can't you see he's in agony?*

But the right words wouldn't come to her, and she was too fearful of using the wrong ones. That was the mistake Kitty had made and she'd suffered dearly for it.

"Then talk to me," she pleaded. "As you did by the stream in Ambleside."

He shrugged. "How can I? We were friends then. . . . You weren't flinging cruel and unjust accusations at me."

"I didn't mean to be cruel. I was making a point. You saved me, Morgan, twice over, and I will never forget that. I also recall that you told me it would be intolerable to you if I never walked again. And then you kissed me and made me think that it truly didn't matter . . . but it was a lie. You couldn't overlook that I was just the clever, broken doll that might never be mended—"

"Stop it!" The words tore out of him as he spun to face her. "You don't have any idea how wrong you are. It's true that I don't want you bound to that chair, but—"

"*That* chair," she repeated ominously. "It always boils down to that chair, doesn't it? It's come between us so often, you'd think it was the size of Gibraltar."

"If you'd let me finish—"

But the anger and hurt were already rising in her blood. "You hate everything this chair represents—the flawed frailty, the shattered dreams, the empty future."

"No! I only hated how much it seemed to limit you. And damn it, Miranda, if you'd stop raging at me and listen, your future won't be empty." He left the window and came toward her. "Although I think it's you who should hate that chair. Because it's become your unnatural haven, your place to hide—"

"How can you possibly say that?"

"You tell me," he shot back. "I'm done with trying to prove the things you already know."

"All right, you want miracles?" she seethed. "Watch this!" Hands gripping the arms of the chair like a vise, she raised herself—with sheer impassioned fury—until she was standing. "Need to see more?"

"Miranda, enough!" he choked out. "You don't need to do this!"

She pushed away from the chair, stood there wavering but upright.

"Am I still intolerable?" she baited him.

Then her strength gave out, and he watched horror-struck as her legs crumpled beneath her. He dove forward onto his knees and caught her, holding her upright with his arms locked around her thighs.

"It doesn't matter," he cried, pressing his face against her side. "God, how can it matter . . . when I can't eat or sleep or even breathe for wanting you?"

His head fell back; she was canted above him, eyes full of uncertainty and a fierce determination not be hurt again.

He lowered her to the chair, keeping hold of her hands and laying his brow upon her knees. "I don't even know when I began to love you. . . . It just flowed into my daily life at Palfry Park. And then I grew afraid. I wasn't sure if I was strong enough, brave enough, to take you as you were." He looked up at her. "I wanted to protect you from harm, Miranda, yet I was the one person who had the best shot at really hurting you."

"So you drew back."

"I tried . . . I tried not to desire you, but I did. I tried not to touch you or kiss you, but by the time we took the horse out together, I was—" He smiled at her roguishly and a bit sheepishly. "Well, you saw how I was."

She combed her fingers through his hair. "You made me feel more normal that day than any other we spent together."

"I was starting to realize it was my father's voice I was hearing, not my own, insisting that you were too marked, too different. So I forced myself to stop listening. And that day, in that circle of stones, all my reservations fell away. You were simply Miranda to me, without labels. Your infirmities became just another part of you, like blue eyes or brown hair."

"And that was the day the General sent you away."

"Mmm," he murmured, rubbing his cheek against her hand. "Blast his infernal old hide."

"Then why didn't you say anything about all this after you came back?"

"I thought you knew. God, the way you kissed me that night in Kendal, the way you just melted into me, I was sure you understood how I felt about you."

Miranda rolled her eyes. "The talkative Mr. Pearce suddenly turns terse when it matters most. All you managed to say was that you wanted me in Cornwall. And that my coming to London was, in your own words, 'just not something I can deal with.' That played right into my worst fears."

"Damn it, Miranda, did you truly think I was sending you away forever, because I was *ashamed* of you? Let me tell you, my girl, men generally don't become ... aroused ... over women they pity."

She blinked several times. "I never thought of it that way."

"And as for the warning about London, I was talking about Kitty's blasted wedding. She's turned the whole household upside down ... and my uncle is still recovering from his illness. I couldn't keep an eye on things there and still have time to watch over you—"

She set her hand on his mouth. "Morgan, do you get paid for all this vigilance?"

He stared at her.

"By my count, you've been watching over me, Ronald, Phillip, Kitty and your aunt and uncle. Anyone I missed?"

He lowered his eyes and looked away. But there were definite lines of amusement around his mouth.

"Because most boys collect puppies or tadpoles when they want something to look after. You seem to collect people."

"I told you, I'm done with it. Except maybe for Cyrus. The rest of them are on their own."

"What about me?"

He drew back dramatically. "I wouldn't presume to look after you from here on, Miss Runyon. You're now officially cut loose from my care."

She ruffled his sleek hair. "Maybe I'll look after you for a while."

He leaned into her touch. "I think I could get used to that. And just so you understand about sending you to Cornwall, the instant this wedding nonsense was over, I was going straight off to Nasrannah, in spite of feeling lately as though I *live* inside a post chaise, and I was going to—"

"What?"

"I was going to have Mrs. Southey bring you down to that cave you spoke of . . . Prospero's cave . . . and . . . and I was going to be waiting there with a gift for you . . . just as your parents always did."

"Oh, Morgan, I've told you, I don't need any gifts from you."

"You need this gift, Miranda. It's the only thing I have to give you, in truth, not having a house of my own and a very uncertain career in publishing due to my frequent and lengthy absences from the firm—"

He was half laughing now, somewhere beyond giddy, but trying to stay serious.

She pressed her hands to his face. "What gift, Morgan?" she whispered.

"My heart, Miranda. You've had it for so very long now, I thought it was time I made it official." He drew her hands down. She could feel him trembling. "Marry me, Miss Runyon of Nasrannah in Cornwall."

Her eyes grew wide and then filled with tears. She tumbled forward from the chair into his arms. He caught her, hugging her so hard that she feared for her ribs.

Finally she pushed back from him, needing one last question

answered. "But why were you so stricken just now. I swear I nearly swooned from the empty look in your eyes."

"I visited Phillip late last night, and he showed me your letter, the one that could have wrung tears from a marble statue. He said he'd asked you if I was the man in the letter, the one who taught you about the meaning of love . . . and you told him no. That was a blow, Miranda. I spent half the night trying to shake it off."

"I couldn't very well tell Phillip how I felt when I'd never even told you."

He touched his brow to hers. "Tell me now."

She gazed into his eyes, so close, so dark and bright. The right words came to her this time, easily, effortlessly, as she quoted, " 'I would not wish any companion in the world but you, nor can imagination form a shape, besides yourself, to like of.' "

He traced her mouth delicately with his thumb. "So speaks Prospero's daughter."

"You brought the magic back to me, Morgan. And my parents' gift that I thought I'd lost, the ability to give someone the thing they desire most. I knew what you desired from me . . . to awaken, to mend, to live. I did it for you, Morgan. I did it for myself. . . . I did it for love."

He shifted his face to nuzzle her cheek. "So did I, sweetheart."

Since there wasn't a great deal more to be said after that, they were both content to remain entwined on the floor of Ronald's parlor, occasionally kissing, certainly sighing, and generally wondering why anyone would waste time fighting when this was such a superior pastime.

Eventually Morgan drew back, and with great seriousness said, "I suggest you put on your best gown, ma'am. We've some business to attend to this morning."

She cocked her head.

"Something we both had a hand in," he continued, "so I think it's only fair we deal with it together."

"What, Morgan?"

He gave her a smug, narrow-eyed smile. "What do you think, Miss Runyon? We're going to church."

*   *   *

There was a handsome phaeton waiting at the curbside, with a pair of lively black horses in the traces. Miranda was surprised when Morgan lifted her onto the seat.

"This is most impressive . . . for a hired secretary."

He grinned as he threw a coin to the boy who'd been tending his horses. "A present from my uncle when I returned from Spain. He's another one who always knows the perfect gift." He set the horses in motion and then turned to her. "And speaking of gifts, is there anything in particular you would like as a token of our betrothal?"

She was about to remind him that she'd already had a surfeit of gifts from him, but then a mischievous notion popped into her head.

"There is one thing," she said coyly. "Your friend, Mr. De-Burgh, says you have not complimented me enough. I think that would be a very nice gift, indeed."

"Yes," he drawled, "that sounds like something he'd say. Blasted meddler."

She laughed outright. "Well?"

"Hmm, where shall I start to list the delights of Miranda Runyon?" he mused, keeping his eyes straight ahead. "Let me see. . . . There is that adorable stubborn cowlick above your brow that is quite gold among the brown and makes me long to touch it ten times to the hour. And a certain tiny mole beside your mouth that demands constant kissing. There is your nose, of an elegant length that ends in a delightful swoop, ditto kissable, and your eyes, of sea-swept hues that shine with intelligence, which haunt me day and night."

"Go on," she said softly. This was far better than anything she could have conjured up.

She saw him rein in a grin. "And your bosom—"

Her brows rose. "You've never seen my bosom."

He shrugged carelessly. "Ah, you're not taking imagination into account here." He sighed and closed his eyes for a moment. "Mmm, lush and lovely."

"Hmm, maybe we should stop now," she said with some starch. "Before you start imagining other things you've not seen."

"Too late," he said as he set the phaeton through a narrow opening in the street traffic. "Now where was I? Your hands . . . delicate; your fingers . . . maddening. Your limbs . . . recalcitrant but resilient. Your earlobes . . . perhaps the only reason for a man to abandon your lips, save for your throat, which is long and white and rises from your shoulders at an angle that intoxicates me."

His voice lowered and his glibness faded. "And there is a dent upon your cheek and a tracing of scars there that have become so dear to me, so much a part of who you are, that, though I rarely note them, when I do it reminds me again of how brave and resolute you once were, and have now become again."

Miranda tucked her face into his coat for a moment, touched beyond words. "There are other scars, Morgan," she said softly.

"I know . . . and we shall have an interesting time of things some day soon, comparing our battle wounds. I think I might win."

She nearly laughed in relief. Leave it to Morgan to turn her worst fears into a sort of lighthearted game.

He slowed his horses as they approached the church. "Do you want to feel the permanent bump on my crown where Kitty coshed me with a dragon paperweight when she was three?"

"No . . ." she giggled. "At least not here."

She suddenly grasped his arm. "Morgan, who is that man on the church steps? He is looking at you so oddly."

Morgan glanced up and then felt himself blanch. So the old jackal had dragged himself to his daughter's wedding after all.

"Wait here a minute," he said tersely as he set the brake; then he whistled for a nearby sweeper to hold his horses. He was five steps away from Miranda before he turned back to her in confusion. She was gazing down at him, wearing a wide smile.

"I can't believe I said that . . ." he muttered with a kind of wonder. "It never occurred to me that you couldn't just climb down and follow me."

"Bravo, Morgan. That's definitely the best compliment of the morning." Then her eyes clouded. "That's your father on the steps, isn't it? I see where you and Kitty get your fine looks."

"And fine tempers, too."

"You're not going to knock him down or anything, are you? This wedding's already going to be the talk of the *ton*."

He came back and gripped her hands. "Tell me you love me, Miranda."

"I love you with all that I am and all that I might become."

He smiled up at her. "Then nothing else matters."

Ronald found Miranda in the crowd at the front of the church. He had brought her Bath chair, tied to the back of a hackney, half across London. Miranda reflected that this chair had probably already covered more miles in one day than the chair in Palfry Park had in three years.

As Ronald pushed her through the crowd, he remarked that it was jolly well amazing how quickly people gave way for a Bath chair. "Ought to take you to the next mill I attend," he said thoughtfully. "A fellow can rarely get close to ringside."

Miranda reached around and smacked him on the arm. "Have a little respect, Ronald." Then she added with a straight face, "You could at least make it a race meet."

Morgan went up the steps, weaving his way around the guests who loitered there in the bright June sunshine. The season was winding down and they were taking advantage of the fine weather to catch up on the last bits of juicy gossip.

"Just wait," he murmured to the crowd at large. "You've not seen anything yet."

His father watched him approach, then broke off from the group of men he'd been standing with. Morgan had to give him credit; the old fellow didn't seem at all discomposed.

"Sir," Morgan said in a clipped voice as he bowed once.

"Morgan." His father returned the salute. "You are looking fit."

"I could say the same."

His father patted his brocaded waistcoat. "I still ride every day. . . . Keeps a man in good trim."

Morgan scuffed his boot toe several times against the stone step. "Kitty's not coming. I just wanted to let you know . . . before I tell the others."

His father's face tightened. "She's not ill? Surely I'd have heard of it—"

"She going off with Phillip . . . to Scotland. I assume you knew what happened to him in Spain. And that he's been abed since then."

"I had heard—and thought it a damned bloody waste. That young man had no business going off to war. Far too much promise to end up as cannon fodder."

Morgan looked away. He thought he'd gotten past the pain, he truly did. But his father's thoughtless words stung him.

There was a hand on his arm, gripping it hard. His gaze swung around. His father's blue eyes met his, brimming with unspoken regret.

"But at least he came home. I thank God for it . . . that you *both* came home."

There it was—a few words, a look, and Morgan felt like his world had righted itself. Or at least had begun to.

"And you don't mind, sir?" he asked in a low voice, still trying to comprehend this change in his father. "That Kitty is creating a scandal and marrying a man who will never be whole?"

His father rubbed his knuckles along his jaw. It was Morgan's own mannerism to the life.

"I don't care to lose her," he said. "Roselinden is like a tomb when she's not about. DeBurgh can give her children, it's to be hoped. That's something to factor in . . . weighs fairly heavy in the balance, actually. A man gets older, he wants his grandchildren, his *family*, about him now and again."

Several people jostled them; the crowd was now making its way up the steps toward the entrance of the church. Morgan knew he had to get back to Miranda. "I must be going, sir."

His father reached out to detain him. "You've done well, lad," he said gruffly. "You've a look about you, an air of command, that draws the eye."

"Blame the war."

Morgan saw him reach deep. "No, it was always there. I . . . I was just too set on having my son follow in my own tracks to see it."

Morgan realized then, for the first time, the mistake he'd

made as a youth, that in rejecting his father's chosen world, he'd somehow been seen to be rejecting his father as well.

"We were never very good at reading each other, sir. Especially not at the end."

"No, you had your own ideas and I blasted you for them. I couldn't grasp that you were meant for other things."

Leaning toward him, Morgan said, "I still am, I'm afraid. I'm not giving up Grambling House, just so you're forewarned."

His father smiled grimly. "Crafty old Cyrus. Your mother's brother always wanted a son—a pity he had to take mine."

Morgan steeled himself—this rift had lain between them for too long—and said intently, "You should never have married her, you know. When she realized she couldn't make you happy, it broke her heart."

His father looked off into the distance and swallowed hard. "You can't tell a man who's in love that he's being a fool. As for the other, no, she didn't make me happy. She kept herself closed off from me most of the time, like a damned cipher. You didn't know that, did you, boy? You only saw *me* withdrawing, because she never shut you out like that. But it takes two people to make or break a marriage. You'll learn that someday."

Morgan thought he already had. Acceptance and openness were his new watchwords.

The crowd was thinning now; Morgan saw Miranda in her chair near the foot of the stairs, Ronald manning the helm.

"Father," he said, "speaking of marriage. . . . See that young woman down there in the Bath chair? She's going to be my wife."

Elliot Pearce studied her with narrowed eyes, and then he frowned. Morgan immediately girded himself to defend Miranda, but his father merely said, "She looks to be a quiet, docile sort of girl. Are you sure the two of you will suit?"

Morgan's shout of laughter startled the pigeons on the roof of the portico, sending them spiraling upward in flight. He watched them circle around the lacework of the spire, thinking he had never been happier in his life.

"You're in for quite a surprise when you meet her, Father.

But first I've some business to attend to. Bailing Kitty out of another scrape."

Morgan carried Miranda up the nearly empty steps, with Ronald dragging the Bath chair behind them.

"I was surprised to see your father here," Ronald said, puffing breathlessly as he reached the landing. "Thought he wasn't coming."

"He apparently had a change of heart," Morgan said as he returned Miranda to the chair. He laid one hand on her shoulder. "Know anything about that, Miss Runyon?"

She tipped her head up. "How could I?"

"Oh, I don't know. Except that you're the one who likes to write stirring letters to lost souls."

"No . . . but I wish I'd thought of it. It looks as though he came here all on his own."

Morgan leaned down. "Are you sure you weren't behind this?"

Miranda winced. "Not me, I promise. Only . . . Oh, bother . . . I wish he'd never told me."

"I'll shake it out of you," he threatened. "You know I can."

Ronald harrumphed. "Not while I'm here to stop you."

"Oh, shut up, Ronald," Morgan muttered. "As if I would ever harm her. Now, Miranda—"

"It was your uncle Cyrus," she blurted out. "He told me last night that he'd written to your father over a week ago. He wanted him here, Morgan, for Kitty's sake, but mostly for you. 'Nothing like a wedding to help bury the hatchet,' is what he said. I promised not to spoil the surprise."

"My father hates Cyrus Grambling," he muttered. "At least he used to."

"People change, Morgan. And with Kitty shuttling between the two houses, it makes sense that they would get a glimpse into each other's world. Through her. You've maybe been too busy holding the past at bay to notice what's been happening in the here and now."

"*Me* holding the past at bay?"

She grinned up at him. "I know. I was no better. I wouldn't

look back at the good and you wouldn't look back at the bad. I think we've both been a bit shortsighted."

Ronald suddenly stepped forward and hissed, "Here comes the groom!"

Sure enough, Lord Waverly was making his way slowly up the stairs, unattended by even a single groomsman.

Morgan had gone to his town house last night and was told his lordship was out indulging in his bachelor's carouse. Since Morgan had left behind Kitty's letter of explanation, he'd never thought to see the poor fellow here at the church.

He went down to meet him, with Ronald a step or two behind. "You didn't get my message, Waverly?"

The young man nodded. "Sadly, yes. Not that I was surprised. It was all that crying, you see. She blamed it on the books, but I knew what was behind it."

"Then I'm not sure why you're here," Morgan said under his breath. "I was just about to go in and make the announcement."

Waverly nodded. "I wanted to be here so that no one would think I was angry at Kitty. She's the dearest girl, you know, Pearce. But with perhaps an excess of sensibility."

When Waverly caught sight of Miranda sitting alone at the top of the stairs, he drifted upward, away from the two men, and greeted her with a bow. "Lord Waverly, ma'am. I say, has someone left you out here? Would you like me to give you a push into the church?"

"Thank you," Miranda said as Morgan came up beside her. "That's extremely kind of you. But Mr. Pearce will see to me."

"Just come this way, your lordship," Ronald said, hooking Waverly by the elbow and drawing him into the vestibule. "We'll sneak in around the side aisle and you can pop up at the altar. And I think what you might require after this is a nice restorative trip to the Lake District. M'father's got a lovely place up there. Scenic vistas, dashed fine fishing . . . and did I mention, I have a sister. . . ."

"He's far too nice for Ariadne," Miranda murmured, and then, "Did you see that, Morgan? His lordship didn't even turn a hair over me."

"Yes, but then he thinks the ironclad Kitty is too full of sensibility, so he's obviously dotty in the head."

She made a face at him, and he flicked the tip of her nose. "Ready?"

She nodded. He propelled her to the double doors of the church, and then paused.

She looked over her shoulder. "Are you sure about this? You could leave me out here. . . ."

His eyes danced. "What, like a garden gnome?"

"A gargoyle would be more apt considering the location."

"No, I'm not leaving you anywhere, ever again."

She smiled and said impishly, "That's reassuring. Though I'll probably be hitting you with a stick before long to give me some time to myself."

His mouth widened into a roguish grin as he purred, "Not for a very, very long while. I promise you."

He leaned down and kissed her on the tiny mole beside her mouth and then gripped the handles of the Bath chair. "All right, here we go. Off to face the lions."

Miranda thought Morgan did a manful job of explaining Kitty's change of heart.

The guests in the church had already begun to talk among themselves when there was no sign of the bride, and the hubbub had grown to a dull roar when Morgan appeared pushing Miranda down the aisle. He'd set her to one side, near where Lord Waverly and the rather baffled minister stood, and when he began speaking in his field officer's baritone, the congregation soon quieted.

"I apologize for the natural surprise you all must feel when I tell you that my sister, Miss Pearce, and her betrothed, Lord Waverly, have mutually decided that they will not suit. Lord Waverly extends his regrets"—his lordship nodded briskly at this point—"and Miss Pearce sends her sincerest apologies. Those of you who are connections of Lord Waverly and were to attend the wedding breakfast, are now invited to his home to share a meal of good fellowship. Those who comprise my own family and friends, I invite to Fanshaw Gardens this evening, where we will celebrate my betrothal to Miss Runyon of Nasrannah in Cornwall."

Morgan stepped down from the dais and returned to Miranda, whose face had gone pale.

"You wretch," she said with a shaky grin. "What on earth is Fanshaw Gardens?"

"A pleasure grove, Miss Runyon. With a lake and boats and a pavilion on the water."

"And ducks?"

"I shouldn't doubt it."

"And you planned all this since this morning?"

He nodded. "Mrs. Southey and Hodges are out right now, making the final arrangements. You see, I wanted you to know, without the slightest doubt, that I would go anywhere with you, be seen anywhere with you."

"I believe this morning proved that. But, oh . . . a pleasure grove. I think I should like it enormously."

Then her face fell. She had nothing to wear to such a place. It required something frothy and flowing with a picture hat, perhaps, and—

She realized Morgan was laughing at her, as if he knew exactly what was going through her mind.

"You're not the only one who can make plans, sir," she said. "I need to visit a . . . Where do women go to buy gowns in this city?"

Morgan, who had clothed a few courtesans in his time, murmured, "Madame Chrien, without a doubt."

Ronald, who had overheard this last part, bustled forward. "You ain't dressing my cousin from a shop that caters to lady birds, Morgan. Madame Chrien's gowns are . . . well, they are . . . far too fast for Miranda."

She tugged on her cousin's hand until he looked down. "Shut up, Ronald," she said.

The sunset sky was awash with color, soft blues and vivid oranges, as Morgan wheeled Miranda along the central path that wove through the pleasure grove. Japanese lanterns were strung along the trees, like fireflies dappling the silken shadows. The lake spread before them, tranquil except where it was disturbed into chevron ripples by the oars of rowboats.

They might have been back in Windermere, she thought, except for the faint din of the metropolis, which furnished a humming counterpoint to the soft strains of a small orchestra.

Every so often, people wandered over for introductions, acquaintances of Morgan's, men connected with Grambling House, friends of Kitty's who looked at Miranda with open envy for having co-opted such a prize.

This was a new experience for her and she attributed it to the handiwork of Madame Chrien. The modiste, on short notice, had managed to fit Miranda with a daringly low-cut, diaphanous gown of pale gray and paler green gauze, overshot with gold thread. She'd topped it off with a circlet of green-and-gold leaves.

Miranda felt positively sinful. The way Morgan looked at her made her feel even more wicked. She was Titania, Gloriana and the Queen of the May.

She was Circe.

Morgan had barely stopped touching her all evening, a flick of his fingers over her cheek, a swift caress on her shoulder, a long stroke down her arm. She was fairly simmering for him to kiss her by the time they reached the shore of the lake, where blankets and wicker seats had been provided for the guests. She eyed the blankets longingly as they progressed along. It didn't take much to imagine Morgan's lean body stretched out over hers on a soft, grass-scented quilt.

But Morgan kept on around the lake till they came to the deserted pavilion. Not an Oriental folly in this case, but a more imposing classical Greek temple.

"I've had this dream a long time," he said as he raised her from the chair and carried her inside. The interior was shadowy, cool, the long bench where he set her down, covered with brocaded pillows.

"What dream is that?" she asked as he slid beside her.

He ran his mouth along her collarbone and whispered against her throat, "To get you inside a pavilion—after dark."

Miranda chuckled. "Not during that first week, I wager."

"You might be surprised."

She leaned back and rubbed the side of her face against his shoulder, admiring the lantern lights on the dark water. "You're always showing me lakes. Have you noticed that?"

"Next I'll show you the duck pond at Roselinden."

"You mean where you sailed the yar little boat you made? I'd like to see that."

"I will, if you promise to show me the sea off Nasrannah."

"Mmm . . ."

She knew what he was after, some assurance that she would pick up the pieces of her old life. She hadn't yet told him that she'd decided she could do it. Someday.

"And very soon, I hope," he added.

"It still hurts, Morgan."

"I know. But if you wait till the hurt goes away, think how many new memories you might be missing."

"Suppose I do go back and discover it's too painful? Maybe if I wait, there will be less chance of that."

"Maybe if you wait, the hobgoblins will multiply."

"I cannot imagine being in that house and not missing my parents dreadfully."

"But what if it's only in that house that you can come to terms with your grief? Away from the place, you carry only reminders of the tragedy. Back there, all around you, are tokens of better times."

"That is my point—how can I view those things every day, and not weep?"

He thought for a moment. "Because twenty-one years of happiness ought to balance out three years of sorrow. It won't make things right for you, Miranda, but it could make them easier. Where love once dwelled, you always have the reminder that it can come again."

"It has come again," she said, turning her face up to his, seeing him as if for the first time, elegant, polished and stirringly male. Her friend first, and now her lover. More than that, she thought, her life's mate. If she took him to Nasrannah, she'd be bringing that same strong unity into the house that her parents had brought.

His head lowered, his lips above hers. "Then take that love with you," he whispered. "And find the 'magic of place' that you lost. Because it's in you, Miranda. It always was."

She nodded, brushing noses with him. "Phillip was afraid that Kitty would be disappointed if things didn't resolve easily for them. I, at least, know better. It's what we have to fight for that we cherish most."

"I know."

"So I will go back to Nasrannah, back to my home. As soon as you like."

"Thank you," he said. "And I could remind you that you won't be going there alone."

"No," she said dreamily.

He pulled back, out of range, and said, "Ronald asked me specially if he could come along."

"Morgan!"

His eyes were bright with mischief. "*Specially*. That was his exact word. It seems he's got this notion that he is now responsible for looking after *you*."

"Do you know," she grumbled, "I wonder no one's ever killed Ronald Palfry."

"Don't worry, he's not coming near the place. Not until you and I have explored every magical nook and cranny. And now, enough about your infernal cousin. . . ."

He clasped her shoulder with one hand, the other hand drifting a caress along her throat. She leaned up, not far, and kissed him. Opened her mouth beneath his and felt the first ripples of pleasure undulate through her, like the fanning waterweeds beneath a tidal pool.

Morgan's arms slipped around her, long fingers splayed on her back, drawing her closer, while his mouth danced against hers, teasing, nipping, then settling in with deep, warm, penetrating kisses.

She strained up toward him, wanting desperately to get closer to that warmth.

He pulled back with a slight gasp. "What is that?"

He was looking down over her shoulder. She twisted her head around.

"That is my left knee."

"What is it doing on my . . . thigh?"

She looked at him in wide-eyed wonder and said in quavery tones, "It . . . it moved there. By itself."

"Move it off," he said in a still, quiet voice.

They both watched intently as her knee slid down the length of his thigh until her foot touched the floor again.

His arms tightened on her painfully. "You realize what this means?"

"It might not mean anything," she protested softly, not daring to hope. "I just wanted to get closer to you. I would crawl right inside of you if I could when you kiss me like that."

He bent her back and gazed down at her face, the lights from the garden igniting sparks in his ebony eyes. There was incipient joy—and the answer to every hope—in that dark gaze.

"Then, brace yourself for battle, Miss Runyon," he said with a wicked grin. "Because I'm going do it again."

"It's a hoax," said the General to Mr. Northam of Truro, tossing the letter back at him across the desk.

The solicitor, an unimposing man of middle height and middle years—but with a certain incisive intelligence lurking in his dark Cornish eyes—shook his head. "No hoax. She wrote another letter to me last week. She is staying in London, in the company of your son."

"Then *he* wrote it. Perhaps with his left hand, so that it was shaky and did not resemble his own scrawl."

The lawyer sighed. "I trusted you, Sir Janus. Four years ago I made you promise that Miranda Runyon would have every care."

"And she has!"

"Then how is it that your reports to me speak—right until this past month—of infirmities and paralysis? What are the doctors up here, a bevy of blasted blunderers with their heads up their backsides?"

"I am not going to defend my actions . . . to a lawyer." He'd said the last word with a sort of sneering distaste.

Mr. Northam looked about him, at the ormolu-and-walnut desk, the elegant and masculine velvet drapes, the bronze sculptures and fine paintings that adorned the room. He'd take great pleasure in seeing the man stripped of all his comforts. "A pity then, for I imagine you will be inundated by my brethren once I bring Miss Runyon's case before a magistrate."

Sir Janus reared up from his desk, but before he could utter a word, his youngest daughter came flinging through the door, wailing, "Papa! Make her stop! Bettina won't let me borrow her new pink frock and I simply must wear it tonight at the assembly in Windermere. She doesn't need it now, the wicked, selfish creature—she's already caught herself a titled husband. What about me, Papa? *What's to become of me?*"

Lady Palfry stood in the garden, within earshot of the tumult in her husband's study, but barely noting it. She was staring down with utter disbelief at the overnight infestation of aphids that had decimated her roses.

Daisy had brought her even worse news that morning. The builder who had come to repair the broken window in Miranda Runyon's bedroom had lost his way on the ground floor of the house and made a terrible discovery: There were deathwatch beetles in the wainscoting!